High Wind in Java

A new Richard Mariner adventure

Richard Mariner is out to buy the revolutionary vessel *Tai Fun*, but not if multi-millionaire eco-warrior Nic Greenbaum has his way. The situation is further complicated when the tiny island of Pulau Baya, *Tai Fun*'s final port of call, is torn by a series of unexplained, overwhelming disasters. Helpless and desperate, the islanders go out to pirate and pillage. And the first vessel to appear over their horizon is the *Tai Fun*...

High Wind in Java

Peter Tonkin

Severn House Large Print
London & New York

This first large print edition published 2010
in Great Britain and the USA by
SEVERN HOUSE PUBLISHERS LTD of
9-15 High Street, Sutton, Surrey, SM1 1DF.
First world regular print edition published 2007 by
Severn House Publishers Ltd., London and New York.

British Library Cataloguing in Publication Data

Tonkin, Peter.
  High wind in Java. -- (Mariners series)
  1. Mariner, Richard (Fictitious character)--Fiction.
  2. Cruise ships--Fiction. 3. Ocean travel--Indonesia--
  Java Sea--Fiction. 4. Pirates--Indonesia--Java Sea--
  Fiction. 5. Suspense fiction. 6. Large type books.
  I. Title II. Series
  823.9'14-dc22

  ISBN-13: 978-0-7278-7849-6

Printed and bound in Great Britain by
MPG Books Ltd, Bodmin, Cornwall.

For Cham, Guy and Mark as always

One

Angel Passing

When the silence fell so suddenly the peanut shells began to scuttle soundlessly across the juddering tabletop and something almost spectrally put a little storm of ripples into the teacup in their midst, Robin Mariner looked up at Richard her husband with a frown of worry. He grinned at her reassuringly, sparkling with energy and excitement, seeming to have missed the tremor that was stirring the shells and the tea. His smiling lips moved. *Angel passing*, he mouthed silently, and turned back to his other companion.

Robin glanced at her watch automatically: twenty past the hour. Just like her mother had told her in childhood. Angels pass at twenty past and twenty to the hour. And everything goes silent then. Perhaps Richard was right, she thought. And perhaps the stirring of the tabletop was nothing more than the traffic on Beach Road or Stamford, or the passing of an MTR train bound in from Raffles Place. That would explain why the shells were marching across the floor just as they were skittering over the tabletop. Why the surfaces of the Singapore Sling and the Perrier beside her fragrant tea were also astir with tiny ripples.

But then the breathless, magically silent, air of the Long Bar within the cloistered confines of the Raffles Hotel itself was abruptly stirred by a rumble of thunder. And that almost put Robin's mind at rest. For thunder to be audible in here, even in a sudden silence, it must have been quite deafeningly cataclysmic out over the hills of Serangoon or the Singapore Strait itself.

The deep exhaustion and lingering disorientation of jet-lag were making Robin almost preternaturally sensitive to her unsettlingly strange surroundings. That and the mild but pleasant confusion born of Richard's steadfast refusal to tell her precisely where they were going or precisely what he was up to. He knew she loved surprises and this one was clearly going to be memorable. But the interim of travelling, even travelling first class on Hong Kong Airlines out of Heathrow, even travelling that alighted in places such as the Raffles Hotel in Singapore within a day of having left the Heritage Mariner offices in London, remained distractingly dreamlike. The resurgent bustle and banter in the Long Bar seemed to flow over her, as vivid but insubstantial as a vision. The animated conversation between Richard and their unexpected companion, the business magnate and eco-warrior Nicolas Greenbaum, babbled like a brook. Her psyche seemed to stretch into the fabric of the building, into the overbuilt rocks of the island itself, seeking for the source of that tiny tremor that made the peanut shells migrate a centimetre or so across the tabletop. But there was nothing.

The thunder rumbled again, more loudly. Perhaps Robin should have sent her imagination up into the black storm clouds she had seen towering away to the south three hours since, as their plane was settling out of the lower sky towards the runway at Changi Airport. Automatically, she raised her eyes as though she could see past the lazily beating fans that only kept the humid, storm-heavy air breathable with the aid of icy air-conditioning.

'So,' said Nic, swinging round to fix her with his piercing stare. 'Richard hasn't told you anything at all?'

'Not a word.' She lowered her steady gaze to meet that of her overpowering interrogator. But she was used to dealing with overpowering men. Her equanimity remained as unruffled as one of Jane Austen's calmest heroines. 'It's going to be a surprise.'

'You must be an unusually trusting woman, Robin. To let him drag you halfway round the world without any warning or explanation.'

'Richard's always been a little impulsive. In everything except his business dealings.'

Nic Greenbaum gave a brief shout of laughter. 'An inspired afterthought. Just in case a part of the surprise involves some kind of a deal with me!'

'Does it?' Robin's golden brows arched above

9

the still grey gaze of her unruffled eyes.

The big American's own eyes narrowed. Lost none of their teasing sparkle. 'It's just too much of a coincidence, you mean, that two men such as Richard and I should just happen to be passing through the Long Bar at the Raffles Hotel at exactly the same moment in time?'

'Heading in the same direction, into the bargain. Up to the same business. You're either making some kind of a deal or you're rivals in some kind of a deal, I should guess. But then again, keeping some travel plans secret from me is one thing. Keeping a deal with Greenbaum International or Texas Oil secret is something else again. Richard's good but he's not that good. So you're likely to be rivals. And that's pretty damn interesting in itself. Because I'm just gasping to find out what on God's green earth is so uniquely desirable that it would set you two at each other's throats. And at each other's throats in person. I'll bet it's something that really is worth coming halfway round the world to see.'

'And even if the surprise isn't worth it,' added Nic cheerfully, with just the tiniest edge in his voice, 'maybe the fight will be.'

'Oh, it'll be worth it,' rumbled Richard. 'It'll be worth it either way.'

Another little silence fell, giving Robin an instant to compare her husband and his rival. Both were big men. Richard's Celtic genes were overwhelmed by some Viking giant in his Scottish Border ancestry so that nothing remained except the blue-black hair above the ice-blue wave-wanderer's eyes. Nic Greenbaum's Texan drawl reminded her unsettlingly of John Wayne at his most western, while his white hair and neat beard made him resemble a very large, surprisingly lean and very tough-looking Santa Claus.

There must have been little more than five years between them, Robin thought, but Nic looked a generation older. His white locks were beginning to thin. Richard's remained thick and black except above the ears. Nic's eyebrows were becoming wiry; Richard's perhaps were beginning to lengthen into devilish points at his temples. Nic's face was just beginning to lose definition. Richard's remained angular. Chiselled. Especially down the broken blade of his hatchet nose and the lean line of his square, determined jaw.

But Nic's five years in age were reflected in well over five billions in fortune – even calculating in pounds sterling. Nic was super-rich. Personally super-rich, not just in terms of corporate interests and company shares. And at least five million pounds more than even Richard was. He was up there with Bill Gates just as his business empire was up with Microsoft – in oil, shipping, transport and real estate. And, latterly, in the burgeoning worldwide green economy, where Greenbaum was a name with universal respect and credibility.

But, since his groundbreaking deal to sell decommissioned supertankers to Russia for

11

ecologically profitable recycling, Richard's star was on the rise again. The *Financial Times* in London and *Forbes* in New York spoke of him in the same breath as they spoke of Richard Branson. And Heritage Mariner was fast becoming the Virgin of the seaways. And after all, Richard was the kind of man who learned dazzlingly quickly. By the time he was Nic Greenbaum's age, Robin knew he planned to be much more than five million pounds richer; well up with Nic's five billion overall.

It might, indeed, be interesting to see these two go *mano a mano*, as the Italians had it – head to head like two bull elephants fighting for control of the same great herd. As long as no one really got hurt, of course, either personally or financially.

Robin stirred herself out of her reverie, suddenly aware that the silence that had caused it was lasting far longer than she might have expected. And it contained unsettling undertones almost as fundamental as the stirring that had moved the peanut shells. Even at her own table, she had ceased to be the centre of attention. The whole of the Long Bar was focused on a newcomer who had silenced them as surely as the threat of a thunderbolt, tsunami or earth tremor.

She stood six feet tall, or would have done so had her determined stride faltered. From the crown of her head to the shoulders of her silk jacket, her hair fell in an ash-blonde cascade saved from being utterly white by the slightest

12

tint of gold. There was no question of 'Maybe she's born with it, maybe...' Born with it she was. The perfect oval of her face was widened almost imperceptibly by the angles of her cheekbones and the squareness of her jaw. Above the cheekbones sat eyes that were exactly the same shade as a summer sky at moonrise. Above the line of her jaw there rested a pair of carmine lips whose depth and sheen struck the only false note in the Nordic perfection of her Ice Queen countenance. The breathtaking head sat on a long neck lengthened in turn by the fact that she wore no blouse beneath the black silk of her severely tailored jacket. The cleft of her chin was echoed much lower and much more arrestingly by fifteen centimetres or so of power cleavage, which was all that kept the lapels of the jacket apart. And gave a whole new meaning to the phrase 'double breasted'. The waist of the fastened jacket was at once impossibly slim and obviously loose. And yet the clinging material was pulled out into fullness almost at once by the flare of her hips. The line of the jacket ended exactly level with the tops of her thighs, but the suit itself extended down in a perfectly cut pair of trousers weighted with turn-ups where the impossibly long legs just brushed against the insteps of her high-heeled, open-toed business sandals.

As the vision moved through the Long Bar, every eye seemed to rest upon her, every head to move in unison as though the patrons were all watching some kind of an angel passing.

13

My God, thought Robin, reaching automatically towards the suddenly garish-seeming jumble of golden ringlets on her head even as she tried to readjust the rubbery brushed silk of her travelling blouse, which suddenly now seemed as crushed and wrinkled as used tissue paper, I hope she's not coming anywhere near our table!

But no sooner had Robin's desperate prayer formed than the vision became even more breathtaking as she smiled – no, beamed – and waved. 'Nic!' she called in a Scandinavian contralto deep enough to cause shivers. 'And Richard! I have both of you together! What luck! At the very least that will save on one Rolls-Royce.' She stopped with her thighs scant centimetres from the table edge; close enough for Robin to see that there were broad white pinstripes in the absolute black of the cloth; broad ones, almost wide enough to be chalk stripes but not quite wide enough to balance the black itself. Of course, she thought; it was the stripes that helped define so perfectly the outward swells on either side of the power cleavage, the casual drape of excess material around that wasplike waist, the generous flare beneath. The newcomer frowned suddenly, as though picking up on the atmosphere Robin had been lazily preparing to enjoy. 'As long as you don't mind sharing,' she said, uncertainly.

'I don't,' said Richard at once. 'Robin. Do you mind?'

It was only when Richard turned to speak to

Robin that the Ice Queen seemed to see her. Midnight-blue eyes met a grey stare that was suddenly almost steely. 'Fine with me, darling,' answered Robin equably. 'If Nic's amenable.' 'Well,' drawled Nic, 'I guess I am amenable at that.' He grinned suddenly, the same wide boyish excited grin that Richard used on occasion. He exploded to his feet, seeming to spark with restless energy, and the other two rose with him, pulled erect almost by his personal magnetism. Peanut shells scattered hither and yon as they moved. 'On the one hand I simply couldn't drag myself away from two such lovely companions. Robin Mariner, may I introduce Inge Nordberg, the daughter of our host, who, I assume, awaits us. Inge, Robin Mariner, director and co-owner of the Heritage Mariner shipping company.' He drew breath as the two women shook hands like duellists standing on form.

'And on the other hand, Robin my dear,' he continued with overwhelming cheeriness, 'I want to be there to see the look on your face when Richard shows you his *next* surprise.'

Two

Landing Site

There were two new green Rolls-Royce Phantom limousines waiting at the Grand Entrance. Although designed as coupés, the cars had their hard tops firmly in place. And they needed them, for the storm Robin had first seen more than three hours ago as she had landed at Changi Airport as a black line of thunderheads over the Singapore Strait had well and truly arrived. The thunder was now a continuous cannonade overhead, and rain was pounding down in a truly tropical deluge. The two great cars, scant metres outside the tiled portico, seemed to be on the point of melting beneath the relentless pounding of the rain and washing away towards Beach Road; their outlines blurred by spray, seemingly only hanging on to their paintwork by a very temporary miracle. As the little group hesitated under the great awning outside the main doors like explorers trapped behind a waterfall, a uniformed doorman approached with a golf umbrella. Without thinking, Nic and Inge stooped beneath its protection and hurried outwards towards the

16

nearest Rolls. They had taken perhaps three steps before the wind and rain destroyed the bright waterproof canopy and left them defenceless against the deluge.

Another doorman approached and Richard grabbed the umbrella himself. With one hand high on the shaft right up by the straining spokes and the other tightly round Robin's shoulders, he clasped the umbrella handle firmly in his armpit and threw them forward. But Inge had slammed the door of the first Phantom as soon as she was in it and the driver was already easing forward while the soaking doorman with his wrecked umbrella was turning away, his feet washed by the spray from the immaculate black tyres.

Richard headed for the second Rolls, therefore, and Robin pulled the back door wide. So they tumbled inwards, Richard swinging back at the last moment to hand the umbrella to the drenched doorman, who took it with every sign of relief. Then the door slammed shut with that satisfying sound that only the most expensive car doors make.

Robin was settling back luxuriously, making the calfskin seat-covering groan ecstatically. 'I love this car,' she said as the Phantom surged forward like a jet on a runway.

'You want one?' asked Richard, settling into the fragrant warmth of the passenger compartment beside her. 'MNO.'

MNO was a term that Nic had introduced them to when Robin reacted with simple horror to the price of the Texan's Singapore Sling. 'You could get a room in a decent hotel for less than that!' she had said.

'True. But I don't want one of those. I want one of these,' he had countered, raising the glass and winking at her over the rim. 'And there are times when I just have to have what I want, MNO.'

She raised her eyebrows. He sipped and put his glass down grinning.

'MNO,' he repeated. *'Money No Object.* I guess that's a technical term that you and Richard will have to get used to using, if what *Forbes* and the *Wall Street Journal* say about Heritage Mariner can be believed.'

Robin opened her mouth to give him a piece of her Puritan conservative, socially responsible mind. But shut it again without saying anything. Questioning any decision Nic Greenbaum made about money, morals or social responsibility would be childish arrogance, if what *The Economist,* the *Ecologist* and the Archbishop of Canterbury had all said recently about his funding of work in the developing world could be believed.

'MNO,' she echoed now, raising her voice over the throbbing roar of the rain on the roof. The way she said it was every bit as sensuous as the manner in which she settled into the pale hide of the seat. 'That is a dangerously seductive concept, Richard.'

'Only to the super-rich,' he countered. 'We have lots of calls upon the income that Heritage

Mariner generates for us. Independently of the reinvestment programmes into the business itself.'

Robin glanced up, her grey eyes limpid beneath the dark gold of her lashes. 'And what is this little jaunt, then, my darling? Reinvestment or MNO?'

'It's a surprise,' he countered. 'Wait and see.'

The Phantom followed its mate out of the hotel's gates and on to Beach Road, swinging right down the hill towards the river.

'You've earned a rest,' he persisted, able to speak more gently because the rain began to ease. 'Your adventure in Archangel was hard on you, even if the outcome was good for the company.'

'One night alone on a derelict hulk with four assassins licensed to kill by various governments and a freezer-full of corpses,' she countered lightly. 'Every girl should try it. Especially if it's going to turn into a money-making machine for her doting hubby.'

'And it's not as if you've had much of a chance to catch your breath since,' persisted Richard, frowning with genuine concern. 'What with your father and stepmother moving off to that ramshackle old place of hers in Grimaud and inviting my mum and dad out there with them. Leaving us to sort things out in Cold Fell and Summersend. Two bloody great houses at either end of the country; neither of them anywhere near our own home. And yes. By *us* I mean *you*. Staying on top of one house is quite

19

enough. Staying on top of three...'

'And the flat in town,' she reminded him. 'Ashenden may be easy enough to run – that's why we bought it. But Summersend is a Grade Two listed country mansion and I think Cold Fell actually counts as a castle. What I need is *staff* not holidays, Victorian though that sounds. If we're going to make use of the houses for corporate entertaining, and turn them into a kind of Chequers, Chevening and Dorneywood like the British Cabinet does, or like Windsor, Balmoral and Buckingham Palace, then I really will need staff. A decent butler or two. Or three, in fact. God, what I'd give for just one Jeeves.'

'Jeeves was Bertie Wooster's *gentleman's personal gentleman*,' said Richard at his most pompous, straying dangerously where angels might fear to tread. 'A valet, not a butler.'

'But Bertie said Jeeves could buttle with the best of them,' replied Robin coolly. 'And I think he did buttle on several occasions. For Gussie Fink-Nottle amongst others. Including J. Washburn Stoker and at least one terrible aunt, if memory serves. But it's not like you to be so picky. What's up, lover?'

The Rolls slowed to a stop and the lights at the corner of Bras Basah Road shone in to reveal Richard at his most deviously shifty.

'What's up?' she repeated, with more of an edge on her tone.

'Well, it's part of the surprise, but I don't see any point in waiting any longer,' he admitted. 'So. While we're away, recruitment have been

20

directed to find you your Jeeveses and at least two sets of staff.'

Nic would have appreciated the look of wonderment on Robin's face as the next layer came off the Salome's Dance of a Surprise.

The recruitment section at Heritage Mariner was almost as high-powered as the movements and commercial intelligence sections; second only to the crewfinders section itself. Headed by the fearsome Captain Rupert Bligh, and consequently known as the *Bounty* to all who served in it, recruitment specialized in finding and employing the best officers and crews in the world. Watch officers and engineering officers, cadets and so forth. Training them and employing them on long-term contracts too – not short-term emergency-fix 'any crewmember anywhere in the world replaced within 24 hours' stuff like crewfinders specialized in. Recruitment specialized in finding more than officers. It found ship's architects and engineers capable of designing, building and improving every kind of ocean-going vessel. And it had its work cut out. Heritage Mariner financed, built, contracted, crewed and employed vessels from pleasure boats for weekend sailors to VLCCs. From the Fastnet-winning *Katapult* series of racing multihulls through the SuperCats that ferried passengers across the Channel, the Great Lakes, the mouth of the Amazon and beyond. Through the *Atropos* dangerous waste transport vessels and the *Sissy* series of ocean-going tugs to the *Titan* series of crude-carrying submarines and the massive *Prometheus* series of supertankers. Recruitment scoured colleges, schools, universities, navies, competitors and personnel sites worldwide, 24/7, 365 days a year. Rupert Bligh would be less than happy to be employing his crack team to find a couple of butlers, some housekeepers and a flock of parlour maids. 'Like using a Maserati as a muck spreader!' Robin said.

'Do you know, that's exactly what Rupert said,' laughed Richard. 'But I told him how important it was. And he knows which side his bread's buttered on.'

'Hmmm. I'm sorry to have missed out on that conversation. Did you actually mention bread and butter? Not salt beef and hard tack? No one raised the cat o' nine tails?' There was a brief silence as the pounding of the rain eased further and the gloom within the car eased further still. 'So this little trip is actually a cunning plan to get me out of the wrathful Rupert's way, is it? Or to stop me interfering in recruitment, making sure they want to find me the kind of staff I'd want to employ myself?'

'They'll have a short-list for you when you get back. Then you can interfere all you want. And you know Rupert's bark is worse than his bite.'

'Tell that to the poor souls in the *Bounty*!'

The Rolls was sweeping down St Andrews now, like one of the lesser Queens leaving her berth. Robin's view was of the towers of City Hall and the Supreme Court behind the frontages they shared with the Raffles of tall palms and strictly regimented tropical undergrowth. Richard looked across the Padang, where rain had stopped play, between the Recreation Club and the Cricket Club to where the veils of misty downpour were withdrawing towards Connaught Drive.

'Wherever, whenever and whatever this surprise is, I hope it involves something to eat quite soon,' said Robin. 'Peanuts and Lapsang Souchong in the Long Bar won't help this girl recover from the better part of twenty-four hours of airline food. Even Hong Kong Airlines food.'

Richard leaned forward and snapped open a panel beside the opposite seat. A little bar folded out. 'Sorry,' he said, rummaging around within. 'Looks like more peanuts. Roasted and salted.'

'That'll do to be going on with,' Robin answered brusquely. 'And is that a baby bottle of Bollinger beside the Perrier there?'

As Robin nibbled the nuts and sipped the champagne, the Rolls swept along the steaming expanse of Parliament Lane between the back of the Parliament building and the frontage of the theatre. The Empress Palace Building loomed on Richard's side, and beyond that, at the bottom of the slope, the expanse of the Singapore River, also steaming in the post-downpour afternoon humidity.

Richard knew Robin would have had a shrewd suspicion of where they were heading.

23

None of the buildings they had passed held any obvious attraction – not even the theatre and music hall, and Robin knew Singapore perhaps even better than he did himself. Though the last time she had spent any time here was at the time of the Hong Kong hand-back when she had come here trying to prove him innocent of murder. In those days this had been one of the stop-off points on the circular routes of the China Queen shipping company which Heritage Mariner had briefly owned as part of a slightly longer Far Eastern venture. But Heritage Mariner had never quite made it into the Noble House league alongside Jardine Matheson; and Richard had never quite become Tai Pan. Although, Sir Francis Drake's treasure chest, which Richard had brought back from Tiger Island soon after, still resided in the vaults of Coutts & Co., his bankers in London. And it was still full of treasure. Perhaps *money* was indeed *no object*, just as Nic had said.

Certainly, Robin showed no surprise at all when the Rolls drew up alongside its companion at the very start of North Quay Road, where Parliament Lane swung right along the river's edge with the white statue of Raffles standing determinedly at the Raffles Landing Site. Here, beside the statue itself, an exclusive little covered pathway led down to a private pier. 'You didn't bring me all this way just for a really good meal, then,' she said as Richard hurried her forward through the suffocating humidity. Oblivious to the steamy heat, she

24

held back a little, looking longingly at the restaurants and bumboats which were beginning to stir with early night life all along either side of the river from here to Clarke Quay. Then she gave in and let him pull her back on to the air-conditioned walkway. 'This had better be worth waiting for, buster,' she finished threateningly.

But in fact, by both of their calculations, the sight that awaited them down on the landing stage was well worth waiting for. Nic had wisely chosen to clothe himself in linen, money being no object and the heat really quite testing. Well-pressed linen with just a hint of stiffening here and starching there can hold its shape like the sturdiest worsted, though it becomes fashionably wrinkled in places. If a linen suit gets wet, however, it holds its shape and style slightly less forcefully than a bath-flannel. Nic Greenbaum looked less like Santa Claus and more like the Snowman, suddenly; but at least he seemed to see the funny side of his predicament.

Not so the glorious Inge. Silk, like cotton, can become treacherous when wet. Now the white stripes that had defined her curves so stylishly were pink ones that revealed them all too clearly. Showed with every movement of her lithe form, the way she had shoe-horned herself into a black lace basque, uplifting enough to deepen her cleavage and tight enough to narrow her waist. And, had Richard not been a gentleman born and bred, he might have noticed like the

25

revengeful Robin just how precisely the black thong that Inge favoured below the clasp of the basque was defined by pink stripes clinging and straining before and behind. Especially behind.

'Here you are,' snapped Inge. Then she added, after a beat which just might have contained the phrase *at last*, 'Now we may proceed.'

'After you,' said Richard automatically. Only to find himself on the receiving end of an amused glance from Nic and an old-fashioned look from Robin.

Inge led them across a little pier and down a short gangway into a roomy slipper launch. She was handed aboard by an imperturbable Indonesian sailor in a white cotton uniform. An inscrutable Orang Laut who did not even seem to notice how much of her was on show. He and his three companions settled all their passengers safely aboard before casting off and revving up the powerful engines until the launch was bouncing out into the steady flow. Like something that might indeed have taken Jeeves and Wooster across Southampton Water – or the East River for that matter – the launch sped away from the landing stage. Sir Stamford Raffles, rendered in white stone, watched them from his plinth as they roared along the waterfrontage of the Empress Palace building and under the wrought-iron frontage that announced this as the Cavenaugh Bridge. Then Raffles passed out of sight behind them as they swung left with the river and under the Fullerton Road Bridge immediately beyond.

After the Fullerton Building and the Road Bridge, the launch swung sharply right around the point at Merlion Park, before scudding determinedly out of the river mouth. For an instant, Robin thought they were going hard round into the Telok Ayer Basin, where the container terminal was, and the anchorages for the container ships such as the Sulu and Seram Queens – ships that had come so close to killing both her and Richard back in the days of the Hong Kong handover.

But no. The launch swung to the left again as one of the crewmen spoke rapidly into his hand-held radio, communicating with the harbour master or someone at their destination or both. The shipping of a busy anchorage came and went before them. Even the ships at anchor seeming to take motion as the launch raced past. Container vessels of every design, shape and size, with their attendant lighters, tugs and bumboats pushed in and out of the basin. Ferries came and went to and from Clifford Pier. Further out in the roads all manner of shipping was sailing from the East Anchorage to the West and back again, or around to Pasir Pajang and Jurong.

Beyond the ships, boats, yachts and junks, the Singapore Strait and the Java Sea heaved a restless, stormy grey. And above the waters hung the retreating ranks of the thunderclouds, falling southwards back to Sarawak.

Robin glanced across at Richard and was simply shocked by the childlike excitement in his face. Like her, he was searching the timeless dazzle of the shipping out in the roads, almost as though he expected to see Lord Jim hailing down from the foredeck of the doomed *Patna*. Or Almayer, Tom Lingard, McWhirr, Marlow or even Joseph Conrad himself might sail past, ghostlike, somewhere near, and sometime soon. But then she realized that, incurably romantic though Richard was, his excitement now went beyond the avid reading and endless dreaming of his youth. His excitement was for something more vital and immediate. And when his eyes met hers she knew. It was her surprise. He was looking for her surprise.

And, suddenly, unexpectedly and overwhelmingly, she was excited too. She surveyed the bustling seascape anew, no longer a tired and world-weary sailor butting across yet another crowded port, but a little girl again on Christmas morning looking amongst the bright wrapped mysteries beneath the Christmas tree. And, just with the very thought, like the fairy lights coming on, the sun burst through the overcast. Blades of brightness chopped through the scene, sweeping like spotlights over numberless, nameless vessels, turning them into a kind of maritime magic show.

Until, there, right in the middle of the anchorage dead ahead, the westering sun illuminated one particular vessel. Robin was on her feet, legs spread and thighs tensed against the rocking, thudding pitching of the launch as it raced towards the bright white vision. Her right

28

fist closed with thoughtless force upon the merino of Richard's tropical-suit shoulder. Her breath held pent in her breast and her eyes wide. Such was her focus dead ahead that she had no idea that the others were watching her.

'What is that?' she breathed. But her words were snatched away by the gusting headwind, the rushing wake and the grumbling throb of the motors. 'What is that?' she repeated. Although she already knew the answer.

Nic laughed aloud, sharing her simple joy, not mocking her stunned expression. She had an impression of Inge standing beside her, hair whipping back in the wind, like a Valkyrie heading for Valhalla. But it was Richard who answered.

'That's the next bit of your surprise, darling.'

It was simply the most beautiful vessel that Robin had ever seen in her life.

Three

Tai Fun

Tai Fun swung easily at her mooring, secured to the buoy assigned to her by the Singapore harbour master's office when she first made contact last night. She had arrived with the dawn, sent some tourists ashore in the launch soon after, had restocked by mid-afternoon, retrieved her drenched and dripping shore party by teatime and was all set to sail now. As soon as the last few guests arrived aboard. Guests worth waiting for: the owner's daughter and the passengers destined to occupy the Royal Suite and the Presidential Suite that sat on either side of the Owner's Suite. The three huge new suites made an exclusive trio on the aft upper passenger deck behind the Starlight Bistro which stood in turn behind the navigation bridge. The suites all had exclusive balconies and overlooked, in steps down one, two and three decks below, the after sun deck, the main pool and the water sports platform aft of that.

Luggage, marked Hong Kong Airlines via Changi International, had arrived with the supplies at noon and the Filipino stewards had

30

already unpacked and stowed the contents in drawers, wardrobes and cupboards that would have accepted twice as much with ease.

Everything was going like clockwork, precisely to plan and bang on schedule. And yet Nils Nordberg was uncharacteristically nervous. He turned to Captain Olmeijer, but the Dutchman had crossed to the far side of the open bridge to talk to the radio operator. 'How long, Captain?' he called.

'They report that they can see us, Mr Nordberg. We will see them in a moment.' The owner and his captain spoke in English and addressed each other formally on the bridge. In private they were Nils and Tom; sometimes they spoke Dutch and sometimes Swedish. Sometimes they drank advocaat and sometimes schnapps; but more often Amstel beer. They had known each other and *Tai Fun* since the ship had slid like a swan down the slipway of Ateliers and Chantiers shipyards at Le Havre. The three of them, it seemed, had been good friends ever since. *Tai Fun*, star of the High Wind shipping line, had never had another name, another owner or another captain. And if, on this cruise, she gained a new owner, Nils Nordberg was keen to ensure that the captain stayed the same. But even considering selling *Tai Fun* was all too close in Nils's mind to prostituting his beloved daughter. He had not expected things to become so complicated, so personal or so difficult. He swallowed and found that his throat was dry.

'We have them in sight, Mr Nordberg. They will be aboard in a quarter-hour.'

'Very well. Lower the port-side accommodation ladder when you see fit, please, Captain.'

'It has been lowered all day, sir.'

'Of course. How could I have forgotten? I will greet them there.'

He had forgotten, he realized, because of his gathering, hopefully groundless, worry.

Ten minutes later, Nils Nordberg was standing on the little welcome platform that projected through *Tai Fun*'s side two decks below main deck level. At his feet, a gangway reached down two more decks to the surface of the anchorage where another little platform held the launch safe while its four passengers disembarked. Disembarked and embarked both at once. Inge came up first, which was unusual. Her face was dark with some ill-contained irritation that compounded her father's concern. But she stepped past him on to *Tai Fun* and stopped. Turning courteously to make her formal introductions – as though anyone here could be unfamiliar to the others. But there were formalities to be observed; and in any case, wasn't there a famous film star who always introduced himself in spite of possessing a universally recognized face? It was a way of breaking the ice; of putting people at their ease.

Robin Mariner came up next and paused to give Nils an infectious grin as Inge introduced them. 'This is simply the most beautiful vessel I have ever seen,' said Robin. Her grey eyes were exactly level with Nils's and they sparkled with an open excitement that he found charmingly irresistible. Until it occurred to him what an excellent business ploy such apparent openness might be.

'Absolutely,' agreed Richard, who succeeded her almost at once, towering over his host and pumping his hand exuberantly. 'Even more graceful in the flesh than in the pictures I have seen.'

'She's just as lovely inside,' promised Inge, gesturing him aboard.

'Looks like an expensive lady,' concluded Nic, with a twinkle and a glance that seemed to take in both *Tai Fun* and Inge at once. 'But I'd bet my bottom dollar she's worth every cent.'

'She and all her sisters,' confirmed Nils like the proudest paterfamilias.

'I thought you were an only child,' said Robin, following Inge up towards their suites. For different reasons, each of the women wanted to shower and change as a matter of some urgency. At the very least, neither felt ready to face the officers, crew and other guests at drinks or dinner, the one due within the hour, the other within two. The rain, wind and spray had not been kind to hairstyles. Robin still felt as though she was dressed in a plum-coloured tissue-paper bag; and her travelling slacks were very much the worse for wear. Inge's flesh and underwear were still all too obvious beneath her damp business suit, and her open-toed sandals were on the verge of falling apart. The one followed the other, therefore, through the gathering bustle of the common parts as the accommodation ladder was raised, the launch attached to its falls and brought aboard and *Tai Fun* prepared to cast off and come under power. Robin was content to follow the statuesque girl, certain of their destination without further question. The men had gone off together like a gang of boys about some adventure, no doubt to watch or oversee some part of any of the activities leading towards *Tai Fun*'s imminent departure. *Boys and toys,* she thought. Still and all, *Tai Fun* was one hell of a toy.

'I am an only child,' Inge answered Robin, flinging the words over one shoulder. 'Father was talking about *Tai Fun*'s sisters. They're all named after great winds. There's *Mistral*, *Sirocco* and *Monsoon*. There was another sister, poor *Chinook*, but she burned in San Francisco harbour last year.'

Robin nodded. 'The High Wind fleet. Yes, I know them.'

'I should think you would,' said Inge, her tone unreadable. Her face unreadable also as she stopped on the top step of the gangway and turned fully to look down into Robin's enquiring face. 'Especially as you've come all this way to buy them.'

So both Nic and Richard missed out on the flabbergasted look on Robin's countenance as she digested the next element of Richard's big surprise.

As they rode up in the lift, Robin stood frowning and silent. She simply did not know what to say – any more than she knew what to think. When she saw *Tai Fun* it was love at first sight. If she had thought anything then, as she stood entranced in the launch, it was that Richard had found her the most perfect holiday, MNO perhaps. He was hardly noted for his sensitivity or insight but every now and then he certainly could give her something she hadn't even realized she wanted. At first glance, this seemed to be the case today. He had pulled her out from under a load of work that, in her still exhausted post-Archangel state, was threatening to overwhelm her. He had whirled her halfway round the world to what appeared at first glance to be her idea of utter, blissful heaven. But this was something else again. To buy her a holiday was one thing. To buy the whole sodding fleet...

What was the bloody man thinking? That he could make a great deal here, obviously. A great deal and a great deal of money.

Well, at least it explained Nic Greenbaum.

'The lift's incredibly quiet,' she said, just for something to say.

'Electric motor,' answered Inge. 'Generated onboard. We use almost no hydrocarbons or fossil fuels. We're completely self-sufficient with regard to power and everything else aboard except for chandlerage and supplies.

And even that's all local – no air-miles whatsoever.' Inge looked across at Robin, her face suddenly full of simple pride. 'This is the greenest ship in the world,' she concluded. 'The most environmentally friendly form of transport ever designed.'

And suddenly everything began to make perfect sense to Robin.

So that when Richard tapped on the door of the Royal Suite and caught her in her terry-towelling robe halfway to the shower, she was able to cut straight to the chase.

'This is very comfortable,' he said approvingly the moment that she let him in. 'Functional but neat. Roomy. All mod cons and then some.' He picked up a banana from the basket of complimentary fruit on the table. 'Red bananas,' he said, peeling it. 'They're a local delicacy, I understand.' He crossed to the windows at the rear of the suite and looked down over the balcony there. 'No one on the sundeck,' he observed. But there's a die-hard or two in the pool. Nice view of Singapore. Have you looked?'

'You reckon these vessels are wave of the future, don't you?' demanded Robin by way of answer. '*Katapult* multihulls turned into cruise ships? The Archangel business sent afloat?'

'They're everything Heritage Mariner has stood for for years,' he replied, happy to pick up the conversation as though he had been privy to the thoughts that engendered it. 'They're part of

36

our corporate image. Or could be at the drop of a hat! Big but ecologically friendly, that's us. The best for our clients, our employees, our partners, stakeholders and shareholders. But most of all *best for the world that we live in*! And the High Wind fleet fits right into the heart of all that. We couldn't have come up with anything better if we'd designed them and built them ourselves! Don't you see? Heritage Mariner has to grow or die. Your father admitted that when he handed over to me and went off to the Château du Four in Grimaud for a well-earned and sybaritic retirement. And cruising is a growing market as long as you can soothe people's worries about the carbon footprint of flying. But this is the perfect package. Carbon-neutral airlines – as near as they can be – getting people to Singapore, San Francisco, Santander or Suez. *Mistral, Sirocco, Monsoon* or *Tai Fun* to pick them up! Cruise them up to Alaska, all around the Caribbean, up and down the Med and right through the Java Sea. Down to Oz and back if we can swing it. And they're not even carbon neutral! They're *carbon positive*. Even allowing for the flight out, every single client will be in carbon credit by the end of the first week. It's amazing!'

Tai Fun heaved gently in the first deep-water swells of the Singapore Strait. Other than the rolling of the waves, there was utter calm. The departing storm had left dead air between here and Sarawak. And almost complete silence. Robin cocked her head, making a pantomime of listening to something, and raised an eyebrow. There was the faintest whine of electrical power, the familiar grumble of motors. 'What about that lot?' she said. 'Engines and electrical motors. Doesn't sound all that carbon positive to me. And look at all this lot.' She gave a speaking gesture that encompassed the Bose radio iPod-and MP4-player-compatible sound system, the laptop ports and Bluetooth network system, the Internet, the TV and DVD system. All state of the art, all very power-hungry. 'And look.' She crossed back to the bed and passed her hands over sections of the consoles there. Lights came on and dimmed, curtains swept shut and open again across the big double doors leading out on to the balcony whose rails seemed to contain the lights of Singapore like the frames on a three-part panorama of stars in the night sky. 'Carbon positive?' she demanded sceptically.

'But it is!' insisted Richard. 'I'll show you after dinner. It's not something I want to waste time explaining. It's something I want you to see!' He began to strip off his travelling suit with restless impatience. 'Have you showered?'

'Just going to. You'll have to wait a moment.'

'No, I won't. I've a shower en suite as well. But I'll come in and shave while you wash off.'

'As long as shaving is all you have in mind, buster. I know you and showers of old. Dinner's in less than an hour and this girl has no intention of turning up late.'

Four

First Night

Richard and Robin missed drinks, but made dinner right on time. Richard had not come here unprepared. Keeping secrets from Robin made his preparations more difficult, but he had taken care to be as thorough as usual. He had been through the design plans of *Tai Fun* long ago – and the plans of her sisters come to that – as well as the last published accounts of the High Wind shipping company. So he knew his way around the beautiful vessel as certainly as he knew his way round her owner's finances – it was as if he had sailed aboard many times before. And even if he hadn't been so confident of the way, once he and Robin reached the common parts on the next deck down, all they had to do was follow a couple of hundred of their fellow passengers to the restaurant.

Richard didn't drink, and Robin had been content to sip something from the contents of her bar fridge as she sat and perfected her makeup at a vanity table worthy of the pickiest Hollywood starlet. They set out for the restaurant as soon as the dinner chimes sounded, therefore, and had no trouble at all finding the place or, once they were there, their host and his captain.

The other voyagers assigned to the captain's table had assembled half an hour earlier for drinks in the Casino Bar, however, so Richard and Robin suffered the fate of late-comers at any social event. They seemed at first to be presented with a group of people who all already knew each other, and had apparently been acquainted for years. Although some of them clearly knew each other well, others did not. Richard and Robin just had to work out which group was which, and fit themselves in accordingly. Adept though they both were at breaking down such barriers and establishing themselves as amusing and companionable guests, an uneasy feeling that all was not quite as it seemed here lingered, in Robin's mind at least. Lingered until she began to think it was more than a mere impression. Lingered until she really began to suspect that there were people amongst this group of apparently relatively new acquaintances who were hiding a different and deeper relationship.

Robin's first glance around the assembled group explained Inge's care with her looks and her suit this afternoon at once. For there, gazing at Nils Nordberg with a focus of interest that bordered on the worshipful, was the most beautiful woman Robin had ever seen. Thick locks of hair, so brown as to be almost black, coiled down on to a perfectly sculpted shoulder like the Serpent of Eden embracing Eve. Broad shoulders rested on a breathtakingly formed, athletic-looking frame that the diaphanous green silk of the sari-style couturier dress did little to conceal. 'Ah, Richard and Robin,' called Nils as they approached, and the girl beside him turned to reveal a face that would have graced a big-budget movie. Opposite Brad Pitt, maybe. The eyes were almost as dark and sensual as the hair, but they had highlights of gold and green. Eyes like that belonged in a jungle, thought Robin. In the face of a tiger or a panther. 'Introduction time,' continued Nils. 'Firstly, this is Gabriella Cappaldi. Robin and Richard Mariner. Gabriella is our new entertainments officer and seems to be settling into her position quite admirably. This is Captain Olmeijer and his newly appointed second officer Lieutenant Eva Gruber, who is also our navigator on this voyage, I understand. You know my daughter Inge, of course...'

Robin drifted through the rest of the formalities on autopilot, her focus on the breathtaking duo of Gabriella and Inge. Individually each was breathtaking. Together they set each other off like ice and fire. Like the competent-looking but achingly young and dumpy Eva Gruber, she suspected, she would have been happy to hate either or both of the women for their head-turning beauty alone. Even before she took into account the manner in which the pair of them seemed to turn all the men into drooling schoolboys and render all other women there – herself included – somewhere between irrelevant and invisible. But there was quite enough tension between the pair of them already. It would be pointless to add her own petty spite to what looked suspiciously like a duel to the death.

Captain Olmeijer had a table of eight. All the rest of the tables in the restaurant were for two or four. The captain sat at the head. On his right sat Robin and on his left Inge. Beside Robin sat Nic and opposite him, beside Nils's daughter, sat Richard. Beside Richard sat Gabriella who was separated from Eva, sitting opposite, by Nils at the table's foot.

'So, ladies,' began Richard at once, looking left at the two officers. 'One of you decides where we are going and the other decides what we do when we get there.'

'Well...' began Eva, brightening, like a debutante unexpectedly addressed by the most eligible bachelor in the room.

'Not just when we get there,' purred Gabriella overriding her. 'I must keep you entertained on the way, as well you know!'

'As a matter of fact...' Eva tried again, flushing to the roots of her mousy hair but egged on a little perhaps by the sympathetic smile that Richard shot her.

'Particularly,' persisted Gabriella, 'as most of the locations that we are scheduled to visit have many attractions of their own. At Singapore, for instance, all I had to do was make sure there was a ride into port and a guide to meet our travellers.'

'A guide with a large umbrella, I hope,' inserted Nic with a laugh, glancing from Gabriella to Inge and back again. 'Did you go ashore yourself?'

'Not on this occasion. I know Singapore well, of course, but I had a meeting with Mr Nordberg and we felt I had better prepare an itinerary of particular interest for the next ten days or so, as we were expecting you and Captain Mariner aboard.'

As they talked to each other, they had been glancing through the bill of fare. Conversation waned a little as Filipino waiters arrived to take their orders. As Nic was leaning slightly forward, hanging on Gabriella's words and apparently trying not to fathom her cleavage too obviously, Robin leaned back and caught young Eva Gruber's eye. 'But you are the one who decides where we actually go?' she asked quietly.

Eva smiled self-deprecatingly, looking more like a schoolgirl than a ship's officer. 'Oh, no! The schedules are drawn up at Head Office in Stockholm...'

'We combine planning for the interests of our guests,' explained Captain Olmeijer, leaning forward earnestly, 'with the requirements of keeping *Tai Fun* stocked with fresh local produce. Would you prefer wine or champagne, Mrs Mariner?'

'Wine, please. But I suppose that wine can hardly be really local...'

'Limestone Coast shiraz, Mrs Mariner. Australia is the nearest major wine producer. And we have it shipped – literally shipped, not flown.'

'The champagne? They don't make Bollinger in Australia. Nor Indonesia as far as I'm aware.'

'Shipped again,' supplied Inge earnestly. 'With such things it is the regularity of supply that is paramount, not the speed of delivery. Though of course we remain aware of distance.'

Captain Olmeijer took up the explanation gracefully. 'The whisky, for instance, is Suntory, shipped from Japan, and most of the spirits behind the bar come from Japan or China. But the food is local.' He glanced at Inge and she nodded, emphasizing the point. Robin glanced across at Richard. He appeared to be listening to Gabriella but she was certain he was missing nothing of this either. 'The meat and poultry come from the larger islands that we visit,' Captain Olmeijer continued, 'from carefully monitored local suppliers who work to the highest health and safety standards. The fish comes from a much wider range and allows us to pass some of your tourist euros and dollars to much less industrialized locales.'

'I see you have elected to begin your meal with the tiger prawns,' added Inge. 'They are farmed in a bay near one of the islands we shall visit in a week or so if all goes well. It is called Pulau Baya. It is a tiny place and largely unspoilt, but it nevertheless appreciates the work and finance we bring. And the ruler, Prince Sailendra, makes the best possible use of it all,

I am told.' She looked at Captain Olmeijer, who took over the explanation once again

'Certainly, Pulau Baya is becoming a well-established source not only for the prawns but also for island rice – literally Pulau rice – and commercially useable seaweed. The starfruit, guava, mangos and zuzurat you may have noticed in your fruit bowls came from the same source. They also produce durian, which is available on request. You may have noticed the red bananas in the complimentary fruit basket in your suite. They come from the same island. But the Prince has also just completed some less traditional work. There is now a decent-sized pier which protects a promising-looking marina. Also there are protected facilities for our water-sports enthusiasts, independently of the white-sand tropical beaches further along the coast. They set some film or other there recently. That brought in yet more foreign currency. It is one of our most popular ports of call. A considerable commercial combination, Pulau Baya and Prince Sailendra. And one that we are happy to support...'

Inge leaned forward a little, her face flushed with the wine. 'The Prince is apparently something of a pin-up,' she half whispered. 'Western-educated, but strongly traditional in many ways. I saw the publicity stills from the film in a magazine. He fitted right in with all the film stars, men and women!'

The tiger prawns arrived. They had been coated with a tempura batter full of coconut and chilli vermicelli and deep-fried to crisp, golden perfection. Presented on a bed of succulent palm leaves, they seemed more like art than food. But they tasted even better than they looked. As she ate, Robin persisted in her attempts to get poor little Second Officer Gruber to finish a sentence. She stood a better chance now, as the conversation at the table had become more general and interruptions therefore less likely. 'So the First Officer's on watch? Don't you run a standard watch system?'

'Yes. And yes, we do. Though that is a contradictory answer, I know. We run standard watches. The Captain and First Officer normally attend dinner between seven and nine. It is my watch six to midnight, though we will sometimes dog it, I suppose. I have only been aboard a week or so; I am not used to everything yet. I am not used to ... all this...' Eva waved a pair of chopsticks, impaling a prawn, and vaguely signifying the restaurant with its crowd of diners.

'Really? You surprise me,' answered Robin drily. 'So why the change tonight? Balancing numbers at the captain's table? Three boys need three girls? Or is it your input as navigating officer that's required?'

'Perhaps. But the First Officer is sailing master and he's needed on the bridge tonight.'

'I see,' said Robin, although she didn't really.

The empty salad plates vanished. The main-course choices began to arrive. Robin had selected Indonesian lamb, expecting the satay

46

sauce to be peanut-flavoured. Honey and curry came as a surprise, but not an unpleasant one. She was glad to have gone for coconut rice, though, rather than the Singapore noodles popular with the rest.

Five

Sailing Plans

'So, Navigating Officer, where do you plan to take us?' Richard joined in the conversation suddenly, leaving Gabriella and Nils fixated on each other to the exclusion, apparently, of noodles, lamb and Australian shiraz alike.

'*Tai Fun* averages ten knots, Captain Mariner. The electric motors allow us relative freedom from wind and current, so we can draw up fairly reliable itineraries. Our current destination, for instance, is Pontianac in Kalimantan. We have tonight, your first full day at sea tomorrow and then tomorrow night. When you awake the next morning we will be making landfall. During day two, after some fun and games aboard, guests may visit Pontianac and explore the city as well as the river there while we stock up again, especially with coffee. We plan to over-night there...'

'You will be surprised at the night life. The food in the Korem is fantastic!' inserted Gabriella. 'But of course everyone will return aboard to sleep.'

'And when you awake next day, day three, we

48

will be cruising down to the Tanjung Puting National Park,' continued Eva, her voice raised slightly against the interruption. Her Singapore noodles waved colourfully at the end of chopsticks that set the beat of her words as though she were conducting what she said.

But once more Gabriella inserted her tourist-guide information. 'We have arranged to register our park visit for everyone aboard at Pontianac instead of Pangkalanbun. For the adventurous wildlife enthusiast the Tanjung Puting National Park is heaven on earth. Un-spoilt virgin rainforest. Orang-utan, especially at Camp Leakey; owa-owa, proboscis monkeys. All manner of snakes and reptiles. Monitors. Three-metre crocodiles in the rivers. Some say five-metre ones have been seen and even larger than that. And the bird life...'

Eva reasserted herself again. At the point of her chopsticks she had impaled a chunk of lamb as though it were the heart of her opponent across the table. 'That night we will head due east across the Java Sea, once again enjoy a full day's sailing on day four and overnight aboard, so that you will awake upon your fifth morning as we come into port at Makassar.'

But Eva stood no chance against Gabriella, whose nostrils flared at the mention of Makassar like those of a thoroughbred at the off. 'We will spend the day here allowing our histori-cally orientated guests to explore Fort Rotterdam and the old city. Those who are missing Singapore already will go through the

Chinese Quarter. Anyone wishing to acquire more expensive souvenirs at reasonable prices can immerse themselves in the gold markets of Jalan Somba Opu district. We have arranged in particular pete-pete transport for everyone up to Paotere harbour so that we can prepare you for later sections of the voyage by introducing you to the Bugis native islanders and their great ocean-going praus, once upon a time the most feared pirate vessels of the Java Seas. Now, alas, simple trading boats. Finally, for those who wish to linger, and crave a little night life, there is Pantai Losari. The roadside food stalls must be experienced to be believed. Then we sleep aboard, of course...'

As Gabriella set out her plans for Makassar, the plates were cleared away again and great bowls of fruit were placed on the table. There were sorbets and ice creams flavoured with local delicacies – mango, pawpaw, pomegranate. And, inevitably, thought Robin, coffee. And there was, of course, more coffee still to drink. Thick and black and as fragrant as perfume. This was, near as dammit, Java, after all...

'Before departing with the morning tide of our sixth full day,' Eva completed brusquely, lifting a fragrant cup to her lips, 'to sail south round the isthmus of Pulau Selayar and away again eastwards into the legendary Banda Sea. After that it's up to you.' She glanced across at Captain Olmeijer, suddenly aware that she had become a little carried away; emphasizing yet again how new and unfamiliar all this was to her. 'The winds and the currents will influence things too, of course.' A final, almost furtive glance at the owner sitting immediately to her right. 'And there will, naturally, be input from Stockholm.' Then she turned back to Richard and Robin, her face still aglow with the romance of what she was promising. 'But we have the freedom of the sea after Makassar.'

'What about this place Pulau Baya that Captain Olmeijer was telling us about?' asked Robin. 'That sounds like it's well worth a visit.'

'That's south across the Java Sea from Makassar,' said Olmeijer. 'And we'd normally call in on the way back on a round trip. I don't know what Mr Nordberg has planned after Makassar, but we can certainly keep Pulau Baya in mind. The Moluccas, the Ceram Islands, even Irian Jaya, all lie only a few days' sailing further east...'

'And Prince Sailendra,' said Robin dreamily. 'He sounds like someone I'd very much like to meet.'

'It does sound romantic, darling,' admitted Robin half an hour later in their suite. 'I haven't even heard names like those outside the works of Joseph Conrad. And look at this!' She gestured grandly if not absolutely soberly towards the windows at the end of their accommodation. The tall double-glazed panes were full of velvet blue-black sky strewn with massive, pearly stars.

'But do you think it'll sound romantic to the
51

average cruising enthusiast? Is the romance as saleable as the eco-friendly message?'

'Well, let's get this conversation over and done with. I don't want it hanging over the promise of all the rest of our cruise together. I'd say so. Yes. It should appeal to all those people who loved *The Beach* – book and film. All those who want to come to Indonesia but are worried about the bombs in Manila and whatnot. *Tai Fun*'s a wonderful environment, though it could do with less *organizing* in my opinion. I don't know what the fares are like, but if you could offer something to the back-packers as well as the more mature adventure seekers, then I think you'd have cracked it. Why isn't Nils Nordberg coining it in, though? He seems to be pretty fast on his feet. And he can see the potential for these vessels just as clearly as you can. As clearly as Nic Greenberg. What's gone wrong for poor old Nils?'

'For a start, he seems to have been too much too soon. He's timed it badly and had a bit of bad luck. He's got the goods all right but he's ove-extended himself financially and can't afford to go the extra mile that'd move it into the main stream. And from what I can see, the loss of *Chinook* in San Francisco hit him really hard. Lost him the two big American markets he was after – up to Alaska and out to Hawaii. And he had insured his own bottom, so the loss was absolute. He's hard against the wall and looking for help.'

'But what he's got is you and Nic Greenberg

in something between a bidding war and a feeding frenzy.'

'Yup. That about sums it up, all right.'

'Would you rather bargain or buy?'

'If Nic wasn't here, I'd be cutting a deal. Heritage Mariner would want it all long term if we felt it was right for us. But short term, it'd be like it was with the *Katapult* series. Rights and royalties to the designers and original builders, with us moving in eventually and running it lock, stock and barrel. Nils could hang on to as much as he wanted for as long as he wanted, and vary the price accordingly. But Nic is a wild card. I don't know what he's up to.'

'At first glance he's not likely to be up to a hell of a lot, is he?'

'What do you mean?'

'Well, I know we do things differently to most. We still think small business rather than corporate giant. We go in, take a look and make up our own minds. Like we're doing now. But I can't see Nic Goldberg doing that. Richard Branson probably wouldn't and I'd bet my bottom dollar Bill Gates wouldn't. If they were even thinking of being serious, there'd be corporate lawyers from here to Honolulu, there'd be accountants, advisors, industrial-enquiry agents...'

'Good point. But I still think Nic's up to something...'

'He's as far up that Gabriella Cappaldi as she'll let him get.'

'Robin!'

'And I hope he's brought a ladder, 'cause I don't see her slapping him down at all.'

Robin collapsed almost spectacularly on to the big, crisp cotton-sheeted bed. 'I shouldn't have had so much coffee,' she announced. 'I don't feel sleepy at all.' She wriggled a little and her skirt slid almost magically up over her thighs.

'It isn't *coffee* you've had too much of,' Richard countered teasingly. Slipping off his jacket and easing his tie, he crossed to the star-packed French windows at the rear of their suite and slid them open. At once the atmosphere changed. The clinical calm of the air-conditioning was washed away by a wave of tropical humidity. The new wind was full of sea smells and spice. It heaved more restlessly than the waves over which it was running. It breathed, it whispered, it sang.

'Robin!' called Richard, turning. 'Quick. Your surprise!'

'There's *more*?' Robin sat up and slid forward, revealing even more underwear – much of it silkier and briefer – than Inge had done in the rainstorm.

'*Quick!*' Richard was at her side and reaching down.

'Oh all *right*,' she huffed, allowing him to pull her erect so that gravity could dress her properly again.

Side by side they hurried through the door and out into the short passage that joined the three uppermost suites. Richard almost ran

54

Robin through to the nearest door and, through it, on to the uppermost outer deck. Several metres in front of them was the bistro, a more casual dining area that housed any overflow from the restaurant below. The bistro opened on to an open deck area which in turn came up against the aft of the open bridgehouse.

At this time of night, only the bridgehouse was still occupied. The last sleepy waiter had piled the last bistro chair on the last bistro table. The final pair of casual diners had drifted below to sample the dregs of Gabriella's entertainment for the night. Apart from Richard and Robin, it seemed, only the stars were out. Apart from the pair of them, it seemed, only the wind was up. Robin found the restlessness of the tropic night more powerfully romantic than anything she could have imagined. Had she been lazily aroused before, now she was almost afire. All in an instant. *God! He knows me so well*, she thought, and swung towards him, reaching out for him almost blindly. 'Richard!' she whispered, scarcely louder than the wind.

'Sssssshhhhhh!'

'What?'

'SSSSSHHHHHH!'

His arms closed around her, but not in an embrace. He did not hug her, or kiss her or *take* her there and then as she had somehow most poignantly hoped he would. He bundled her across the deck into the shadow of one of *Tai Fun*'s tall masts. For, she suddenly began to realize they were not alone after all.

The ship heeled a little as the warm, fragrant wind intensified. In the brightness of the starlight two more figures were revealed. Nic Greenberg and Gabriella Cappaldi stood so close to each other that their heads were joined by one shadow. What they were whispering was lost beneath the growing business of the night breeze. And, had Richard and Robin felt like eavesdropping, they had no chance, for the other couple parted almost instantly and walked in opposite directions – one to port and forward towards the bridge, the other starboard and aft into the bistro.

'Richard...' Robin was still very willing to be overwhelmed by the utter beauty of the night. But even as she spoke, he took her in his arms precisely as she had desired.

'Darling...' She closed her eyes and pouted her lips and raised her face to his like a flower seeking sun.

'Wait!' he hissed. 'Watch. It gets better. *Your surprise!*'

Robin opened her eyes and blinked. Immediately above her towered the second of *Tai Fun's* four huge masts. It had been these tall white spears that had robbed her of her breath in Singapore's anchorage. That the ship they had come aboard could have the grace of an old-time clipper ship as well as all the modern conveniences of a cruise liner seemed just wonderful to her. It combined the luxury of modern cruising with the elegance of old-time sailing. But until now the masts had been bare. The diesel motors had chugged her off her moorings and the electric motors powered her since then. But now, as Richard had known they would, at the first sign of a steady wind, the sails themselves unfurled. Somewhere in the bridgehouse forward beyond the bistro, immediately behind the first of the four great masts, the sailing master pressed the button of his computerized sail controls. And with eerie speed, superhuman precision and breathtaking elegance, the four great sails spread out across the wind and snapped home. At once the whine of the electric motors stilled, the long hull leaned over like the *Cutty Sark*, and sped like an albatross across the Sunda Strait. The only sounds audible were the whisper of the wind, the snap of the sails and the rumble of the surf at her cutwater.

And the passionate gasping of Robin's breath. 'If you don't get me back to our cabin pretty quickly, buster,' she whispered, almost perfectly ecstatically, 'then you'll probably be too late!'

Six

Pulau Baya

Prince Sailendra was concentrating on the new map of his island so completely that he did not notice that the ground was shaking until the publicity photograph of himself and Johnny Depp on the white-sand, palm-fringed expanse of Bandar Laut beach toppled off his desk. No sooner had the sound of it shattering on the floor jerked the young prince out of his reverie than the door burst open.

'What is it, Parang?' demanded Sailendra. 'Some kind of earth tremor?'

'No, sir. I believe it is something worse. You must come.' Sailendra's secretary Parang was, like himself, young and Western-educated. He wore the same basic Western outfit as his employer, a silk shirt, cotton trousers and leather sandals. He had been appointed to his post because he was university-educated, son of a local family and utterly unflappable, and yet he was clearly shaken now. And not just by the movement of the ground. No sooner had the thought entered the young prince's head than a distant echoing rumbling began. Sailendra left the vision of Mr Depp and himself in sarong and turban looking very much like brothers among the shards of shattered glass and ran for the door.

The two men ran out of the prince's palace and into the compound outside. This took almost no time at all, for the palace was a one-storey building of traditional design, rendered palatial mainly by the acreage it covered. Palatial also in the position it had occupied since time immemorial, on a ledge of the mountain foothills that legend said had been carved by hand out of the living rock. Certainly, the ledge had been perfectly fashioned or wisely chosen. The palace looked over the tops of the tallest rainforest trees which still crowded the slopes below, commanding a view on the one hand of the lower mountain slopes and coast right round to the ancient but burgeoning city of Baya and on the other the lower, flatter teardrop tail of Pulau Baya over the banana groves, fruit farms and lower rice paddies towards Bandar Laut bay. Here, of course, Johnny Depp's film had been shot so cleverly that there was never any suspicion that the waters were actually an enormous prawn-fishery.

In the compound behind the palace sat Sailendra's current earthbound pride and joy, a massive Toyota four-wheel-drive all-terrain vehicle. No mere SUV, this was designed for genuinely hard off-road driving. Which was fortunate – the roads in Pulau Baya were still largely designed for use by men on foot or bicycle herding animals of various kinds. It had only been during the Second World War that wheeled vehicles powered by anything stronger than bullocks had come to Pulau Baya. Almost all the important routes for trade and communication here still had to cross the Java Sea. Sailendra was planning to take the Toyota up into the remoter areas of his island, looking for yet more ways of dragging Pulau Baya further into the twenty-first century, but that was something for the future. In the meantime, there was yet another crisis to overcome. And at least a part of it hit Sailendra in the face as soon as he raced outside like a challenging slap from a duellist. Solid though the big Toyota was, its outline was blurred by the shattering downpour all around. It was a tropical storm of truly epic proportions and utterly overwhelming power. Not only was the rain threatening to strip the paint off the Toyota's chassis, noted Sailendra grimly, it was tearing at the hard mud of the compound and threatening to rip it away. Then he was out in the full force of it himself and was all but knocked unconscious by the icy, agonizing weight of the water on his head and shoulders.

In the days of Sailendra's father, there would have been guards here – a ceremonial contingent at least. But Sailendra was of the opinion that his island princedom could ill afford such luxuries at the present time. In the absence of an actual army of any sort, honour guards were better employed in more productive ventures.

60

Or in strengthening the island's little police force and emergency service contingent at least. But he had a driver, and he too was pounding across the compound, alerted by his prince's sudden appearance in the thunderous down-pour.

'Where are we going, Parang?' demanded Sailendra, swinging open the nearest door – the rear one on the driver's side – and clambering in.

'The heliport,' called the secretary, following him. 'I'll give you more details as we go. The cellphones are down, for some reason. I know what I know from the radio.'

The third man leaped into the big Toyota. He was built like a Japanese Sumo wrestler but he had the dark skin of a Bandar Laut – a seafarer burned by the sun through countless genera-tions. His sarong was sopping and his turban dripped rivulets down the back of the seat. But his driving boots were made by Doc Marten and they were heavy on the pedals. The driver gunned the motor and they were off down the hill from the palace towards the coast. 'Where?' he bellowed with a traditional island lack of subservience.

'The heliport,' Sailendra answered. *To my other new toy*, he added in a cynical after-thought.

Like the Toyota, the helicopter and the facility needed to fly and maintain it were a present from Luzon Logging, one of the few business ventures Sailendra was hesitant about inviting

61

into his island paradise. One of the few businesses that felt the need to try a little low-key bribery, to get a foothold on the island, therefore. He was as well aware as anyone of the commercial value of the huge stands of mahogany and other, rarer and more valuable woods in the virgin rainforests up on the mountain slopes. But he was also aware of the speed with which neighbouring islands – far bigger and more powerful than Pulau Baya – had been stripped of their forests in the final years of the last millennium of Western time so that once-green ridges stood grey and naked now. For, by its very nature, virgin forest was almost impossible to renew. Sailendra had no firm grasp on how uncontrolled logging up on the peaks of his own princedom would damage the island's environment. And until the arrival of the chopper and the Toyota, there had seemed precious little practical chance of finding out. It seemed ironic that the men he refused so absolutely to allow on his island had sent him the means of exploring it further. It never occurred to him that by sending him driver and pilot as well as the vehicles they controlled, Luzon Logging could also keep some kind of control over where he went and what he saw. Such as the high forest, for instance.

Only some local tribesmen had really explored the wild and impenetrable upper areas along the peaks that were the backbone of the island since his grandfather's time, when they had briefly been full of Japanese and American soldiers fighting the Second World War. And the shy tribal elders had reported wreckage, corpses and strange magic spells that made the ground beneath the feet of even the wariest walker on the jungle tracks explode with deadly force.

'Well?' demanded Sailendra as the Toyota leaped down the hill from the palace like a frightened goat.

'Whatever it is, it seems to be on the western slope of Guanung Surat.' Parang looked up at the largest, closest mountain looming precipitously on their left, whose lower slopes formed the coast here. Formed the coast for the whole of this end of the island, indeed, its ridges becoming headlands, its valleys becoming bays. 'That's what Radio Baya reported just before it went off the air, at any rate. Before it went off the air *again*. We still have work to do with the new radio station...'

Sailendra closed his eyes, dismissing Parang's worries about the radio station, recalling the map he had been studying just before the crisis struck. It showed a curving teardrop of land some thirty kilometres long, ten wide at its broadest. It lay like a giant rocky tadpole in the Java Sea. The head of the island was formed by the great mountain of Guanung Surat, which rose precipitously into a series of ridges that reached like the spines of a dragon down to the tail. The map, one that Sailendra had recently commissioned, showed the towns and villages nestling round the coast and reaching hesitantly up into the rainforest. It showed the fisheries and the seaweed farms off the coast, the plantations that were opening up the lower spines below the towering Guanung Surat. It showed the one city, the port and capital of Baya, that they were heading for now. The city nestled at the mouth of the Sungai Baya River which itself came cascading down the mountainside and only gave a couple of kilometres of river plain to build upon before it plunged again into the deep-water bay.

'It is steep up there on Guanung Surat,' Sailendra said after a while. 'Could it be some kind of avalanche?'

The Toyota was at the coast now, swinging on to the best road on the island – the coast road into Baya City itself.

'It would need to be a big one to make the ground shake,' said Parang thoughtfully.

'It's been known,' supplied the driver. 'In the time of my grandfather, when the forests on the upper slopes had been damaged by American bombing. There was an avalanche in the year—'

'What the Westerners call 1945,' supplied Sailendra thoughtfully. 'My own grandfather told me of it. I remember now. But there has been no bombing. The rainforest is untouched.'

'There is rain like we have never known it,' pointed out Parang redundantly. 'It is this global warming everyone talks of and does nothing to stop. I have never known such rain. Nor has my father. Nor has my grandmother, who remembers General MacArthur standing on the beach at Baya.'

The beach at Baya appeared through the driving rain like the blade of a distant scimitar on their right hand now, as the first houses of the city itself appeared on the lower slopes on their left. The dome of the nearest mosque seemed to float hazily in the air above the greenery behind them. 'We will stop at the police and emergency services station first,' decided Sailendra. 'If there is anyone there, we may learn more.'

'You don't think the chief of police will have commandeered your helicopter by now?' asked Parang.

'I doubt it. He is a suitably law-abiding man and he knows as well as you do that it needs an order of permission from the council for anyone but me to take the chopper up. I really think some of those old men believe the thing is worked by some sort of evil magic.'

'Change has been slow to come to Pulau Baya, my prince,' soothed Parang with unusual formality. 'And now we have so much change happening so swiftly, it should come as no surprise that the wise heads of our elders sometimes yearn for the old ways of their fathers and their grandfathers.'

Even as the secretary spoke, the Toyota swept past the council building like a boat sweeping along a narrow river beside a tribal longhouse; which was, in effect, what it was. A figure leaped out from under the shelter of the overhanging, palm-thatched roof and slid into the beam of the headlights. The driver stamped on the brakes and the Toyota skidded to a halt. The figure wrenched the front passenger door wide and clambered aboard. His sarong and turban were almost as wet as the driver's but he was also wearing a heavily embroidered traditional jacket that seemed to have some waterproof qualities.

He turned round as the Toyota pulled away and looked back over the seat, his thin, high-cheekboned face twisting with disapproval as he saw what the prince and his secretary were wearing. But the matter of royal responsibilities and traditional costume could clearly wait. 'You go to take the *machine*?' he demanded. He spoke in language as traditional as his clothing. There was no word for helicopter in the traditional vocabulary and he refused either to use the Western alternative or to coin a new one as the others had done.

'Yes, Chief Councillor Kerian. It will take us to the source of the trouble most swiftly.'

'I thought as much. The chief of police has been to the Council House demanding the right to employ the machine on just such a mission.'

'And did you give him permission?'

'I am the servant of the council,' answered Kerian formally. 'Although I lead it, after your-self, of course Prince Sailendra, I cannot speak for it. No, I did not grant permission. He has gone about his business in his own official vehicle.'

'The Land Rover is a powerful piece of work,' said Sailendra. 'It will get him close to what is going on, I am sure. But why have you condescended to join us, Kerian?'

The chief councillor's reply never came for another figure leaped out into the headlights, gesturing. This one held a flashlight that he waved wildly and pointed towards a temporary road sign saying danger. The driver crushed the brakes to the floor and the Toyota skidded to a stop. The figure pounded at the window and the driver lowered it to reveal the streaming face of one of the young emergency officers trained to turn his hand to fire-fighting, police work or, in this case traffic management. 'Sungai Baya River has burst its banks,' he bellowed. 'The bridge is at great risk from the flood.'

'We have to reach the heliport,' called Sailendra decisively. 'If the bridge is still standing, we will risk it.'

'Very well, Your Highness. But proceed with the utmost care. And do not expect to come back along this road if the rain persists like this.'

Sailendra nodded and slapped the driver on the shoulder. 'Are you sure you want to remain with us, Kerian?' he asked as the Toyota eased forward. 'It would be a pity to wipe out the royal line and damage the council all at one blow.'

'As far as the landing place,' grated Kerian. His tone told the others he meant the landing place of the unnameable machine.

The Toyota was up to its axles in rushing water by the time it reached the up-slope of the big broad bridge. The driver gunned the motor and eased the rugged vehicle up on to the shaking span. Then, seeing clear road ahead over the hump to the other side, he gunned the motor and raced forwards as though this was the start of a race. And Sailendra, looking up-stream as the vehicle roared forward, saw that it was a kind of race indeed. A low wall of water was washing downstream with disturbing speed. Its oncoming face was brown and strewn with debris. Its crest was ivory yellow and carrying more than mere detritus from the lower forest slopes and the upper city. Any moment now it would smash into the balustrade of the bridge itself. It was impossible to calculate how much damage the weight of muddy water would do to the structure. But, the prince saw with utter, unbelieving horror, such a calculation was totally redundant. For on the crest of the oncoming wave, like battered, shattered, stout and war-scarred battering rams, sat the trunks of four great wild-forest trees.

And, in the moment of stark horror which was all that time allowed before they hit the bridge with the force of artillery shells, Sailendra realized that, in spite of what he had said and had believed up until now, they had all been carefully cut and trimmed. Someone was secretly logging up on the high mountain slopes after all.

Seven

Land

'Go!' shouted Sailendra, tearing his throat.

The driver needed no second bidding. His black Doc Martens kicked against the Toyota's floor plates. The big vehicle leaped forward on to the downslope of the bridge with enough force to hurl the passengers inside back against their seats. Chief Councillor Kerian and Secretary Parang both felt their backs and necks complaining at the impact. It was Sailendra's left shoulder that took the force as he stared horror-struck at the oncoming wall of water and the telltale naked logs at its crest.

'Did you see that?' he shouted to no one in particular.

'What?' shouted Parang, looking over at his prince but not yet registering what Sailendra could see.

'On the river...' shouted Sailendra so forcefully that even Kerian turned.

But in that moment, as the two men began to focus their eyes on the outer world, so the Toyota hit the flood-water on the far side of the bridge itself and a great muddy wave obscured their view.

'What was it?' asked Parang.

'Logs! In the water. *Logs!*' Sailendra slewed round in his seat, looking back up the slope of the bridge they had just come down. The moment that he did so, the first log hit the structure like an ancient battering ram. Both the ram and the bulwark shattered at the impact. The log itself reared up out of the wreckage it had caused but it could have been any tree trunk now, its suspiciously neat and trimmed shape battered away by the sturdy wood and brick-work of the span. Then the others rammed home as well and the bridge, the road, everything was whirled away through the southern section of the city towards the sea. Sailendra offered a silent prayer of thanks that this section of his city was still under construction. Precious few as yet lived downriver in the path of the flood.

'Logs?' called Kerian, when some semblance of calm returned after the grinding shriek of the bridge's death. 'They just looked like tree trunks to me.'

Sailendra swung round, frowning darkly. He closed his eyes as though he could rewind and replay the memory like a movie on the backs of his eyelids. But he could not. He saw only blackness and the picture would not come again. He had been certain. And now he was less so. But he knew how he could check on what he thought he had seen. Indeed, if there was logging going on secretly high on the mountain slopes, he was about to get into the

70

machine that would help him find it the most swiftly and certainly of all.

The helipad was the newest addition to Pulau Baya's increasingly busy building programme that was erecting and defining infrastructure all around them to foster and house the economic boom that was seemingly already promised to the island princedom. It was rudimentary, for Luzon Logging had given the chopper and the pilot, not the complete suite of facilities needed to maintain it. And Sailendra was reluctant to break into his carefully calculated budget – especially as it had been so difficult to get so much of it agreed with Kerian's more reactionary council members. But at least there was a security fence with a manned gate, a modest palm-thatched hangar and a proper concrete pad built out into the bay. The gate opened as soon as the Toyota loomed into the guard's vision and the helicopter itself was ready to go the instant the four-by-four slid to a halt beside it.

Sailendra knew little about such things but he understood that this was a Bell, among the smallest of their range. It would take three as well as the pilot. But Sailendra suspected one seat at least would remain empty. Still, he had to offer. 'Councillor Kerian. You are welcome to come and survey the damage...'

Surprisingly, Kerian seemed willing, if not precisely keen. 'It is my duty, Your Highness,' he answered ponderously, his voice straining under the triple assault of the Toyota's motor,

71

the cataclysm pounding on the roof and the gathering pulse of the chopper's rotors close above. 'I bear a heavy responsibility for the welfare of the island. Almost as weighty as your own...'

Sailendra was so surprised that it did not occur to him to be suspicious until very much later.

So the three dripping men piled into the Bell and the pilot gunned the motor, lifting off into the battering downpour as they strapped themselves in. 'Where to?' he demanded, his *baha indonesia* words coloured by his native Japanese accent.

'Up there!' Sailendra gestured towards the mountain slopes that stood louring over this section of the city immediately on their left.

'Are you sure?' The pilot seemed about to enter into a discussion, then he saw the look on Sailendra's face. He glanced back at the equally grim chief councillor, nodded, and they were off, without the need for radio contact with any airport authorities, flight controllers or air-traffic control, because of course there was none. The game little machine simply shrugged off the weight of water trying to crush it to the ground, skipped across the wind trying to blow its destruction and skimmed across the rooftops towards the all too near hill slopes.

On one side of the river lay the new buildings, still raw and largely untenanted, in stark contrast to the older sections of the city that reached up along the eastern bank. To the west, beyond the foaming torrent, the city looked like a cross between an out-of-town trading estate and a building site, all square, brutal and practical, its concrete brutality chopping into the steeper jungle slopes. To the east, the jungle-clad gradients, still almost steep enough to be called cliffs, closed over the outskirts more naturally, seeming to flow naturally in between the buildings. In contrast to the brutal west bank, on the east, palm-lined domestic thoroughfares broke up into more isolated neighbourhoods. The pattern of the city fragmented into individual buildings that climbed the green-clad buttresses, neighbourhoods becoming villages. Villages becoming individual houses. Houses giving way to mosques and temples. Then all sign of civilization giving way to the rearing green canopy whose only clear feature was the wild, foaming tumble of the swollen river.

Sailendra looked down broodingly. He knew well enough that there were roads, pathways and tracks below that seemingly featureless green on the west bank as well as on the east. In childhood, young manhood and more recently still he had followed so many of them, at first simply exploring what would one day become his, with a sense of pride and possession. Often as not at the side of his grandfather or father. Always with a contingent of bodyguards armed against the wild pigs, the long-horned deer and the clouded leopards that preyed on them. Armed, near the river, against the massive crocodiles. And securely booted – even on horseback – against the snakes and scorpions that swarmed in the undergrowth. In later days he had gone equally well dressed but less well escorted, trying to make some sort of a catalogue or asset list; keen to know his princedom for himself and unwilling to trust the all too helpful strangers who would offer to do the work for him. Strangers like Luzon Logging.

Independently of the bewildering range of precious woods that the trees represented, there was enormous wealth within the jungles. Wealth that needed husbanding and protecting, for it was at once enormously tempting and terrifyingly fragile. It was here he had discovered the sweet-and-sour red bananas they now grew in plantations further south. Here were the almost priceless and irreplaceable orchids whose carefully garnered offspring grew in the carefully guarded commercial enterprises nearer the coast. The various canes growing in the undergrowth, from bamboo to rattan; the fibres, from coir to hemp, old fashioned though they sounded – biodegradable, renewable and saleable again. They'd soon have gutta-percha and gum-dammar back on the market, he thought wryly. Well, they still shipped enormous amounts of Macassar-oil in the newly renamed Makassar away to the north across the Java Sea.

And that was all before he let the chemical companies and the loggers in. But no sooner had the thought arisen in his mind than he saw with simple horror that he had failed his virgin-rainforest protectorate after all.

'Parang, do you see that?' Sailendra called, scarcely willing to believe his own eyes.

'Loggers!' spat Parang, as horrified as his prince.

'Kerian?' Sailendra was so shocked that he forgot to accord the prickly councillor his full title. No doubt he would pay for the solecism later.

'How is this possible?' cried Kerian, seeming as horror-struck as the others.

'Down!' ordered Sailendra. 'As low as you can without landing!'

'I wouldn't land there anyway,' answered the pilot, addressing the prince as informally as Sailendra had addressed Councillor Kerian. 'If we go down too low we'll never get her up again.'

But the Bell settled lower on his word, allowing him to make out some details in the streaming darkness. Right along the upper ridge, though still well below the rearing thrust of the watershed peaks that towered above their right shoulders still, a swathe of jungle had been simply torn away.

'Down more!' yelled Sailendra, straining to make out detail in the pelting darkness. 'I need to see...'

The little Bell settled lower, until it seemed to Sailendra that her rotors beat between the tree-tops and her undercarriage hung beside the lower branches, tilting forward as it did so.

Then the pilot hit a switch that Sailendra could not see and the Bell's landing lights came on, illuminating the whole scene like searchlights. The two things combined to give Sailendra a grandstand view through the wildly whipping wipers. Huge tree trunks lay in regimented rows like the corpses after some unutterable disaster arranged for identification and disposal. All along the black-brown nudity of the obscene scar, there was evidence of secretive human activity, though the relentless downpour was doing its level best to obliterate all signs of everything, as though it too was employed by the logging companies. One long, lingering fly-past was enough to explain it all to the horrified young prince. At one end, the clearing was opened into a makeshift landing field that looked large enough for a couple of big workhorse helicopters to grab the carefully piled logs and swing them seawards.

Palm-roofed, almost perfectly camouflaged lean-tos the size of the Bell's makeshift hangar housed bulky machines – tractors, trucks, whatever they needed to do their work down there. Under the light their paintwork gleamed bright yellow and red. At least there were no signs as yet of the great logging machines he had seen at work on the Discovery Channel that do to forests what combine harvesters do to wheat fields. Nor, indeed, was there any sign of the men who worked here. With their helicopters, no doubt, safely and secretly aboard some anonymous ship at anchor just off the coast.

But the explanation for the destruction of the bridge below was made all too obvious by what was happening at the far end of the terrible scar as well. Here the mountainside sloped steeply eastwards as well as southwards, for it was on the side of a spur that became the west side of the river valley. Here, where the angles were sharpest and the soil was thinnest, the ground was beginning to wash away, carrying anything that lay upon it down into the wild torrent below.

'Do you see that? Parang...' called Sailendra, struck suddenly with poignant regret that he had not brought a camera or even a cellphone to record the horrific destruction like a war correspondent at an unsuspected massacre.

'Yes!' answered Parang. And, 'NO!'

Even as the Bell swooped over the restless, rumbling area, Parang, Sailendra and Councillor Kerian all saw the earth begin to tear away from the naked rock beneath. Roots of headless trees lost their grip on mother earth and reared, thrusting up their hairy limbs like giant spiders slithering down the hill. Logs the size of factory chimneys rolled down the precipitous valley-side like a bundle of toothpicks. The jungle on the slopes below them began shaking and shifting as though it was turning liquid under the relentless downpour.

A buffet of wind made the helicopter dance and twirl, the pilot fighting at the controls and swearing quietly in Japanese. The panorama beneath Sailendra's bulging eyes rolled unsteadily back towards the ridge-top. And, running westwards, as swiftly as the prince's horrified gaze itself, the gaping rent in the straining soil tore wide. Along the line of the felled trees, the living soil seemed to be simply ripping open, spewing semi-liquid mud in a wide boiling black flood. The whole of the slope below the ridge, above the western edge of Baya City itself, slid into ponderous, unstoppable motion.

Eight

Under Sail

Richard and Robin rose unusually late next morning. They had made love twice the night before – once, quickly, for her; again, more lingeringly, for him. Then they had lain side by side in the rumpled cotton sheets under the lazy motion of the fan. Feeling the stirring of the cool air on their sensitive, glowing skin. Feeling the restful sway of the ship as she leaned into the steady breeze that filled the sails so close above their heads. Looking past their up-turned toes to the panoramic windows that stretched above their balcony and towered over the three-deck-deep hill-slope to the stern, like the face of a tall glass cliff. Watching the shooting stars come tumbling down the velvet sky below the gleaming diamond constellations, so close behind *Tai Fun* that it seemed they were being extinguished in the fluorescent foam of her wake. And they talked.

It seemed to both of them that for the better part of twenty years they had hardly been able to complete a sentence or a thought – children, company, crisis after crisis had all come between, imperiously demanding attention. But now, here, as timelessly under sail as Achilles bound for Troy, or as Ulysses wandering homeward, they had peace and time at last.

'I love this ship,' said Robin, sleepily at last. 'I want her. I simply have to have her, like Nic says: MNO. But you knew I would, didn't you, darling? That's why you brought me out to her.'

But Richard answered with a gentle snore. So she rolled over beside his massive body, placed her thigh across his loins and snuggled herself against his shoulder. Asleep in an instant. And the moment her breathing deepened into the familiar rhythm, Richard's eyelids stirred and for an instant in the darkness his eyes gleamed as bright as the stars outside as he smiled with excitement and contentment. For even this was only the beginning of his plan.

And so it was that the moment they were up and dressed next day, Richard was dragging Robin off on a guided tour of the ship. Not that she was reluctant to go, insisting only on a fleeting visit to the breakfast bar for some coffee first. She found herself irresistibly reminded of the first time they had looked around Ashenden, their rambling, heavenly home on the cliff-tops of the South Coast overlooking the English Channel. They had bought Ashenden together nearly twenty years since, running from room to room like children in a toy store, almost too excited to speak; adding, Richard teased later, another hundred thousand pounds or so to the estate agent's asking price. It was a house they loved, which they missed more and more each time they were away from it. But here and now, her only thought was that she was as happy and excited as they had been that day. And so was Richard.

They began their daylight inspection precisely where they had left off the night before, gripped by excitement of a rather different kind. On deck, between the twin houses of their own accommodation and the bistro, which backed on to the open access bridge further forward still. Richard was keen to start there, the one cup of thick black Java they had snatched so far seemingly gone to his head. But Robin paused on the very spot and stood looking upward, simply entranced, her slim figure outlined by the breeze moulding her light cotton dress to every curve and sending the French blue stuff of the skirt straining between her legs like another little sail.

She saw at once what had put the notion of Achilles and his Troy-bound Myrmidons into her head. *Tai Fun*'s sails had black panels; no mere decorative checkerboard design but huge central sections framed by gleaming white. No – not gleaming – *glittering*. The black-hearted sails were huge. There must be the better part of two thousand square metres of sail. Four triangular monsters bellied and strained to contain the breeze, one before each soaring mast, and a stern-most one, slightly smaller, reaching out along a boom behind the last. The masts themselves were massive aerofoil constructions, like

81

gliders' wings that had been pulled longer and pushed thinner until they were like feathers. They reared the better part of fifty metres against the hard lapis blue of the wind-scrubbed Indonesian sky. And on the very distant top of each one sat a little windmill, its sails racing into a circular blur beneath the steady pressure of the wind. The whole set, windmills and all, seemed to be pushing nearly two hundred metres of stiletto-slim hull towards Kalimantan at well over twenty knots.

'Awesome, isn't she?' demanded Richard, sounding exactly like his university-student son. Looking like him, too, she thought, in his tropical whites. The starched cotton of the shorts and short-sleeved shirt, innocent of epaulettes or badges, gave him the air of a young cadet rather than a mature, widely experienced captain and international business leader.

'And then some,' agreed Robin, maternally indulgent.

'Almost orgasmic,' he teased.

'But why the black sails?' She changed the subject swiftly.

'They aren't just sails! Haven't you guessed? They're solar panels! And the windmills generate more additional wattage than you'd expect, as do the waterwheels along the hull below.'

'Waterwheels! To what end?'

'Everything aboard is electrically powered. A ship this size, a yacht – she is technically a high-tech cruising four-masted sail yacht – would need a keel to steady her and a pretty

82

sizeable ballast to force her sails into the wind. *Tai Fun* has a specially designed aqua-dynamic hull with a draft of only five metres, and instead of water ballast she has moveable batteries – super-upgrades of the huge batteries they use on submarines. An hour in bright sunlight can power up the batteries for the next twenty-four. A day's sailing can power her up for a week or more of cruising. And when she's running free like this the windmills and waterwheels give her all the power she needs to service all her functions from ceiling fans to fan-assisted ovens, from computers to Jacuzzis, without tapping into the main power sources at all.'

'But what if she gets becalmed under cloud for a week?'

'It'll never happen. And even if it did, you know cloud cover doesn't stop solar panels from generating power. Still and all, if her electrical systems did fail for any reason, there's a generator aboard that would easily power the bridge computers, basic essentials and life-support – and diesel motors capable of getting her the better part of a thousand miles at eight to ten knots. The motors are used for working her in and out of port, usually. They are the only part of her apart from the systems in the life-boats that aren't at least carbon-neutral. And,' he insisted, with the passion of the newly-converted St Paul arriving in Damascus, 'it's only to make assurance doubly sure in any case.'

'Sort of belt and braces, anyway,' she accepted, deflating his high-flown passion a little, like the practical Northern lass that she sometimes was at heart.

His eyes crinkled into their ready laughter-lines. 'I knew I could count on you to keep my feet firmly on the ground,' he teased. 'Even in the middle of the Java Sea!'

'Ha! You are admiring my beautiful sails, I see!' struck in a new voice, rich, deep and resonant.

Robin turned and found herself confronted by a deep-chested, short-backed Viking. 'First Officer Larsen,' the newcomer introduced himself, thrusting out a great red-furred paw the size of a large York ham.

'First Officer and sailing master. It is a pleasure to meet you, Mr Larsen,' answered Richard, as Robin shook the proffered hand and gazed unbelievingly at the wild red beard and wild blue eyes. 'I am Richard Mariner, and this is my wife Robin.'

'As if there could be anyone aboard who does not know you!' Larsen gave a booming laugh. 'Are you come aboard to fight Mr Greenbaum for the hand of my lovely lady here?'

Robin found herself looking automatically around, half expecting that there was indeed a Viking princess to be fought over. With double-bladed axes no doubt. But no. The first officer was simply talking of his ship with a pride that verged dangerously close to infatuation.

'Mr Nordberg and Captain Olmeijer have made no secret of it,' Larsen continued expansively. 'And you do not think the lovely Inge comes aboard on every cruise, I suppose?' Again he gave that booming laugh. 'I tell you no. She only steps out of her ice palace when there is money to be made or contracts to be signed. Deals to be done!' His Norse accent lingered over the 's's in his last few words as though he was hissing in disapproval or disgust. 'Perhaps I should bring her up to look more closely at my sails, eh? They would melt her if anything could. And literally, too! You see the glittering of the wires in the white sections round the edges of the solar panels? Specially designed! Not only must they conduct the electricity into the main conduits in the masts themselves, they must do so at nearly five hundred degrees Celsius.' Oddly, there was no hissing as he said the words. 'These sails are unique to these vessels. They are supposed to be able to withstand heats in excess of one thousand degrees! Think of it! One thousand degrees! That would start to thaw our *Ice Princess*, eh?' And the sibilance returned for the final two words.

No sooner had he hissed his last, however, than the ship's alarms began to sound. Captain Olmeijer's voice boomed out across the seas, 'Report to your emergency stations, please. Emergency stations if you please, everyone.'

Richard and Robin looked at each other, almost horror struck. In all the bustle and excitement of various kinds they had entirely forgotten the most basic safety precautions. They had no idea at all where their emergency station

85

was. But Larsen, seemingly noticing nothing untoward, swept them along with himself. 'You are in my boat, of course,' he explained, hurrying them along the deck. 'And you need have no real concern. It is a drill only – or I would be in the bridge taking care to furl my sails! I can get them up and down both within two minutes, you know! Two minutes. Hot or cold! There was some lively debate, I can tell you,' he continued unstoppable as he swept them towards the foremost port lifeboat, the better part of a hundred metres further along the deck. 'But with the owner and his daughter, Mr Greenbaum and the lovely Miss Cappaldi, together with the passengers assigned at the earlier stages of the cruise, the captain's boat is full. He did not think that such experienced sailors and captains such as yourselves would be too upset to be in the lifeboat with the men and women who *work* the ship.'

As Larsen offered them this heartfelt if backhanded compliment, a new element suddenly came into play. The wind, which had been blowing steadily on their quarter, from a little to the north of west, suddenly gusted strongly from dead on the port bow. The great sails creaked under the added weight of wind. The rigging sang ecstatically and the whole vessel began to heel over. But at once the straining deck began to tremble. 'Ha!' bellowed Larsen, stopping for an instant, looking up. 'Five degrees! What do you say, Captain Mariner? Five degrees – maybe six, and my computers tell the internal motors down below to shift the ballast! She will come back up in a moment!' And so she did, swooping back into motion as the wind settled back on to the port quarter.

'In any case, you will be much more safe with me or Eva Gruber,' Larsen continued, rushing them forward once again along the nearly horizontal deck. 'She knows where we're bound for and I know how to get us there. Let all the rest look after themselves eh? Owners and captains and *entertainments officers*.' Again the accent lingered disapprovingly upon the four 's's. Particularly over the last two, Robin noted with some amusement. Apparently there was no attraction of opposites between Norsemen and Mediterranean women. And no love lost either between red-bearded sailing masters and the ash-blonde daughters of the ship's owners, come to that. Not aboard *Tai Fun*, at any rate. She was more than enough to fill the big sea-farer's heart. Mere women of flesh and blood, no matter how lovely, would stand no real chance against her.

Richard noted none of this. As he strode along beside First Officer Larsen, he was taking in a host of new details about the ship he had come here to buy at almost any price. He noted that beside each of the four masts there hung a brace of lifeboats, port and starboard – eight in all. Apart from the navigating watch, and, he supposed, whatever engineers were needed to oversee security below, everyone aboard was assembling beside one or the other of these. The crews were unleashing the lines, swinging the davits round, going through the ritual of preparing to launch. But the gently swinging lifeboats looked as though they would hold twenty rather than thirty. And there were certainly more than one hundred and sixty souls aboard. There were supposed to be nearly two hundred passengers alone. The ship's launch might take ten more, he supposed, but that still meant four or six big inflatable life rafts somewhere. Another interesting little secret to be winkled out of *Tai Fun* within the next few days before he really started going head to head with Greenbaum.

He would check every little detail of her safety equipment as well as testing the facilities further – from library to lido, from cinema to scuba diving, from washing facilities to wind-surfing, from the bistro and the strange ballast of moveable batteries to the backgammon, blackjack and baccarat tables.

It was all he could do to stop himself skipping with excitement at the prospect, like a youngster out on his first hot date.

Nine

Once Over

Lunch followed soon after *Tai Fun*'s emergency drill. As far as Richard was concerned, that was a very good thing, for he had not eaten heavily last night, too deeply involved in conversation and by-play to pay much attention to dinner. He had eaten no breakfast this morning and, what with one thing and another, he found he had stoked up quite an appetite. And, as things were to turn out, a well-lined stomach proved a good basis for dangerous action to come.

But once again, the passengers assembled round the captain's table, even in the absence of the captain and his officers, managed to become quite distractingly involved with matters other than eating. It was Nic who started it. Pushing aside a half-eaten spring roll as though it was some kind of gastronomic disaster instead of the exact opposite, he announced, 'You know, I'm not sure I like cruising at all. I could get bored out of my head pretty quickly, even aboard a sweet ship like this one.'

'Isn't that where Miss Cappaldi comes in?' asked Richard, a little distractedly as he eyed the repast. 'Isn't she supposed to keep you entertained?'

'*Us all* entertained,' chimed in Robin, and Richard realized that his thoughtlessly innocent phrase might be open to misinterpretation.

'She's given me a schedule of events,' allowed Nic, less than happily. 'But the only thing I fancy is this Dr Hirai's talk about volcanoes. And that's not scheduled until tonight.'

'We'll be about seven hundred kilometres north of Krakatoa then,' said Robin, who, to Richard's surprise, seemed to have found time to look at her copy of the entertainment schedule. 'That's as close as we go – unless we swing south on the return leg of our voyage.'

'If we come back that way,' agreed Nic, his mind apparently wandering a little. 'And if we're still aboard when she does.'

'You're not planning to stay for the whole cruise?' asked Robin, surprised. Richard finished his first spring roll and reached for the salad of avocado, beansprouts and wind-dried duck.

'Definitely not. I have businesses to run. And any case, I've a time limit on whatever I want to do while I'm out here. And, hey! Like I say, I get bored easy. Short attention span, I guess. Got to keep a little spice in the old life, you know?'

'What sort of thing does entertain you, Nic?' asked Richard. He was genuinely interested. But he would have asked the question anyway, because his only worry about the trip so far was that Nic and he would be all too likely to find themselves going head to head if a bidding war started. And it really looked to him as though he and the third richest man in the world were about to start competing for *Tai Fun*, her sisters and the whole of the Nordberg Line. And if Nic wasn't planning to stay aboard for the whole cruise, they were going to have to get things settled sooner rather than later. So, at the very least, Richard would need to know his enemy. As things stood, however, he had taken a liking to the Texan and wanted to know more about the man rather than the reputation.

'Excitement,' answered Nic without hesitation, his eyes sparkling.

'What kind?' Richard probed gently, and popped in a mouthful of duck and avocado, hoping for a long reply.

'Any kind.' Nic's expression was open, apparently ingenuous.

'Sounds risky. I knew a fellow once whose idea of excitement was jumping out of helicopters at the top of virgin snow-slopes wearing skis – and a parachute in case things got too rough,' said Robin, coming to Richard's aid as he chewed a little desperately.

'Extreme skiing. Base jumping,' said Nic. 'Yeah. I tried all of that when I was younger. Went off-piste at Aspen, came down the Matterhorn. Jumped off Angel Falls. Got the T-shirts somewhere.'

'That was this chap's nickname,' continued Robin, allowing Richard a moment or two more alone with his spiced duck salad. 'T-shirt.

Everyone called him that because no matter what you mentioned, he'd been there, done it, got the T-shirt. We met him skiing down glaciers at the South Pole.'

'I go for a different kind of excitement now, mostly,' said Nic. 'Something where the risk is more intellectual, less physical.'

'Ah. Perhaps that's the problem with Dr Hirai,' probed Richard, round a more modest mouthful of bamboo shoots. 'His talk on Krakatoa is on at the same time as the casino's open.'

'They call it Krakatau down here,' corrected Nic gently – though Richard made a mental note that he hadn't corrected Robin earlier. 'And no. Not that kind either. Though I do play a mean game of backgammon. And anyway, the slot machines are open 24/7.' His lean Santa Claus face clouded with an instant of disapproval. Or perhaps of something deeper.

'It can't be hunting,' observed Robin. 'Not a man of your green credentials – though you do look a little like Ernest Hemingway in certain lights.' She caught Richard's eye in one of those moments of intimate communication that some married couples share. He had been about to start on Nic's reputation as a bachelor. According to the gossip columns, Nic derived a great deal of excitement from playing the field. Everything from Hollywood film stars to Hoboken fishwives, it seemed. From aristocratic European debutantes to exotic Eastern dancers.

Nic focused his attention back on her for a

moment, his eyes crinkling with wry amusement. Explaining to Robin at least why he seemed to have managed so many conquests with so little bitterness and recrimination. So many speculative gossip columns, so few banner headlines. 'You can see right through a guy, can't you?' he purred. 'Yeah. Given only that I use a camera rather than a gun, yeah. The thrill of the stalk, creeping up on something magnificent and wild...' Nic paused thoughtfully, suddenly aware that he too had strayed into double meaning here. He glanced at Robin again, something almost dangerous in his eyes.

Richard's nostrils flared as though he was scenting the air.

'Something big and dangerous...' purred Robin in return, bringing the conversation firmly back to hunting animals.

'OK, I admit it.' Nic's tone became less seductive but he stayed right on the narrow path between double meanings. 'Getting into position. Going for the perfect shot. Then mounting ... *pictures* instead of *heads* up on the wall. I still get a kick out of that. But I hardly ever do it any more. Can't afford the insurance – even in MNO mode. That's part of the problem with fast cars too ... Formula One is out of the question nowadays. Even Nascar.'

'It must be business, then,' concluded Richard. 'That seems to be all that's left. Mergers and acquisitions. Hunting in the financial jungle. Taking on the big corporate beasts and out-thinking them. Going for the perfect deal.

Mounting yet another company scalp in your business portfolio.'

Nic's full focus rested on Richard now. Like a duellist unconsciously mimicking his opponent, the Texan picked up his fork and attacked his recently discarded spring roll. 'Yeah,' he admitted after a moment. 'Something like that.'

Richard opened his mouth to take things further, though he was not absolutely certain what he was going to say, especially as Robin caught his eye and gave a warning frown whose message he could not quite read. But Captain Olmeijer arrived at that moment. 'Ladies and gentlemen,' he said, as though the three of them were a considerable crowd. 'Mr Nordberg has suggested that you might like a tour of the ship. I am about to perform my full captain's inspection. Would it amuse you to accompany me?'

Richard and Robin had conducted more captain's inspections than they cared to recall and even Nic had been round a ship or two in his time, but none of them had been even faintly like this one, so the guided tour was something of a revelation to all of them. Revelation leading to life-or-death action, as it turned out. At least it began on the bridge – territory that should have been familiar enough to the Mariners. But *Tai Fun*'s bridge was like nothing that either of them had ever commanded. It was an open, airy, popular and bustling place, as full of passengers as it was of officers. Its clearview windows commanded a breathtaking view past the foremast and over the bowsprit to the awesomely distant almost indigo horizon, with everything, including the edge of the world, sitting at a little less than five degrees of angle. The roof of the bridgehouse was glazed as well but rather than let the sun steam in, the skylights were shaded by blinds hand-made of rattan rolled in hemp twine. It was just possible to see through the long thin splinters of cane to the belly of the sail on the second mast, whose trunk reached down through the after section of the charthouse, where the sail-handling computers were located.

Larsen was standing at the helmsman's shoulder, like Erik the Red in tropical whites, every inch the sailing master, relaxed and confident, chatting to Navigating Officer Eva Gruber about their speed and heading, their progress towards their destination. And then, with hardly a breath, passing the same information on to the passengers who flocked here, eager for the experience of seeing a ship handled under sail.

Even Captain Olmeijer was not above pausing to pose for a photo with what he grandly called 'his guests'. Likewise, the crewman in charge of the helm – a wheel that might have graced a Mississippi paddle-steamer – was content to settle eager hands upon the spokes. And explain how to hold her on a heading, gesturing with a straight-faced frown towards the compass in a big brass binnacle that might have come from the *Titanic*.

Richard was highly relieved to see that Eva

Gruber at least consulted a series of screens that seemed at a glance to combine state-of-the-art GPS system, Kelvin Hughes Coursemaster and the most advanced radar sets – both under-sea and collision-alarm – that he had ever seen. But she only did this in passing, so to speak, as she conducted eager tyro navigators to her chart-room, where she showed them their position marked with chinagraph pencil on a Perspex sheet over the white, sand and blue of the relevant British Admiralty Chart. Those that were really keen double-checked in the Admiralty Pilot NP 36, for the Waters off Indonesia (Volume 1). She glanced up and caught him watching. 'A pity you weren't here an hour ago,' she said with a smile. 'I'd have let you use my sextant.'

He grinned. 'Sorry to have missed that. Maybe tomorrow.'

She made a moue of almost Gallic regret. 'Tomorrow we shall be in Pontianac. It is no fun to shoot the sun at anchor. It must be done...' She made an expansive gesture which took in the limitless sea, the infinite sky and the black-hearted sails straining across the winds between.

Larsen bustled in then, with Olmeijer at his side. 'The sail-handling computers are fine, Captain,' he was saying. 'If you wish, I shall demonstrate, though it seems a pity to lose the wind. There has been no repetition ... The work at Singapore has settled everything perfectly, I think.'

'Very well,' Olmeijer acquiesced, but Richard suddenly got the impression that had Robin, Nic and he not been there observing, the sails would have come off and gone on again a couple of times, and let the wind go hang. For there was something not quite right here after all.

'I expect,' said Olmeijer pleasantly to Robin, 'that when you have completed your inspection of the navigation on the bridge of one of your famous supertankers, you would proceed to your engine room. Well, I have done this, you understand, by consulting my sailing master. What would be next?'

'The cargo,' she replied without hesitation. 'Cargo and stowage.'

'Precisely. And so it is aboard *Tai Fun*. Except that our cargo is comprised of the passengers aboard. And they are *stowed*, if I may use the word, in our leisure and entertainment facilities!'

'Good,' said Nic. 'This is what I came to see.'

Ten

Fire Down Below

'Very well, then.' Captain Olmeijer led the way out of the bridge and into the bistro, quiet now and preparing for afternoon tea followed by sunset drinks and starlight dinner. Out of the bistro and towards the forecastle instead of sternwards into the forward sections of the aft accommodation. There was a lift here – the forward lift – that opened just behind the chart-house. The captain pushed the button and the doors wheezed open as though they were as much at his command as the rest of the vessel they were inspecting. The lift-car was big enough for all of them. The captain pushed more buttons and they slid down – that one or two disturbing degrees off the vertical. 'Two decks down to the main public areas,' he explained. 'Two more down to the main work areas, where we will find the most important crew-members. We will check with the purser, the chief steward and the chefs in due course. And, eventually, two decks further down again, with the computing and engineering officers in charge of the main computer systems, the electric motors and the engines themselves. But my next most important conference must be with the casino manager and the entertainments officer.' Both of whom were waiting for them at the lift doors, each equally keen to show all of them over their respective domains.

During the next two hours, utterly ignorant of the impending crisis, the four visited all of *Tai Fun*'s interior recreational areas and talked to the men and women in charge. The entertainments officer and the casino manager came and went. He was succeeded by the purser, whose main function seemed to be to oversee the little shops and concessions that sold everything from perfumes to bikinis at prices that might have shamed Harrods or Bloomingdales. She was temporarily replaced by the fitness consultant, then by the physiotherapist. Then came the theatre manager and his director, the chief steward, the coiffeur and make-up consultant, the salsa coach and line-dancing instructor, but both the casino manager and the entertainments officer still succeeded them from time to time.

Apart from the view through windows and portholes, the angle of the floor and the sense of surging motion, they might as well have been looking over a modest but expensive hotel in Las Vegas, thought Richard, awed. A hotel catering almost exclusively, it seemed, for the leisured in their later years. He saw no faces that looked as though they were naturally aged less than seventy at any of the facilities they visited. And every step they travelled seemed to emphasize to the tanker-man just how thinly populated the vast vessels in the Heritage Mariner fleet really were. The only amusement really afforded the frowning man was the sight of Fritz the casino manager archly flirting with Robin while Nic the hunter got further beneath Gabriella Cappaldi's obviously weakening defences as she came and went and came again.

Richard's interest was not really re-awoken until, leaving the crowded casino, empty cinema, bustling gym, aerobics room (complete with over-eighties' Pilates class), health spa, beauty salon and hairdresser's, ship's hospital staffed by two nurses apologetic for Dr Hirai's absence, massage parlour, Internet café for those with more modestly equipped cabins, library where the good doctor was discovered reading up on Krakatau for tonight, the theatre (with rehearsal for the *Follies* that would follow the doctor's lecture), the gourmet restaurant and galley replete with not one chef de cuisine but two, they went down the next two decks into the heart of the vessel. Leaving their two guides reluctantly behind and falling more formally under Captain Olmeijer's command again.

And yet even here Richard found it hard to maintain his interest for long. In the relatively untenanted corridors too boring even to tempt the passengers, a series of nerds and geeks it seemed to him oversaw the vital computers whose programs did everything that general-purpose seamen and sail-hands ought to be doing aboard, from deploying and furling the sailing master's sails to monitoring the navigating officer's screens. It was as though they had passed from the Montecito Hotel to the headquarters of Microsoft. It made Richard increasingly uneasy that there seemed to be almost no actual sailors aboard – simply computer whizzes and glorified hotel staff. But he held his tongue. And Robin, clearly, was holding hers. Nic was seemingly interested, however; and so he might be, thought Richard. Here, it seemed, was a vessel that could be run by half a dozen seamen and a hundred landsmen trained in greeting, gambling, catering and general service.

But in the lowest inhabited sections of the vessel Richard at last found what he was looking for – someone whose responsibilities seemed familiarly nautical to him. An engineer whose main concern was with engines. Just the simple diesel smell of the tiny engine room filled him with nostalgia, and the hairy and lugubrious little Frenchman who worked there really was a chef, but a chef de marine, not a chef de cuisine.

'The motors are one hundred per cent, Capitaine,' he insisted, dismissing his visitors from his mind the instant introductions were complete, maintaining courtesy only in that he spoke in rushed English with a near-impenetrable accent. 'They worked perfectly as we manoeuvred out of Singapore, did they not? And they will answer perfectly when we take aboard the pilot at Pontianac in the morning. In

101

the meantime, I am using them to power the hydraulics. I realize we can move the platform with the electrical system and needless to say the batteries are charged to optimum. But it will be a good test, you understand? And we have more than enough bunkerage, even allowing that I have used it to fuel all the water-ski boats.'

'We will take on bunkerage along with everything else we need in Pontianac in any case,' allowed Olmeijer. 'But you do not want anyone from ashore to double-check?'

'Who will there be? No one who knows the system as well as I! You may rest assured, Capitaine.'

'Very well.'

'Trouble with your motors?' asked Richard as they hissed upwards once again in the aft lift that he and Robin had used last night.

'No. The chef believes there was water in the bunkerage. That is all. Power fell away unexpectedly as we came into Singapore. It was nothing...'

Captain Olmeijer's words were lost suddenly beneath the hissing of heavy hydraulic movement. It was sudden enough to make the three passengers look around in some concern, but the captain hardly seemed to notice it. The angle and surging motion of the hull around them straightened and slowed, making things seem even worse for an instant. Captain Olmeijer simply raised his voice over the hydraulic clatter. 'Ah, good. Now we will see the after sections in their fullest working order. And meet the rest of our passengers. The ones who do not yet need to lift their faces – or anything else, indeed! So your first impressions may be reversed a little, I think, Captain Mariner!' and the moment he completed this little speech, the lift stopped.

More like a conjurer than a commander, Captain Olmeijer pressed the button to the lift doors and they sighed open, revealing what seemed disorientatingly like a completely different ship full of utterly different passengers. They were looking out over the sun-bathing area surrounding a sizeable swimming pool. The deck swept away under the stepped cliffs of two U-shaped terraces, the uppermost of which contained Richard and Robin's balcony. The open end of the U faced sternwards and here the pool deck stepped down again to a hydraulic platform it was just possible to see at sea level, all a-bustle with young and active figures. The chef must just have completed lowering it into the optimum position to allow some serious water-sporting to commence. One group of figures was pushing a big black-sided Zodiac inflatable into the iris-coloured water where it sat among the indigo and golden wavelets on a short line. Beside these, more youngsters were shoving the jet-skis le Chef had just fuelled into the gently heaving water, flinging themselves astride and starting to power away from *Tai Fun* into the featureless vastness of the Java Sea. A

103

third group was pulling scuba gear free of its restraints, and strapping it over wetsuits or swimwear, ready to explore the mid- and lower reaches of the apparently untouched and timeless waters.

But just for an utterly distracting moment, Richard saw nothing of this at all. What he saw was the three tiny handkerchiefs of Inge Nordberg's bikini. Or rather what they so spectacularly failed to cover. 'Ah ha!' she called to him, bouncing forward and taking his hand as he was nearest to the door. 'Welcome to the *Youth Club!*'

Richard stepped out into the disorientating dazzle and bustle. He had just got used to feeling that he was – by the better part of a generation – amongst the youngest aboard. Now he felt positively geriatric. Inge was by no means the only young woman nearby. In fact there seemed to be nothing much else to look at between here and the Java Sea. The only man he could see above the hydraulic platform was the lifeguard, who seemed to have just stepped out of *Baywatch*. And Inge was certainly the most modestly dressed person there – by a long chalk!

'Stop gaping, dear,' said Robin helpfully. 'Did you realize that your eyes were out on stalks?'

'Aw! Give the guy a break,' said Nic cheerfully, stepping out of the lift at her side. 'This is one heck of an awesome view! Just smell the air – *Ambre Solaire*! And it's a genuine pleasure to see you again, Miss Nordberg...'

'Boys!' snapped Robin. 'Sometimes I just despair!'

Captain Olmeijer seemed to notice none of the byplay. 'It is the hydraulic platform that I wish to show to you,' he said enthusiastically. 'We offer such a range of water sports and related activities, you see...'

Inge swung round with a flirt of the hips that was just short of a declaration of war and oiled off with Richard on one arm and Nic on the other. The only consolation Robin could find as she fell in beside Captain Olmeijer was that neither of them was in any position to see how little of her unnaturally tanned and shapely rear was covered by the lower handkerchief.

At either side of the pool deck's rear edge, two expanding gangways stepped down on to the hydraulic platform. They were at their fullest extent now, but were so well designed that the five of them could climb down on to the busy platform. Here Robin abruptly found herself surrounded by tall, tanned, blond young men with sun-bleached hair and easy Australian accents. She suddenly, and with some pleasure, began to suspect that had she not been with Captain Olmeijer they would have been asking whether she had on a swimsuit under what she was wearing – for there were jet-skis and scuba outfits just waiting for her to try them. And any number of hot young men falling over themselves to lend her a hand.

Richard tore his attention away from Inge and looked around. The expanding gangways – like

105

so much else aboard the amazing *Tai Fun* – had been brilliantly designed by her original French architects. They functioned as outer safety rails – indeed, they were effectively sloping walls – to port and starboard of the platform, so that only the last few metres, where the five of them were standing surrounded by the blond crowd, were completely open. The inner section of the platform was walled by the stern of the ship itself, making yet another U-shaped level below and behind the pool deck. In all available sections there seemed to be a reassuring range of safety equipment. And a glance at the tall and muscular young men surrounding both Robin and Inge assured the thoughtful Richard that they were probably as competent-looking and as well trained as the *Baywatch* boy on lifeguard duty by the pool. And it was pretty clear that the young man in the Zodiac was not just sitting there for his own benefit. Not even the sudden arrival of Navigating Officer Eva Gruber distracted him.

For a moment it seemed to the amused Richard that there was a kind of race developing to see which woman they could get astride the last jet-ski first. And it seemed that Inge only won because she was already dressed for water sport. But then he saw that she was familiar with the controls of the water-borne motorbike. And the young instructor who had inveigled her astride seemed content to take the passenger seat behind and wrap his arms around her slim waist as she roared off to join the other four skinning across the surface of the somnolent sea.

'Lucky son of a gun,' observed Nic, under his breath.

Richard gave a half-smile and looked around for Robin. She had stepped into the Zodiac beside Eva Gruber and begun a conversation with her.

'I need say nothing here,' said Captain Olmeijer. 'This is one area that speaks for itself. Also when we are under power we can water-ski from here and even parascend. This area and the pool are more than enough entertainment for the younger passengers in the day. And as well as lectures and shows for the more mature guests, there are discos for this age group.'

'Do they still call them discos?' wondered Nic.

Richard shrugged. He had no idea. But he had two children who might know. At university on the far side of the world. 'It must be pretty well sound-proofed,' he observed, 'I didn't hear anything last night, at dinner or afterwards.'

'Like everything aboard,' said Captain Olmeijer, with that fatal hint of self-satisfaction which always seems to tempt Fate. 'Everything aboard is proofed against almost everything that can happen.'

Richard wasn't actually looking at the captain as he spoke. He was watching Inge Nordberg and her companion. No sooner had the curving track of their progress across the silken sea curved in to join the other four than all five fell into formation like fighter aircraft. With Inge in the lead, they formed a chevron, its arrowhead pointing toward *Tai Fun*'s stern, and in they roared as though they were attacking the ship. Whooping and shrieking loudly enough to be audible even above the racing engines and the foaming crash of the water they spewed out behind them, the ten young riders came racing recklessly home.

When all at once, around them, the surface of the sea exploded. Thousands of slim silver bodies hurled out into the lower air, battering the drivers and their passengers with an all-too-solid shower. Richard realized in an instant what was happening. Something had spooked a shoal of flying fish so badly that not even the threatening rumble of jet-skis had held them under the water. Muscular little bodies anything up to forty-five centimetres long were pelting everyone aboard the jet-skis, and the drivers and their passengers were being battered off their vehicles and tumbling willy-nilly into the foaming water.

Richard ran down towards the edge of the area, coming all too close to hurling himself down into the water. He looked across at the Zodiac and saw with a piercing shock of relief that it was already in motion. With Eva Gruber and Robin both aboard it was speeding out across the fifty metres or so towards the floundering survivors, who were all equally at the mercy of whatever monster was fearsome enough to spook the flying fish.

But then the fish arrived aboard *Tai Fun* itself in a disorientating and painful wall. More like an avalanche than anything Richard had ever associated with the great waters, they battered in at head height, moving at a fair speed, each one a solid kilo or more of sharp fin, muscle and bone. Richard turned his shoulder to the rain, and saw Nic and Captain Olmeijer doing the same, both simply stunned by the hammering, slithering, slippery squall. But at least they were standing their ground. The younger men were simply running away from the shockingly sudden attack, slipping and sliding as the silvery bodies piled up beneath their feet, flapping, arching and writhing wildly.

Then, as the battering agony began to ease, Richard was able to swing back. And he saw, with a shock almost equal to the onslaught of the fish, that the empty jet-skis were all still headed unerringly homewards towards the platform beneath *Tai Fun*'s stern. Each of them recently filled to the brim with le Chef's carefully quality-checked fuel – every cubic centimetre of which could reliably be expected to explode at the moment of impact.

Eleven

Slide

Prince Sailendra gaped through the window of the helicopter as it skimmed dangerously low above the gathering catastrophe. The sound of it was enough to drown the battering of engine and rotors and come close to deafening them all. A great section of the forest-pelted soily skin of his island was ripping away as though the mountainside was being flayed under some invisible hunter's knife. What should have been bare rock, revealed as the land lost its grip, was flooding at a terrible speed with great washes of mud. But it was the way the forest floor itself seemed to rear up and fall away that really staggered him. At least the prince had the grim satisfaction of seeing the culprits' industrial logging vehicles – huge though some of them were – succumb first to the overwhelming power of the slide.

Beyond words, Sailendra simply hammered on the pilot's shoulder and pointed downwards towards the distant lights of his city. The pilot obediently turned the nose southwards and opened up the throttles. The chopper skimmed lower, picking up speed. But no sooner had it done so than the pilot was pulling back on the control column, wildly exchanging speed for height. The sliding rainforest below them was exploding. The loggers' trucks and tractors were overwhelmed like toys. They had no opportunity or occasion to burn or to explode, though thickening tendrils and clouds of steam were warning of some kind of heat down there. But the trees were a different matter. Towering trunks that had stood for centuries – millennia – were being wrenched from their stands and thrown about like toothpicks. Their trunks and branches shattered in the grip of forces too vast for them to bend to. Like the huge pine trees of the Siberian taiga that explode when the frosts freeze their sap too hard, thirty-, forty-, fifty-metre tree trunks shattered into splinters as though packed with hand grenades.

And all around, the earth itself seemed transformed into thick black oily water. Foaming like the flood crest on the river that had swept away the dam, the mountainside's soil cover rose in crests, throwing upwards a kind of foam made up of boulders and clumps of living soil the size of Sailendra's palace.

The chopper soared up out of the dangerous air with the splinters and pebbles rattling against its underside like bullets, but the game little aircraft lost ground to the landslide. The wave of destruction rolled down the hillside at a speed they could no longer match. Only when the slope of the mountainside began to moderate did the wave of destruction begin to slow. Rather than rolling downwards so wildly, ripping everything up before it, the terrible wall of absolute destruction settled. But it did not – could not – stop. Instead it was transformed. The weight of the still-slipping upper slopes might no longer be overwhelming the deeper, steadier soil of the lower slopes above the city, but like the face of a sand dune, the mountainside continued to slide – less wildly, more decorously, but unstoppably, with a terrible inevitability. And after the jungle and the forest, it took the city with it, sweeping everything that had stood there down into the heaving sea.

But as the chopper at last caught up with the advancing ripple of destruction, Sailendra could see all too clearly that this was no sedate affair. The trees, ripped from their roots by the downward pressure of restless soil, still crashed downwards. If they no longer shattered under the strain, they nevertheless added their massive weight to the onward-rolling Behemoth, as the stripped trunks had added the rams of their power to the destruction of the bridge that the weight of mere water might have left standing. The slower, infinitely more powerful rams of the land-borne trees slid up against the still-building outskirts of the new city like a besieging army intent on destroying an all too flimsy fortress.

It seemed to the horrified prince that it was the trees that battered his half-constructed city into a ruined wasteland – though second thoughts and, later, expert advice would suggest otherwise. The trees swept into the part-built blocks as though intent on avenging the desecration of the virgin forest above. They were a wave of darkness, snuffing out street lights, security lights, factory lights. Tearing down and overwhelming city blocks and the infrastructure in between them. The shells of factories destined to produce island-cotton products, training shoes with genuine, locally tapped rubber soles, electrical products and car parts under licence from Japanese and Chinese business partners, the new Baya Radio and Pulau TV studios due to be opened in a month or so, the editing facilities for the nascent film industry – part of the price for using Bandar Laut Bay as a location – all vanished. The new telecommunications centre beside it – with its wavebands and phone lines so recently transferred from the old post-war Telegraph Office. And with it the masts that allowed TV, radio and cellphone communication across the island and between Pulau Baya and the rest of the world. The new electricity-generating plant that had powered all the ruined infrastructure, replacing for the merest glimmer of time the traditional palm-oil lamps. The heliport did achieve a brief flash of deep red fire, made brighter by the surrounding darkness, as the Avgas tanks went up. But then it was washed out into the new marina and both were buried by a million and more tons of mountain soil. And the unstoppable wall of tree trunks became a huge, tangled armada launched out into the Java Sea as though the Bandar Laut – the sea men of the island – had returned to their old Bugis roots. Had taken to their wooden praus and gone pirating once more under the pale eye of the full, fat pirates' moon. And it was only when he saw the pearl-bright face of it low in the eastern sky that Sailendra knew the rain had stopped at last.

But blessedly, Sailendra slowly came to realize, as though the moon itself was explaining things to him, only the as yet untenanted, almost uninhabited, new city on the west bank of the Sungai Baya River was destroyed. And it was the river that saved the rest – or, if not the river itself exactly, the steep sides of its valley. For the slide had started just below the watershed and the massive eastward tearing of the earth had been brought to a stop high above by the precipitous headwater valley. It had poured its cut logs eastwards into the floodwaters of the swollen river – and a great deal of soil and mud as well. But the water and the valley down which it tumbled had contained it. The great rent in the living topsoil had ripped westward to the edge of the next valley and been contained there too. Only that one great western spur had suffered total destruction – although that was bad enough. And, eastwards of the blessed river, the main part of the old city still stood. Shaken, battered, powerless and flooded.

But it still stood.

'Where do you want me to go?' yelled the pilot.

Sailendra dragged his moon-dazzled gaze back aboard the chopper. Kicked his mind into gear. The heliport was out of the question now, he thought. And the Toyota was gone as well. That loss was somehow more personal – almost painful. 'Wherever you can land. As near to the city as possible.'

Automatically, though still deep in the grip of simple shock, he began to plan and prioritize. Or at least to ask the questions whose answers would order – perhaps – organize things for him. Should he check the surviving city first looking for casualties? His eyes swept over the rooftops as the pilot searched for space to land. There seemed little wreckage except along the edge of the flooding river, though the ground had certainly quaked as the landslide tore down the mountain. Perhaps enough to have registered on the Richter scale like a genuine earthquake. But such things were not uncommon here and the buildings were well adapted. There were no fires visible either, though, in the powerless darkness of the moon-shadows, there were millions of tiny golden flames. Palm-oil lamps.

The west bank had not been utterly unpeopled. There had been workers at the broadcasting facility, at the power station. There had been security guards, others. There had been one or two boats in the marina – though thankfully the main port facilities were over near Bandar Laut

Bay. Perhaps his first priority ought to be to arrange help from the old city to search for survivors there. But the river, which had saved so many, seemed to be intent on damning those lost in the rubble, for its flood had widened and its flow intensified. There was no sign of the bridge – or the slope up to it. Or, indeed, much sign of the roadway leading up to the slope. It seemed as if they might need the trusty old pirate praus that had so recently sprung to his mind after all.

Or – Sailendra's mind began to function more effectively – he could send word to the towns that nestled in the valleys further round the coast. They could probably send help in less time than it would take to get a useful number of people across the swollen flood. But how was he going to contact them? Come to that, how was he going to contact anybody? And, it suddenly occurred to him, the effects of the landslide might well be more than the island could handle unaided. 'Is your radio still working?' he asked the pilot.

'Yeah, I guess so...'

'Well, it may be the only one on the island that is working. Can you put out a general distress call, please?'

'I guess...'

As the pilot began to broadcast the first request for help, Sailendra turned to the two men in the seats behind. 'Parang. You and I must draw up a list of immediate priorities. Kerian, first amongst these must be a meeting

116

of the council. Can you please organize that while I see about more immediate relief work?'

Kerian answered first. 'Of course. The council must be at the heart of whatever we do now. There is much new work to be done, perhaps even a new direction...'

'We will discuss that with the council. Parang, as soon as we get down we must go to the emergency services HQ and the hospital.'

'A pity the new hospital was built over by the glorious new film studios, is it not?' asked Kerian, getting back into his stride.

'A blessing that it was not yet staffed or open for business,' snapped Sailendra.

'It was full of millions of dollars' worth of equipment, though. Like all the rest of the new buildings. All gone now, through the will of the mountain.'

'All gone,' grated Sailendra, rapidly running out of patience, 'because of illegal logging in the rainforest. That's what caused all this! And when I find out who was responsible for *that*...'

'Not that you ever will now,' sneered Kerian. 'There can't be many clues left, can there?'

'Prince Sailendra?' the pilot interrupted. 'I have a contact.'

'Who?' asked Sailendra, realizing with a shock that he had completely disregarded the pilot's vital conversation because he was pointlessly fighting with Kerian. Now there were some priorities he really did need to get straight, he thought.

'A ship,' the pilot answered. 'The signal's not

117

too strong. I didn't catch the name. He's talking in English and mine's not too good. Sounds American.'

'Let me speak to him.'

The pilot passed the headset to Sailendra, who leaned over as far as his seat belt would allow so as not to over-stretch the twist of wire connecting it to the radio. 'Hello?' he said in English. 'Hello?'

'I hear you strength four,' came a faint reply. 'What can I do for you?'

'This is Prince Sailendra of Pulau Baya. We have an emergency here. We need help urgently...'

'Sorry to hear that, Your Majesty, what can we do?'

'What ship are you?'

'Freighter *Miyazaki Maru* outbound from Kagoshima, Japan. Did you say Pulau Baya?'

'Pulau Baya, yes. I am Prince Sailendra...' Sailendra's mind raced like a caged mongoose in an exercise wheel. What help could a mere freighter somewhere between here and Japan offer them? Effectively, no help at all. But then the surging crackle of the dead air warned him that the little chopper's radio was losing the freighter's signal in any case. And if they lost this contact, who knew when they would be able to make another one. And send another plea for help out to the world. *'Miyazaki Maru?* Please listen. We have suffered a catastrophic landslide. We have lost half our city and all our communications. Please pass this message out.

Tell everyone that you can contact that we need help most urgently. Do you understand? Get the word out as fast as you can! It is vital! *Miyazaki Maru*, can you hear that? *Miyazaki Maru*?'

But there was only the surging silence of dead air in answer.

Sailendra handed the headset back to the pilot, who slid it back on his head and listened, frowning with concentration. 'Lost the signal,' he said at last.

'Do you think they heard us?' asked Sailendra, his voice shaking slightly.

The pilot shrugged. And as he did so, Parang leaned forward. 'There!' he said. 'I think you could set down there.'

Miyazaki Maru lay at anchor in the shallows off Pulau Baya's northernmost headland. The last light from the full, fat pirate moon bathed the still-running wetness of her decks, covering her with silver. Her battered bridgehouse looked like a precious ornament. The rusted sides gleamed like some unimagined Cellini salt dish. The piles of teak and mahogany tree trunks, so recently ripped out of the forests on the not-too-distant mountain and stowed on her deck, looked like the purest ingots.

The captain glanced down across their cargo, seeing only profit there, no beauty at all. He turned back to the radio operator, his hard face twisted with ready anger. That this imbecile should have answered the distress call in the first place. That he should have made contact with the prince whose island they were raping. That he should even faintly consider retransmitting the desperate message beggared belief.

'No, you will not pass the message on, you moron!' snarled the captain. 'Forget you even heard it and erase all the records that you can. Then get on to Luzon Logging and tell them we're coming home!'

Twelve

Impact

Most of the jet-skis slowly surged to a stand-still, losing power as their riders' hands no longer pushed the throttles wide. Two, however, were clearly malfunctioning. Even riderless they came onwards and, as luck would have it, they came on side by side. The others wallowed off-line and settled into the regular swell of the sea, steady enough for one or two of their more athletic riders to be attempting to re-mount them. But not the last two. These two seemed to be guided by some invisible hand. Sod's law dictated that they should each turn off-line in the opposite direction – leaning into each other and straightening their combined course with the accuracy of torpedoes.

Richard looked first to Robin in the Zodiac. It would be the work of a moment for her and Eva Gruber to upset the precarious equilibrium of the last two skis if they could get to them in time. But they were all too obviously pre-occupied, trying to reach those erstwhile riders still floundering helplessly in the water before whatever had scared the flying fish decided to come after larger, juicier prey.

Dismissing Robin's help in a twinkling, therefore, Richard turned to fend for himself, his mind racing. What he needed was knowledge. He racked his brains to remember the design plans of *Tai Fun*'s after sections that he had pored over so carefully in preparation for this trip. Where was the control that would raise the hydraulic platform before the swiftly approaching jet-skis rode up and on to it? Where might there be something that might fend them off before they came aboard and exploded? Where was there a hose? The last question was easily answered for he remembered clearly where the nearest fire point was and he was crossing purposefully towards it before he realized he had come to his decision. The only thing slowing him was the care with which he had to place his feet on the thin carpet of twisting, flapping fish. If he could get the hose off quickly enough, its powerful jet would be enough to stop the jet-skis. But the gathering snarl of their approach warned that time was getting very short indeed.

Richard had just torn open the front of the fire point when Larsen arrived. The big sailing master seemed in the grip of some almost inexpressible rage. He exploded on to the deck with the unexpected force of a paratrooper landing. He kicked the dying fish aside and hurled himself towards Richard almost as though he wanted to attack him, his massive fists swinging as though they held a pair of invisible axes. His Viking beard bristled beneath his flame-red cheeks and his blue eyes actually seemed to spark. Richard did not speak any Scandinavian languages and so he had no idea what Larsen was saying to begin with – and that was probably just as well. Side by side, they tore the hose free, Larsen twisting the controls with fearsome power. Then they turned, and tensed themselves to run, side by side, down to the lip of the hydraulic platform. Larsen's brutally obscene monologue slid into something approaching English. And Richard realized it was peppered with orders and suggestions, pleas and exhortations, some of them addressed to him.

Water gushed out of the brass nozzle and washed the fish back on to the sea as Richard and Larsen staggered forward. 'These bloody children have put my beautiful ship at risk. I will swing for them, I really bloody well will. Christ! How could they be so stupid. We will never get there in time. We will never turn the jet-skis. Look! All we are doing is washing away the fucking fish! We should let them fry at least, the stupid things. We must get the water jet on to the accursed jet-skis and hold it there. They will come aboard but we may at least stop them from exploding. If we are lucky! Lucky, HA!'

On that spectacularly unamused 'HA!', the jet-skis did indeed come aboard. With a power that surprised Richard at least, the solid little vehicles – each the size and weight of a motorbike – powered in. Their slick undersides rode up over the lip of the platform which sat at water level, and they slid aboard on the bow-wave of their own relentless progress. They were moving at a speed well in excess of five knots and that, together with their considerable mass, was enough to do some considerable damage. They exploded through the shower of the water from the hose and slid forward with almost disorientating rapidity.

'Aim!' howled Larsen and the pair of them wrenched the water jet back on target. But all they succeeded in doing was knocking the jet-skis over. And the moment they fell, the swan-like elegance of their progress turned instantly into a train wreck, a car crash, as the forces that had been holding them together set about tearing them apart. The least robust parts of their construction were those around the fuel tanks. Lines, hoses, thin metal sides. And at the same time, with their motors racing past maximum revs, there remained, in all too close proximity to the spraying fuel, pistons that were hot from overuse, overheated gears and spark plugs that were still sparking. Even under the deluge from the fire hose, the whole twisted mess, still sliding rapidly across the platform towards the white stern of the ship itself, exploded into flame.

Robin saw the explosion. It looked to her as though *Tai Fun* had become some kind of rocket-propelled vessel, belching fire out of her stern. She shouted in shock, before she even began to realize that Richard was trapped, perhaps fatally, somewhere on the far side of the flames.

Eva Gruber was not looking at the ship, however. She was looking at the water and by the happiest of coincidences Robin's shout alerted her to something more primeval than rocket propulsion. For there, in the water, just beyond the struggling jet-ski riders, was the creature that had scared the flying fish and started this whole adventure in the first place. What sort of shark it was, the young officer could not be certain. But it measured a good four metres from dorsal to tail-tip and that made it big enough to eat swimming people as well as flying fish. And it seemed to Eva in that horror-struck moment that the shark was making an all-too-purposeful line directly for the owner's daughter Inge.

So Robin, still gaping at the outpouring of bright gold fire that obscured the last place Richard had been standing, found herself suddenly being tossed about like a puppet in the bows of the Zodiac and whirled away on a new tack altogether. The throttle was opened as wide as it would go and the solid little vessel roared across the water with desperate purpose. Robin had taken part in too many rescues not to sense the urgency and start looking for trouble dead ahead. So she too saw the sinister pair of triangles that were the shark's main fins. 'It's big,' she shouted back to Eva.

'I see.' Eva answered tersely. 'Do you know what sort it is?'

'Not the foggiest. But we'd better assume it's dangerous.'

'And hungry...'

The Zodiac smashed from wave-crest to wave-crest, showering Robin with cool salt spray as she looked around for some kind of weapon should they have to tackle the shark. But there was nothing more threatening than an old-fashioned wooden oar. She caught this up, thinking that it would be as useful for giving swimmers something to hang on to as it would for bashing sharks on the nose with. But when she looked up again, with the solid piece of no doubt recycled ecologically friendly timber across her chest, the shark had vanished, the triangles of its fins lost among the sharp-edged shadows of the waves. And Inge Nordberg was right beneath the scudding rubberized canvas of the firmly inflated bow.

'Grab hold, Inge!' Robin pushed the oar into the water and the Zodiac seemed to swing right round it, coming to rest with its solid bottom firmly between the girl in the water and the last position of the inquisitive shark. Then Eva was there at her shoulder and the pair of them pulled the gasping Inge aboard. She came out of the sea like a young seal in a shower of drops, and slid gasping into the scuppers. The only real damage done by the adventure so far seemed to be to her already minuscule bikini, thought Robin wryly. Inge's popularity as a pin-up would be vastly enhanced if many of the men aboard could see her almost total nudity now! She turned to Eva Gruber, her mouth open to ask whether they had any kind of towel or blanket aboard, only to stop, her good intentions side-tracked by the impact of the look on the young officer's face. It was unconscious, Robin was certain, and was gone in a fleeting second. But just for that instant, Robin thought that she had never seen such awed wonder mixed with such naked desire in all her life.

Richard was hurled on to his back by a combination of searing force and fish-slippery footing. Larsen came down like a tree half on top of him. The hose whipped away like an escaping anaconda. Something smashed against the stern wall disturbingly close above them and crashed down on to the deck beside the fallen men. The impact seemed to shake the ship to her keel. Richard dazedly expected the masts and sails to join the sailing master piled on top of him. There was a searing smell of blazing petrol overlain with a much more intimate stench of singed hair. The masts stayed miraculously upright. Larsen rolled over, stunned. Richard gathered himself to rise, but the wild writhing of the hose brought the heavy brass nozzle back and it knocked him down again before he could pull himself anywhere near upright. He scrabbled the bludgeoning, throbbing, all-too-lively weight to himself and discovered how hot he had become when the blessedly icy coolness of the water jet inundated him. Only now did he open his eyes.

Past the foaming fountain of the pulsing hose, Richard was able to make out the still-blazing lake of petrol that surrounded the skeletal wreckage of the jet-skis and gave birth to a pirate's banner of thick black smoke that trailed away across the wind. Someone's swung her head round a good few points or all that smoke would be smothering us about now, thought Richard as he began to fight the jet back on to the blazing wreckage. It was only when Larsen began to pull himself erect that Richard realized he was still down on his knees. But knees was as far as Larsen could achieve, and the pair of them leaned together like a pair of ancient octogenarians looking for their Zimmer frames, and held the hose steady. From very, very far away, Richard could hear a stream of Nordic swear words occasionally larded with something more familiar. It was Larsen, of course, bellowing at his shoulder. But, like reality, hearing was slow to return, though blasted away in the merest instant by the explosion.

The power of the hose's water jet began to bite then, and it started to sweep the blazing petrol off the back of the vessel and into the water of her wake. And, as with the smoke, the intelligence of whoever held the helm or directed the course was revealed. For as the floating flames oozed off the deck and into the water immediately behind it, so the carefully controlled motion of the hull ensured that the fire was contained in a gentle curve of wake. There was only just enough to keep the fire underneath its own black plume of smoke and keep it from flooding across the water, but it pulled the flames away to starboard as safely as possible – allowing the Zodiac to skim in to the clear port section.

A distant, raucous cheering erupted as the chubby black rubberized side settled home, and Richard glanced upwards in shock. It was unsettlingly as though a flock of seagulls had taken the voices of a gang of football hooligans. But then the first of the rescued jet-skiers clambered aboard, led by an apparently stark naked Inge Nordberg.

Suddenly there were white-clad legs all around Richard, his head level with the hips of four men. He looked up, still dazed, to see le Chef frowning down at him. The sturdy French chief engineer had brought three more good old-fashioned seafaring men along with him, and suddenly Richard and Larsen were relieved of the hose by an entirely competent fire crew. A couple of sheepish lifeguards appeared and helped the pair to their feet, then lingered, staring across at the spectacular sight of Inge taking her own sweet time about getting to safety and decency. Larsen pulled free without so much as a thank you and limped across to the stern wall of the ship, apparently oblivious to the spectacle presented by the owner's daughter. Richard followed him, amused. Impressed. The white paint was seared and smoke-blackened, but there was no blistering, warping or melting evident. A heavy metal section from one of the jet-skis had smashed into it with enough force to make a dent. Richard remembered hearing the impact. It had been moving at quite a speed when it hit. He stirred the still-smoking culprit with his foot – it was pretty massive, too. He looked up again, surprised that the dent was so small. But other than that, the vessel seemed to have survived the drama surprisingly well, he thought.

Robin appeared. 'Look at you!' she said severely, though her words seemed out of synch with the movements of her lips as though she were acting in a badly dubbed movie.

Richard glanced down then and was surprised to find that his clothes were filthy as well as soaking. Dazed, he looked at his forearm and discovered that he seemed to have been mildly sunburned. He looked at Larsen, whose face was even redder than Richard's arm, and his beard bristled with an almost brittle wildness. He had survived the adventure much less well than his beloved ship, thought Richard.

Then he turned and followed Robin stiffly across the hydraulic deck to the gangway leading back up to the poolside. The cheering began again. This time it was louder and less raucous than it had been for Inge's arrival. And it was not until the first hand clapped him on the shoulder and the first fist closed to shake Robin by the hand that he realized that the cheers were all for them.

Thirteen

Pontianac

Tai Fun swung at anchor, her hull moved by the flow of the Landak River so that her sleek prow looked up south-eastwards towards the bridge at Jalan Gajah Mada with the glittering roofs of the Mesjid Jami and the Istana Kadriyah on the point to the left just below. Sailing Officer Larsen had little time to enjoy the view, however. He was overseeing the bustle of workmen who had come out – as soon as they could do so without unduly disturbing the passengers – to effect repairs to the damaged stern. They had been summoned from the local shipyards further down river, and seemed a thoroughly competent crew, made up of ethnic Kalimantanese and Chinese workmen. As befitted his elevated position, Larsen oversaw them from the upper deck – while le Chef got down and dirty, rubbing shoulders with them as he made doubly sure that the hydraulic platform had survived yesterday's accident.

To be fair, in any case, the air-conditioned confines into which Larsen was happy to retreat so regularly came as a blessed relief. The glittering bustle of the all too modern and municipal city generated an atmosphere that was absolutely stultifying. The air seemed as thick as the muddy river water, and just as difficult to breathe. There was no wind of any description and the temperature combined with the humidity to make the recently singed officer feel that he was frying alive whenever he stepped outside, in spite of much good work done by Dr Hirai yesterday evening. Just as Pontianac stood astride the river, so it also stood astride the equator itself. The shade temperature was in the mid-forties with the humidity more than twice that.

Captain Olmeijer and the owner were on the bridge, entertaining local officialdom over aromatic local coffee and freshly baked croissants while Navigating Officer Eva Gruber, nursing a mug of coffee and eyeing the croissants hungrily, went through the sailing plans with them once again. Apart from the workmen and the officers attending them, these were just about the only senior people left aboard. Indeed, apart from those crew members making sure that the accommodation was up to standard and that the entertainment facilities were ready to go this evening, they were the only people left aboard.

Dr Hirai was at the hospital, trying to restock the salves and ointments that she had used upon the blast victims yesterday afternoon and evening, torn between the Chinese herbal remedies on offer and the much more expensive Western alternatives. The chief steward and his minions were down in Kapuas Indeh market, restocking with everything from cutlery to coffee. The lesser of the chefs de cuisine had been with them to begin with, but he had moved on. He spent more of the day restocking the galleys with local delicacies. These ranged from tender goat and suckling pig available at the Pasar Daging meat market to crabs pulled out of the river and prawns brought across the sea from the fisheries at Bandar Laut Bay on Pulau Baya Island, available at the Pasar Ikan fish market.

Fritz the casino manager was deputizing for the entertainments officer at the BNI bank on Jalan Rahadi Usman, ensuring that there would be currencies of all sorts available to everyone aboard upon demand. But he also had orders to ensure that he called in at the Pontianac City and Kapuas Palace hotels as well as visiting the airline offices on Jalan Pahlavanand and Jalan Gaja Mada on behalf of several passengers leaving the ship tonight and flying home tomorrow. On top of that, he had agreed to talk to the owners of several specific *warung* restaurants on his way back aboard in case anyone wanted to eat ashore tonight. Fritz was grudgingly obliging in this, because he felt that, as usual, he had drawn a very short straw indeed. He had refused point blank to enter into the lengthy, complex and expensive negotiations necessary to get all the passengers that wanted to go there into the great park at Tanjung Puting where they were due to enjoy a two-day visit in two days' time.

Gabriella Cappaldi herself was disposed most decoratively beneath the shade of a palm tree on the white-sand vastness of the beach at Pasir Pajang. Between her voluptuous, bikini-clad form and the distant indigo water, almost every passenger and crew member who could walk seemed to be somewhere on the shore. For in spite of the stultifying workaday atmosphere of a city a-bustle with half a million busy people only a couple of kilometres back along the road, the languorous beach at Pasir Pajang was one of the highlights of the itinerary. On a day like today, the attractions of Pontianac palled. Even the promise of the Dyak longhouse and the Negri Pontianac Museum could tempt no one. But Pasir Pajang was a beach surpassed only by the breathtaking Bandar Laut Bay on Pulau Baya, where they would be lazing within the week. *I might arrange an excursion across town after dark when it cools down a little*, she thought. But she knew well enough that it wouldn't really cool down after dark at all, and the hardy souls remaining ashore were more likely to be heading for Korem Place than Jalang Jend A Yani and the Somay Bandang Restaurant or *warang*. And besides, there was the promise of Dr Hirai's lecture on Krakatoa – or *Krakatau* – postponed from yesterday because of the adventures of the afternoon and the medical needs they engendered. And further, it

134

was absolutely vital that she get as many as possible of her hardy charges into Tanjung Puting National Park – to cover up what she and Nic Greenbaum were planning to do, if for no other reason.

'This is all very well,' rumbled Nic, breaking into her thoughts abruptly and aptly, even though he was talking to Richard Mariner, 'but I could be doing this in the Florida Keys or somewhere in Mexico without having dragged my ass halfway round the world.'

'It's not quite the same, though, is it?' countered Robin before Richard could answer for himself. She rolled over on to one elbow, the dusting of sand like caster sugar on the tanned muscularity of her body. Only the best-trained eye, looking closely enough to risk a slap or a right hook, would have seen the network of scars left by various surgeries necessitated by a range of adventures over the years. By the same token, Richard's long legs looked youthfully untouched, though the metal in his knee joints regularly set off alarms at airport security gates.

'Well, I'll grant you it's prettier than most...' Nic observed, looking at Robin not quite closely enough to see her almost invisible imperfections, but with the dry double entendre so many women had found almost as hard to resist as his massive fortune.

'No. I mean it's part of something wider,' persisted Robin with calculated innocence, fixing him with her still, cool, grey gaze. 'It's part of an experience that comes in a bigger...'

'Package.' Nic finished her sentence for her. 'Yeah. Maybe that's why they call them *package holidays...*' The term was said almost with a sneer. 'Though as often or not it's *package rape* of the environment, one way or another. And all for no real benefit even to the tourist.'

'That's not what I mean at all!' Robin huffed in reply, tricked into an outrage that made her breasts quiver beneath the tiny halter of her top.

'Granted,' said Richard, interrupting her forcefully and uncharacteristically, almost as though he had noticed some of this lazy byplay. 'But think about it, Nic. The last time these people, our fellow passengers, were on a beach it was on Pulau Ubin off Singapore, after they had visited the Bugis Village. The next one they go on will be the beach below Tanjung Puting National Park, if they haven't elected to trek through the park with the rest of us and overnight at Camp Leakey or wherever. Then Bira Beach at Makassar, though – and this is my point really, though I'm labouring it I know – the hardier souls will probably be off to Paotere Harbour...'

'What's there?' asked Nic sharply, with a slight frown and an unconscious glance across to the recumbent Gabriella which perhaps only Robin really noticed.

'More Bugis,' answered Richard. 'Real Bugis this time. What there is left of them. Proper old-fashioned Orang Laut in their praus. Men, women and children who were supposed never to come to land, like the wandering albatrosses of the Southern Ocean. Paotere is supposed to be the closest the Bugis ever get – loading and unloading their cargoes for trading around the islands and their own floating villages and townships. Literally – town *ships*. Not like in the Bugis Village in Singapore, prettified up for the tourists. Paotere may be loud and ill-organized; it may stink to high heaven. But you can really get an idea of the old pirate history of the place. There's something of the old danger still there. Just the hint that if things went wrong...'

'What,' teased Robin, 'you mean the *Bugis man* would come and get us?' She pronounced *Bugis* in the correct way – *Boogey* – as though she were speaking French.

Richard gave a half grin. 'It's where the Boogey Man started out from,' he warned. 'They were the originals. Ruthless, deadly, stop-at-nothing, murderous pirates. Whispering out on the evening breezes from secret bays and secluded river mouths in all the local islands and coasts around the Java Sea, searching for prey. Sneaking silently aboard unwary ships in the night watches armed to the teeth with sword and kris, splitting skulls, slitting throats, stealing valuables and spiriting children away to raise as new generations of pirates. They scared the wits out of Conrad, Raffles, Rajah Brooke...'

'You see?' Robin turned back to Nic. 'You simply don't get stuff like that in Key West or Cancun!'

'Must have given J.M. Barrie a nasty turn too,' countered Nic, refusing to be impressed. 'Sounds a lot like Never Never Land to me. Maybe we'll find Peter Pan in Tanjung Puting...'

Richard and Robin exchanged a secret smile almost as intimate as the glance that Nic had shot Gabriella earlier. It was a kind of synchronicity – the whole conversation. For they themselves had been entangled in an almost fatal case of piracy not far from here ten years or so ago. And, if they didn't know anyone local called Peter, or Wendy or Smee, they really did know a captain whose name was Huuk.

'Krakatau lies at the heart of the Sunda Strait. Here, at six degrees, six minutes and twenty-seven seconds of south latitude, one hundred and five degrees, twenty-five minutes and three seconds of east longitude. I have found that people generally do not realize how close it is to many islands and land masses. I have talked to people who believe that it is simply somewhere in the sea, east of Java, and that the people who were killed and maimed in the most famous series of explosions, those of 1883, must have been living on the island itself. This is to misunderstand utterly the enormity of the actual event. In 1883, the year of the catastrophic explosions of the 26th and 27th August as recorded in Rogier Diederik Marius Verbeek's classic contemporaneous record, people visited the island for a range of reasons, but no one actually lived on it. Krakatau, then, as now, was one of the most active volcanoes of all...'

Richard gave up his search of the faces in the audience for Nic's. Then he eased himself back in his seat as Dr Hirai's earnest words swept over him. Replete with prawn and piglet, he was suddenly sleepy – in spite of several cups of excellent coffee. Feeling him move, Robin stopped looking so suspiciously for Gabriella and leaned in towards him. Their arms and shoulders rubbed gently together, his covered in crisp cotton and hers naked. She hoped he wasn't as sleepy as he looked. The view from their balcony was magnificent, especially now that the moon was rising; and she had plans to make good use of it for some renewed romance tonight, even if *Tai Fun* was riding at anchor with the black sails safely furled.

If the view from the upper decks of *Tai Fun*'s stern was breathtaking, it was as nothing compared with the view from the bridge at Jalan Gajah Mada. The centre of the span here commanded a vista looking north-westwards over the confluence of the Landak and the Kapuas Kecil rivers, down towards the delta of the Sungai Landak and the sea.

On the right hand, the land heaved up into the heights of Pontianac East, falling forward into the point of land where the multiple roofs of the Mesjid Jami and the Istana Kadriyah rose majestically. The traditional buildings seemed to burn amongst the grey concrete of more modern and practical masonry, catching the last of the afternoon sun, then exchanged their gilt for diamond as darkness brought myriads of bright traditional lanterns out. Beyond the point, Pontianac North rose again beyond the busy, boat-filled river confluence that was in many ways the heart of the city.

On the left Pontianac South became Pontianac West and reached out towards the sea. But the confluence, the river and the delta claimed the sight, in a great riverine sweep that reached somehow timelessly away to the sea and the lower sky.

An hour ago, the sun had spent a quarter of an hour tumbling gloriously down the sky in the abrupt, almost casual glory of a tropical – equatorial – sunset. The bludgeoning white-hot disc had taken on shades of orange, almost of ochre. Then, as it settled into the city's haze, it had turned abruptly crimson, gathering to scarlet in the lower sky. The cloudlets that would have told Larsen of an approaching weather system only served to enhance the glory as the sunset seemed to turn them into rubies and garnets scattered across the velvety French-blue sky. The sun seemed to hesitate like a modest bather before it plunged into the curve of sea, transforming in an instant – for an instant – from ruby to emerald as its rays gleamed through the water.

Then it was night.

Nic Greenbaum and Gabriella Cappaldi stood like any tourists awed by one of the world's great sunsets. But their conversation was too earnest and businesslike for them to be mere travelling companions struck by a wonderful view, even though they had bumped into each other here apparently by accident. She was returning from lengthy negotiations needed to arrange for the visit of nearly fifty hardy tourists to the Tanjung Puting National Park in two days' time. He was wandering back, oddly on foot, from a lonely visit to the Museum and the Dyak Longhouse close beside it. Amused, if the truth be told, by the way the longhouse had brought Richard's romantic talk of Bugis pirates to mind. For if there was a people more fearsome than the legendary Orang Laut sea-farers, it was the original orang-utan Dyak forest warriors.

Nic and Gabriella's earnest conversation continued for more than an hour as the sudden, sticky darkness revealed a fairy-tale world of lights where massive, low-hanging stars and stark, workaday street lighting settled cheek by jowl into the broad bright surface of the river. Where ferries bustled hither and thither like hives of multicoloured glow-worms. Where running lights and riding lights reflected each other in inverted constellations. Until the full, fat moon began to rise across the black sky with all the lazy sensuality of the season and the time – equalling in feminine mystery and promise what the sun had so casually and briefly shown in its dying glory. A shooting star curved across the heavens above it like Icarus falling in

141

flames.

'I don't usually sleep with my employees,' said Nic Greenbaum at last. 'But with you I think I'll make an exception, in spite of the obvious risks.'

'With a man of your reputation, it'd probably be more suspicious if you didn't make a move on the entertainments officer. Really get your money's worth in entertainment if nothing else.' Gabriella paused for an instant, a half-smile on her full lips, seeking his hooded eyes in the shadows of his face. Then, 'In the city or back aboard?' she asked throatily.

'Better be the city. I don't want to give too much away. The Mariners already suspect more than I would like. I don't want them involved, unless...'

Gabriella nodded decisively, then turned and led him southwards. 'We'll have to be up early,' she warned him. *Tai Fun* sails with the first tide tomorrow and if we're not aboard then it'll really ring some warning bells.' As she talked, she guided him decisively through the thinning crowd of pedestrians homeward-bound. At the south end of the bridge stood the Kapuas Palace Hotel, a walk of less than a hundred metres.

And she had a suite reserved here for the night, which they would share – after she introduced him to the man from the Luzon Logging Company who was currently awaiting them in the bar.

Fourteen

Council

'Aid? There will be no aid!' Chief Councillor Kerian's voice was shrill with outrage as it echoed around the council chamber above the heads of Pulau Baya's full council. 'How much aid arrived after the great tsunami five years ago? And how long did we have to wait then?'

'Enough to rebuild the old city of Baya, and then to build the new one,' answered Prince Sailendra, almost rising from his ceremonial seat beneath the island's emblematic flag at the end of the chamber. Restrained, perhaps, by the knowledge that it was the new city that had been swept away now. He settled into the carved and gilded ivory under the baleful gaze of woven clouded leopard in its prau. Met the equally baleful gaze of his chief councillor. 'And the fisheries at Bandar Laut Bay,' he continued. 'And oh so much else, and well you know it, Councillor Kerian. And if we had to wait a little while, that was because we were much lower on the list of priorities than some of our neighbours – and lucky to be so!'

'Even so, it is as well that we do not have to

wait for this *aid*! This charity from all the larger neighbours who would rather consume us than help us stand alone. Aid from China, Japan, Europe and America. *Aid at a price...*'

'We are aware, Councillor Kerian, of the speed with which the employees of your various companies have joined the rescue programme. We are aware of how much the council as a whole has already invested in bringing men and machinery from their own private concerns to join the larger municipal and national effort...'

'Helping ourselves, Prince Sailendra. Helping ourselves in the old way, before we began to hold out our hands for *aid*.'

Sailendra leaned forward, quite ready to take Kerian on, head to head, filled with some as yet vague fear that the councillor would lead them all into danger and disaster if he was allowed to have his head. All too well aware that it was Kerian's grandfather who had urged his own forebears to stand alone against the Japanese – and nearly lost the island altogether. But just as he opened his mouth to carry on, he felt a gentle tugging at the island-cotton sleeve of his shirt.

It was Parang. 'News,' said the secretary. 'I think you should come, Your Highness.'

Parang was not technically allowed in the council chamber and technicalities were high on the list of procedure since Kerian had become chief councillor. So the news must be important. Sailendra raised his hand and then stood up, his heart suddenly pounding. Perhaps

144

this was indeed news of the international aid for which he had been praying since the message went out last night.

'I am called away, Councillor Kerian,' said Sailendra formally. 'You must continue this meeting in my absence, of course. But may I urge care and caution.' He glanced pointedly up at the island's symbolic standard hanging limply in the hot morning air above his head. 'Like the clouded leopard which is the symbol of our island, let us not leap into action until we can see clearly where the leap will take us.'

Sailendra turned to follow Parang out of the council chamber, with Kerian's riposte ringing in his ears. 'But remember, fellow councillors, the leopard is only one part of our heritage. We are not only Bayan, we are Bugis. The Bayan leopard stands in the Bugis prau – to remind us that when the land becomes too dangerous, then we can always look to the sea.'

The messenger was the last that Sailendra might have expected. She was a young marine biologist whose main function was to advise the men who maintained the prawn fisheries at Bandar Laut Bay. 'What is it?' he asked at once, frowning.

The biologist's name was Nurul and she had been educated at Jakarta University, completing her doctorate in marine biology at the university's marine department. She considered herself a woman of the world. But of an Eastern world, perhaps. On the one hand, the frown of

145

the prince came close to cowing her. On the other hand, the frown of a man she had last seen standing beside Johnny Depp on Bandar Laut beach almost made her faint. 'You come, Your Highness; you see.'

'I am in a meeting with the full council, Dr Nurul,' Sailendra countered more gently. 'And I am only there because that meeting itself is vital enough to call me away from the rescue work in what little is left of the city beyond the river. Is your information *that important*?'

'Your Highness...' Her expression was more than enough. Kerian, the council, the work in the flooded wreckage beyond the river, all would have to wait.

The Toyota that lay beneath the landslip with the heliport and so much more was merely the best of the vehicles available to Sailendra. It was by no means the only one. There was at the very least the royal Rolls-Royce so beloved of his father – so impossibly expensive to keep in running order that it stood rusting uselessly in the palace garage, beside the Second World War jeep that General MacArthur had left behind. Also, nowadays, hors de combat. But these antiques were not alone. There were several occupied parking spaces in the royal garage. One of which was empty.

Beside the practical little dune-buggy that had brought Nurul there was parked a slightly more regal Mazda limousine. But the post-storm glory of the morning and the romantic inaccessibility of their destination – as well as the look his thoughtless frown had brought into the biologist's eyes – put Sailendra at his most accommodating. 'I will ride with the doctor, Parang,' he said. 'I should be grateful if you would follow in the Mazda so that I also have a ride home when I have seen what Dr Nurul has to show me.'

The road to Bandar Laut Bay ran in the opposite direction to the road that brought them here last night. After the junction with the road up to the palace, it ran away from the precipitous slopes of Guanung Surat and round along the tail of the teardrop-shaped island. The spine of the lower ranges loomed up against the sky on their right hand like a series of high green sharks' fins and the downslope on their left began to gather into the great sea-filled, white-beached, palm-lined amphitheatre of Bandar Laut Bay. The wind whispered in off the ocean, gusting lazily southwards out of stultifying Pontianac, but cooled by the better part of five hundred kilometres of sea. The waves gathered and tumbled as the road sank under the first overhang of palms, with nothing but fifteen hundred metres of white sand between it and the lazy, low-tide surf.

'It still amazes me, how the bay shelves down,' he said conversationally, looking across her at the view. 'The best of all worlds. Deep here – deep enough for visiting ships, though not as deep as the marina or the harbour, of course. Then shelving up to the plateau where the prawn fisheries are. Then coming up again into the shallows of the bathing beaches leading right down to the point.'

She nodded tersely, and gunned the motor, bringing enough of a headwind to stop his idle speculation, and to flatten her blouse across her chest in a manner that drew his gaze in from more distant horizons. That disturbed him; for the doctor was neither in her first blush of youth nor particularly attractive, and even had she been so, his taste in women tended away from the traditional teak-skinned, ebony-haired island beauties, of which Dr Nurul would have been a perfect example – had she held any pretensions towards beauty at all.

But then Sailendra's introspection was disturbed by something in the middle distance. 'That looks like an oil slick!' he said, shocked. 'What is that?'

'That's what I need to show you, Your Highness.'

'An oil slick! And so near to the prawn fisheries! Has there been an oil spillage here? Has there even been any ship nearby?' He suddenly remembered the radio signal the chopper pilot picked up last night. Could the ship that took their distress call have been sluicing out its tanks here? There was no sense discussing the possibility with the taciturn Nurul. Automatically, Sailendra glanced back at the Mazda speeding along in the white cloud of their wake. He had chosen badly. Riding with the doctor had told him nothing and had distracted him pointlessly at a time when he needed focus more than ever before. He undervalued Parang, he thought; took the faithful secretary for granted all too often. He was fortunate indeed to have such a faithful friend and confidant.

This thought too was brought to an abrupt stop as the beach buggy braked. The sand storm behind caught up with them at the same time as Parang in the Mazda. Then the two men ran across the burning sand to the rubber dinghy Dr Nurul had left tethered to the rudimentary landing-stage beside the neat little processing plant. There was room for the men to sit uneasily in the inflated little cockle shell as Nurul gunned the motor, sending the tiny vessel in an uncompromising line directly for the oily darkness of the slick above the precious fishery.

'Where are the boats? Where are the workers? The plant was empty,' Sailendra demanded suddenly.

And suddenly all the words she had kept so closely bottled up in the beach-buggy came tumbling out in an angry tirade whose ire seemed as much aimed at herself as at anyone else. 'I sent them to join Councillor Kerian's rescue teams in Baya City. There was no problem about leaving the fisheries for a day or two while they helped out there. And from what I gathered the need was pretty urgent, what with the landslide and the flooding. I stayed here and I thought I would be able to keep a safe eye on things. Remember,' she shot a dark look at the prince, 'I am not a medical doctor. I'm at home in an aquarium, not an emergency room.

Pressure makes me nauseous. Stress makes me sick. The sight of even a little blood makes me go down like a club on the back of the head, Bugis genes and Bandar Laut ancestors or not. There was no doubt in my mind. The men and their boats were better with you in the city on the floods and up the river, while I was better here. But that was before I discovered *this*.'

As she uttered the last word – spat it, in fact – the bow of the little inflatable hit the edge of the grey-brown iridescent slick. She cut the motor and let the dinghy drift.

It was the smell that alerted Sailendra to the terrible truth. He had been expecting the stench of oil to be pushed into his face by the northerly breeze, but instead his nostrils filled with something else. Filled and flared. It was strange – almost like something half remembered from the school Shakespeare of his Western education. A sweetness that cloyed and sickened. Except that it wasn't sweet. It was savoury. Fishy, in fact; almost as intensely fishy as the nam-pla fish oil they used in the palace kitchens.

Sailendra looked down.

The dinghy was drifting through a thick, lumpy soup composed of a million and more decomposing bodies. From the length of his longest finger to the size of a pin-head, curled like rotten brown flower-buds with their white legs clenched, all the prawns of the fishery floated dead on the tide.

'What has done this?' he demanded, turning on the woman as though the disaster were her fault after all.

'I know what did it,' she answered. 'But I don't know what caused it!'

'What do you mean?'

Rather than answer him, she simply put her hand over the side and plunged it into the stinking waves.

Without further thought, Sailendra did the same. Only to jerk his fist back again, hissing in shock.

The water was hot.

And of course that explained another thing that had been bothering him, bothered him more now he thought about precisely what he had seen on the approach across the beach. The absence of birds. Usually a feast like this would have summoned a raucous cloud of gulls. But there was nothing. And, now he thought of it, looking down past the lumpy soup that had once been a successful enterprise, there were no predatory or scavenging fish either. Everything that could get away had done so. Leaving only the prawns trapped in their nets to slowly cook alive. But how? Why?

The two men stood on a balcony overlooking the distant prospect of Bandar Laut Bay several hours later. The sun was sinking with tropical abruptness into the sea away to their left and the stars were beginning to burst through the afterglow on their right as they looked over the foothill slopes and into the wind northwards to Kalimantan.

Even at this distance the evening breeze brought the sick-sweet fish-oil smell of the rotting prawns up over the restless heads of the palm trees to their nostrils.

'What could make the water of Bandar Laut Bay hot enough to kill the whole prawn-fishery?' The words were uttered in the most intense of speculation.

'I don't know, Your Highness,' answered Parang. 'Dr Nurul suggested some kind of global warming.'

'Like the earthslide. That must have been due to global warming, when all is said and done.'

'Or something like it,' agreed Parang. 'Certainly, the storms we have experienced recently would suggest some kind of disturbance in the natural order...'

'Ah. Yes indeed. The natural order.'

The men fell silent, watching the sun fall like a severed head into the great blood-filled bowl of the western ocean.

'The Westerners believe such misfortunes come in threes,' observed Parang, almost dreamily as he surveyed the awesome view. 'First the landslide, then the prawn fishery, then...'

'And still no contact? From the outside world? The East ... or the West? No offers of aid?'

'No. Nothing.'

'Well, let us speculate a little and see whether that might lead us on towards a plan. What might this third misfortune be?'

'I would check the red-banana plantations as early as possible tomorrow,' said Parang. 'Indeed, beside them and the handling facilities where they are gathered, packed and prepared for shipment to market, there are the exotic-fruit farms, the refrigeration units and the canneries. It is all worryingly vulnerable to global warming. To any kind of disruption...'

'Disruption in the natural order. Yes. Indeed.'

There was just the faintest glimmering promise of moonrise. The evening breeze attained the closest to a chill it was capable of.

'But the council. What did the council decide in the end?' asked Parang.

'Nothing as yet. They remain hesitant. So much has happened in such a short time. They too remain hopeful of some kind of outside aid. And in the meantime, it is easier to take no grand decisions, to take no leadership role or responsibility. They are elderly. Weak. They wait to be led. They *want* to be led. And yet, when leadership is offered, they hesitate...'

'I sometimes wonder if their blood has been tainted, diluted, weakened beyond all measure. They are no longer Bandar Laut. Certainly, no longer Bugis – if any of them ever really were.'

Secretary Parang turned his back on the moonrise and leaned back against the handrail. The huge bright disc outlined his head and shoulder as though he were one of the puppets of the shadow theatre. A shooting star fell across the sky like Icarus falling, but he did not see it; his *dalang* puppet-master saw it, but would never associate it with such a hated Western tale.

'Come in, my son,' said Chief Councillor Kerian – offering a great compliment to the young man, but claiming no real family ties. 'We of the Bugis blood deserve to enjoy the old fruits. As lords of the natural order.'

And there in the sleeping quarters of Kerian's house waited two women. They were young, scarcely more than girls. Their flowerlike fineness and wide-eyed nervousness made them seem even younger than they were. They were both naked, and bound as though snatched as booty in some recent pirate raid.

'Choose one,' hissed Councillor Kerian almost silently at Parang's shaking shoulder, like a devil in the despised Western religious stories. 'They are merely mountain girls, brought down here by some of my ... contacts. They are of no account. Indeed, after last night it is highly unlikely that they have either families or villages left up on Guanung Surat.' He gave an evil, wolfish smile, exuding a disturbing amount of naked lust and power for a man approaching his mid-seventies. 'Choose either one and take her in the full-blooded Bugis way. Then I will take the other.'

Fifteen

Paddy

The south side of Pulau Baya was very different from the north. The north side of the island curved inwards in a long shallow bay. The south curved outwards precipitously. If the north-facing slopes of Guanung Surat were steep at their highest levels, they were still just gentle enough to support the burgeoning Baya City on the lower, river-widened foothills and plain. Before the landslide, that is. On the south-facing slopes there was no such hope. From the watershed that reached in a series of ridges along the whole spine of the island, the south-facing slopes at the higher, western end simply plunged in forested cliffs that tumbled almost vertically into the sea. What vegetation there was clung to the cliff-chopped sides, but such was the scale of the mountain that there was unsuspected depth to the outcrops, and men could come and go amongst them. It was here that the bitterest, most dangerous fighting had been centred in the 1940s, for the dizzy heights of Guanung commanded a view across the Baya/Java Strait that could monitor any marine or airborne activity along the coast of Java from Jakarta to Surabaya, although the great island itself lay just below the horizon, even when you stood at the old Japanese watchtower right at the highest peak. Which nobody except the occasional inquisitive high-forest hunter had actually done for nearly sixty years. And, perhaps, the occasional fearful orang-utan escaping the attentions of a prowling clouded leopard.

Here the vagaries of the monsoon dictated that the greatest rainfall came, though the landscape seemed ill equipped to make much use of it. There were no big rivers – merely precipitous cascades which had never quite managed to cut into the rock. No more had the jungle and rainforest managed sufficient plant cover to make much thickness of soil. And the goodness of such soil as there was – especially at the steep-sided western end – was simply washed away by the relentless downpours. Downpours that ironically kept this side of the island poor while feeding the headwaters of the rich Sungai Baya River on the far side of the high watershed ridge, a few hundred metres further north.

But as the jagged peaks of the watershed fell away along the curving spine of the land towards the long spit pointing eastwards like a pirate's cutlass at the end of Bandar Laut Bay, so the slopes also eased, even on the steep southern side. Eased enough to allow cultivation, if not much in the way of civilization as yet. Here beneath the relentless but reliable monsoons were the red-banana plantations, and the great soft-fruit farms, with the canneries conveniently situated between them. Here one or two island-people villages clung to jungle clearings, their men and women given gainful income by the agriculture Sailendra had brought here. Their children were given the rudiments of education by UNESCO, especially in the years since the last great tsunami brought the whole area to the attention of the charitable West.

Here a track wide enough for the passage of trucks led over the lower ridges to the docking facilities on the north coast. And another, smaller, down to the lesser facilities on the south coast itself, where the water was deep enough to accept big cargo vessels but the infrastructure was not yet advanced enough to make it worth their while calling. And here, clinging like vineyards to the recently cleared slopes, were the steps of the rice-paddies. Each season – and there were three a year – the farmers would bring their unique, increasingly popular and fantastically expensive Pulau rice down in ever greater quantities. At the same time, under the careful, ecologically sensitive direction of Prince Sailendra himself, they fought the rainforest back and back.

Sailendra himself remained involved because the forest clearance remained so sensitive. And yet, if properly handled, it too could yield enormous profit to the island. For every stand of mahogany and teak that fell to the requirements of the paddy fields was carefully logged, recorded and put on to the open market – though never yet via the rapacious Gargantua of Luzon Logging, which had deforested and denuded so many local islands large and small. And any protected species – the native orang-utans and the recently discovered clouded leopards – were carefully and sensitively moved. Usually into remoter island forests; occasionally to top-class zoos, which were also willing to pay enormous amounts of money for the creatures.

Given Sailendra's personal interest in so many projects on the south side of the island it was almost surprising that it took him until the middle of the second day after the landslide to come here in person to check for damage. Especially as he knew, better than most, that if the downpour had been so dangerously overwhelming in the north, it must have been far more devastating in the south.

As Sailendra bumped along in the truck the cannery kept in Baya City for ferrying crates to and fro from the port, he really wondered at the way his priorities had been dictated by events. Even for a prince who kept himself calculatedly free of ceremonial and security, he had been worryingly circumscribed by events. He narrowed his eyes a little, never losing focus on the wide track of the part-metalled roadway that led up to a pass between two low shark-fin peaks on the backbone of the ridge. On either side of them the half-jungle was part-cultivated palm-groves, the nodding trees laden with coconut and dates, interspersed with breadfruit. They could have industrialized this part of the island more – but that would have undermined the wild timeless beauty of Bandar Laut Bay, which stretched dazzlingly from side to side of his rear-view mirror. And what they gained in the production of all-too-readily available produce would have cost them uncalculated amounts in tourist dollars. Just what Johnny Depp's film-production company was contracted to pay for the shoot at the bay behind him would go a long way to fixing the damage done by the storms. And then there were the tourist cruises due, and the dollars they would bring. But the simple fact was that the people's prince felt *cabined*, as Shakespeare had put it. *Cabined, cribbed, confined.*

Sailendra had been active in the rescue work in New Baya City – what was left of it; uneasily aware of a pressure to match Councillor Kerian's much-trumpeted, politically weighty work. He had faced Kerian head to head across the council chamber, not once, but three times now – twice as they tried to make plans after the landslide and again after the scale of the disaster at the prawn fisheries became clear.

Sailendra never doubted that he was doing the right thing. He had never doubted it since he had returned from his Western education to assume the throne after his parents' all-too-sudden death. A simple plane crash had removed not only the ruling generation but everyone

159

on whom they had relied – upon whom the young incumbent could have relied. He had done his best since his accession to bring the principality into the modern era, but things had been hard right through the whole of Indonesia. Since President Suharto's death, seemingly only days before his parents', the regimented system that they had all known, as subjects or as allies, had begun to come apart at the seams. It was like the collapse of the old Soviet Union. Now it was every man – or country, region or village – for himself, and no one held the whip hand any more except the great greedy cash-rich companies like Luzon Logging.

Sailendra had done his best to hold it all together. But such forces as held practical power on the island did not feel firmly in his grip. The council held more sway with the rudimentary civil service, the largely ceremonial armed forces and the emergency policing units. It wouldn't take much more, thought the young prince wearily, to make Kerian the real ruler of Pulau Baya. And the chief councillor knew it. The question was, did he *want* it? The power, yes. But did the impatient old pirate see that with power ought to go responsibility?

'Did you say something, Your Highness?' asked Parang quietly.

Sailendra turned to glance at the young man, looking away from the rocky upslope of the road only for an instant. Parang had been quiet all day, since reporting for duty soon after the sudden dawn. But then, he had been under almost as much stress as Sailendra had himself. Had been working almost as hard. Though, with the early night he had been allowed last evening, he did look well rested.

'I was thinking about Councillor Kerian,' said the prince.

'Yes, Your Highness?'

'If anything else goes badly wrong, he'll carry the council and take control of Pulau Baya altogether.'

'It is possible.'

'Do you suppose he plans it?'

'I believe the chief councillor is concerned about the position we find ourselves in. It is almost unbelievable that in this day and age we cannot find a way of reaching out to the wider world and warning them of our predicament. Or that someone somewhere would have register-ed the tremor that the landslide must have caused.'

The truck ground up between the peaks which seemed, strangely, almost as two-dimensional here in the pass between them as they seemed from the distance of Bandar Laut Bay. 'Fate seems to be against us. Or karma. Or whatever. Perhaps we have done terrible things in past lives...' suggested Sailendra, changing down as the truck's nose fell on to the southern down-slope. Here the road was suddenly muddy, as though the narrow pass had brought them into another climate zone altogether.

'Or in present ones,' agreed Parang drily, leaning back into his seat and reaching forward with one straight arm against the dash. 'But still, the fact that Dr Nurul possessed a cellphone that usually communicates with her colleagues at the University in Jakarta...'

'Only to find its battery dead. And her charger incapacitated by the lack of current in the grid since the power station went down in the landslide!' Sailendra pounded on the steering wheel of the truck. The Baya/Java Strait gleamed wickedly under the bludgeoning afternoon sun beyond the steep lushness of the first soft-fruit farms. 'Has no one on the island got a cellphone or a radio that works?'

'Seemingly not, Your Highness. At least, not with the power grid down. There may be individual generators...' He gestured away towards the distant shanties of the corrugated-iron farm buildings.

'Which do not produce power at wattages needed to recharge cellphones.'

'Or radios...'

'Receivers in plenty. Transmitters, apparently not!'

'Except of course in the Baya Broadcasting building. Beneath about a million tons of mud!'

'And not one ship in the harbour. Nothing. Except that one vessel that promised to pass on our emergency message...'

'I believe we have no more hope of that, Your Highness. Maybe it was a false signal. Who knows?'

'Whoever knows, I hope I meet up with him some day!' snarled the frustrated prince. He eased his over-tense shoulders. 'And your own phone?' he asked for about the tenth time in the last thirty-six hours.

'Reliant on the mast that used to stand almost at the top of Guanung Surat, just upslope from the transmitter mast belonging to Baya Broadcasting. Like almost every other cellphone on the island,' mourned Parang. 'A victim of the modern ways.'

'You sound like Councillor Kerian,' joked Sailendra.

'It must be my Bugis blood,' answered Parang, apparently joking too.

The truck slopped through puddles, spraying up ochre waves on to the luxuriant greenery of the roadside. 'The fruit farms seem to have survived,' observed Parang, changing the subject. 'Though I can't see anyone actually working the fields.'

'They've probably gone to Baya City to help Councillor Kerian's epic rescue attempts, like Dr Nurul's workers from the prawn fishery,' said Sailendra, only half joking, his voice sounding unexpectedly bitter, even in his own ears.

'Possibly, Your Highness.' Parang sounded unconvinced. 'The banana plantations will give us a better idea on both counts. As to the storm damage and the presence of workers.'

The conversation died then and both men became lost in their thoughts as Sailendra swung the truck round to his right and began to toil back up the slope along the increasingly precipitous road that led above the banana plantations towards the high rice paddies.

'It's the rice paddies I'm worried about,' he confided to Parang, after a while. 'Some of the new ones are on pretty steep slopes. I know we've dug them in pretty carefully – and taken infinite pains over the irrigation. But that rainstorm the night before last tore the northern side of Guanung Surat. Helped by illegal logging, fair enough. But there's no knowing what it could have done down here.' He swung round to glance at his secretary once again, the fine features of his face suddenly twisted in naked anguish. 'These people were relying on me. On me personally, man to man. I should have come to check on them sooner, Parang.'

That apparently innocent and fleeting glance away from the road ahead had consequences that were far-reaching; almost fatal. The front wheels of the truck simply jumped into a wide puddle lying apparently still across the road in front of them. Jumped, and, instead of landing on a shallow bottom, fell away vertiginously.

Had Sailendra been paying just that tiny bit more attention, he might have seen that the apparently restful surface was simply a pool in a plunging stream that had in fact torn this part of the road away before cascading on down the hillside. Only a pile of boulders wedged in the precipitous valley held the water back just enough to give the fatal illusion that there was a still pool with a solid roadway beneath it. The truck lurched forward into the wild rush of tumbling rivulet, therefore. At once a flood of dirty water – the colour and seemingly the weight of molten gold – was hurled against the bonnet. It drowned the engine in an instant, and pushed on with the relentless force of blow after blow. The whole vehicle swung round, its left front tyre demolished the makeshift dam that had held the seeming puddle on the road, and the truck itself settled on to the slope beneath. And here it hesitated, with the water still thundering down its shaking length, threatening to spew it down still further into the uppermost plantation.

Sailendra, raised in safety-conscious climes, had worn his seat belt since the off. Parang was still sitting with his arm wedged rigidly against the dash. Both survived relatively unscathed. The truck did not. It was dead and all but buried. Even as they realized it was still, they could feel it slipping into motion once again. With one accord, as though psychically linked, they each threw open their door and prepared to hurl themselves out. Only at the last minute did Parang, seeing Sailendra throw himself to his right, think to scramble across the seats and follow him. So that when the truck was washed away down the slope a moment later, at least the pair were on the same side of the torrent.

'We have to get back to the cannery, Your Highness,' gasped Parang, as soon as the easing shock allowed him to talk sensibly. 'They have more trucks down there. We can drive back to Baya City. Other than that, we walk.'

Sailendra looked at his soaking, shaken, filthy secretary, and shook his head. 'You're right, of course, Parang,' he said decisively. 'But I came here to check on the paddies and that little incident makes me feel that it's really important I do so as soon as possible. The whole hillside here could be coming away as well!'

The roadway held no more unpleasant surprises, except for the particularly prehensile nature of the mud. It was hot, too, for the northerly afternoon breeze was funnelled far over their heads by the hill-crest up on their right. Here, the south-facing slope was utterly airless. It would be, Sailendra realized, until the monsoon came by in a few weeks' time. Until then the wind would gust from the north and the air would sit completely still. And it was summer. And they were only a few hundred kilometres south of the equator. But they were determined, so they proceeded.

The first paddy was only a kilometre further on, but by the time they reached it the two men were giddy with heatstroke, fatigue and dehydration, not to mention the after-effects of clinical shock from the crash and their narrow escape. They were, in short, all too willing to immerse themselves in its still cool water, in spite of whatever damage they might be doing to the precious shoots. And it was only the greatest self-control – and the liveliest sense of self-preservation – that stopped them from drinking it.

But that first limpid pool cleared their heads

and allowed them to look around. The paddies stepped down the hillside in long flights of silver-surfaced stairs. They were carefully angled and irrigated so that even the wild downward rush of the torrential rain that had created the near-fatal rivulet running across the road was channelled and controlled. The paddies ran into each other like a series of gutters on a roof so that the pressure of the water was channelled safely down from one level to the next beneath and so through to the systems in the plantations and the fruit farms and finally out into the waters of the strait itself in a great raw concrete sluice standing between the cannery and the little dock facility.

But the long look that the bathe in that first paddy allowed Sailendra to take showed that the system was by no means working as he had hoped. It did not seem to have handled the downpour at all well: the next paddy beneath them, for instance, was overflowing in a steady cascade, and the next in series beneath it seemed to be faring little better. And these were just the first of many more.

'Come on,' gasped the prince. 'We'll look at those two nearest. They're on the way down to the cannery, at any rate.'

Also short of breath after his long walk and luxurious immersion, Parang nodded, and off they slopped together. They sloshed through the paddy knee-deep in the cool water, being more careful of the rice plants now, and feeling the deep, silty mud pull at their ankles as though

167

the fine dark coffee-ground soil could lead, like some kind of quicksand, right down to the black heart of the mountain itself. At the outer edge there was a low wall made of concrete padded with mud, then a step down of nearly two metres into the next paddy, the first of those that were overflowing. Unfortunately, made clumsy by the weight of water in their clothes and by the exhaustion of their adventures so far, the pair heaved themselves over and began to weave almost drunkenly through the lower paddy. Suddenly Sailendra drew himself up, focusing almost fiercely. 'Look,' he said to Parang. 'There's something blocking the sluice. That's all that's wrong!'

Side by side they stumbled over to the lower end of the paddy, where a simple concrete runway led down into the next in the series, blocked like a whale's throat by a simple filter-grille. There was something wedged up against it, blocking it solidly enough to cause the whole finely balanced system to flood. As Sailendra drew near, he thought dreamily that the block-age must simply be a bundle of old clothes. Then, a little nearer, he wondered whether it might not be the body of some animal washed in here by the deluge.

It was only when Parang and he were stand-ing side by side and their knees, bisected by the silvery surface, were actually up against it that Sailendra realized the truth. The blockage was a dead body. A human body, curled against the grille as tightly as one of the prawns in the ruined fisheries of Bandar Laut Bay. The impression was so overpowering that Sailendra found himself bending to plunge his hand into this water too – to see if it were as warm as the bay had been. He froze halfway through the act, with his fist in the water beside the dead man, struck by the massive stupidity of what he was doing. If the water had been hot, his feet and legs would have warned him long since.

But then he noticed something else. Something that drove a spear of panic like a man-sized icicle right through the middle of his being. The water was bubbling. It wasn't fizzing like champagne. It wasn't boiling as though to make tea. But it was bubbling, like sparkling water. Like Perrier. The hairs on his submerged hand and forearm were covered with silver already. As was the dead man curled against the grating; every fold of his clothing, each strand of his hair, every part of him submerged beneath the surface of the paddy was covered with tiny bubbles that gleamed like mercury. Gleamed, and gathered and bubbled up in their countless millions into the air they were trying to breathe.

It was some kind of gas. Poison gas.

Sailendra straightened and swung round. The sensation of being impaled on an icicle had been so vivid that it seemed natural enough now to have a splitting headache. A headache so fierce that it almost incapacitated him. Almost, but not quite. His wide gaze swept across the paddies. Took in anew the number that were overflowing. Overflowing because their grilles were blocked. If they were all blocked by dead men, there had been a terrible massacre here. He turned further, to share his suspicions with his secretary. But it was already far too late.

Parang was standing behind him, eyes wide, seemingly turned to rock. His face was pale, especially around his mouth, though his cheeks were bright red. The edges of his lips looked almost blue as did the point of the tongue with which he was licking them. His eyes and nose were running as though he had some kind of influenza.

'Parang!' gasped the prince. 'We must get away from here!'

The secretary answered by slumping to his knees.

Sailendra reached down and took Parang by the collar. He heaved him forward like a sack of rice, caring little enough for the fact that he was probably choking him. Then, step after heaving step, Sailendra started to drag him bodily down the slope, crashing desperately from one paddy down to the next, as though they were falling very slowly down a massive, mountainous stairway, in a wild and weakening search for that first life-giving breath of clean, fresh air.

Sixteen

Orang-Utan

Richard for one was surprised the next evening to find Inge Nordberg standing where Dr Hirai had stood the evening before, facing down into the packed auditorium preparing to deliver the after-dinner speech. On the screen behind the owner's classically Nordic daughter was a picture, not of Krakatau as it had stood in 1883, but of Tanjung Puting National Park and Biosphere as it was now. And, perhaps in an attempt to add to the authenticity of her talk, Inge was dressed in a bush shirt, shorts, knee-socks and trekking boots. Oddly, thought Richard, she looked the part – like one of those presenters so popular with wildlife programmes on the television. He glanced around the audience. Nic and he were the oldest here by far. It seemed that it was mostly the youngsters from the pools and the water-sports action that were going into the park. The more elderly were spending a more restful time on the beaches and in the casino instead. But there was no doubt that the Ice Maiden could hold her audience. Even Robin was focused on Inge's

171

serious face as she swept an errant lock of hair out of her eyes and consulted a dog-eared set of notes. And, he noted wryly, if Robin was focused, Navigating Officer Gruber was simply entranced.

'We will arrive at Tanjung Puting in a little more than thirty-six hours,' began Inge, looking up, gazing at her rapt audience and talking with all the confidence of a practised public speaker. 'But we deliver the initial briefing now, rather than tomorrow evening, so that you have plenty of time to double-check and ask questions. Furthermore, we suggest most strongly that even the fittest and hardiest of you relax tomorrow and get an early night tomorrow night. You will require a lot of stamina to get the most out of your two days in the park. And it has been our experience that even those who overnight in either of the hotels there do not sleep quite as well as they do aboard. Particularly as the vast majority avail themselves of the night tours as well as the day treks. So, after the next, hopefully restful, thirty-six hours before our arrival, you must expect another thirty-six to forty hours that are really quite tiring – though, of course, unforgettably exhilarating.'

Inge turned to the map behind her. 'The park itself is huge – over four thousand square kilometres. Some of it is unimaginably remote, especially as it is mostly riverine mangrove and jungle swamp and low-lying forest. Obviously you would never be able to explore it all in ten times the time allotted. But in two full days,

172

with an overnight in the park itself, you can see the highlights. You have already started to make decisions about your visit, I know. Entertainments Officer Cappaldi has had to get your individual passes, with the relevant documentation from your passports. You have had to ensure – and confirm with herself and myself – that you are properly equipped, for there are no shops within the park. You have already decided whether you will be overnighting at the hotels in the park or remaining aboard your kolek riverboats to eat, sleep and explore. You have all been assigned a place in a kolek but as these only take groups of four as well as the native crew of two, you may want to decide whether there is a particular pairing or grouping you wish to be a part of.'

Richard caught Nic's eye at that. The pair of them exchanged terse nods, like Ernest Hemingway agreeing Alan Quartermain as his hunting partner. Which meant, by the look of things, that Robin and Gabriella were spoken for as well.

'All access to the national park is by water and only by water. There are paths, of course, that take you through the jungle to the points of major interest – the orang-utan sanctuaries, the main monkey groupings, the flora and rarest forest sections, well worth visiting because they remain under so much threat, even here and even now. And there are several Dyak villages in the park as well, for the fullest appreciation of which I understand that the indefatigable Mr

Greenbaum has prepared himself by visiting the Museum and Dyak Longhouse in Pontianac yesterday evening.' She shot Nic a shy smile and he returned a broad, self-satisfied grin.

Nic liked being ahead of the game, thought Richard. And he remembered the irritation in the Texan's face when he realized he did not know about the Bugis harbour at Paotere, north of Makassar. Did that mean, Richard wondered suddenly, that Nic was not planning to be aboard when they got to Makassar? There were implications in that thought which might bear some examination. And which might form the basis of a conversation on the kolek riverboat if not before.

But Inge was talking again with that quiet authoritative insistence that commanded full attention. 'Much of the tourist information about the peripheries of the national park will not really apply to us. We will moor as close to the port of Kumai, which is the starting point for almost all authorized visits into the park. By that time you will have finalized your group-ings. You will have been issued with all relevant documentation and will have had your equipment checked. So we will simply transfer you in your groups from *Tai Fun* into your koleks, check with the crew, double-check with the park's guards and rangers, and off you go. You have already paid the standard daily rate for the koleks, which includes food, drink, accommodation aboard as necessary and guid-ing along the trails as you require. Or rather, we have done so on your behalf. To those of you watching your budgets, that's a hundred and fifty thousand rupiahs each, which comes out at about fifteen dollars each. The hotel comes in at nearer seventy dollars. Those of you in hotels, your rooms are reserved, your meals are spoken for and your places on night tours booked. There are no shops in the park itself, remember, so you have no need of money in the park, though if you are staying at a hotel you might wish to take a little. But not much. That is the upside of your need to ensure you have packed everything you are likely to need for your visit. We will take care of any other matters such as gratuities as you instruct us upon your return to Kumai' – she consulted her watch – 'in almost exactly one hundred hours' time.'

Almost exactly sixty hours later, almost breathless with childlike excitement, Richard handed Robin down into the stern of their kolek. This turned out to be a narrow blue-painted riverboat the better part of six metres long. It was fully decked, with a motor nestled under solid planking and a tall, flat-roofed accommodation area midships, looking for all the world like a cross between a Wendy house and a tree house, which he had already learned to call a 'mandi'. It would accommodate four, eating or sleeping, in campers' comfort. Its solid roof would make an excellent observation platform. Indeed, as Richard let go of Robin's hand, he saw Nic already swarming up the ladder, intent on deploying his camera and binoculars at the earliest opportunity. Gabriella talked quietly to the taller of their boatmen, and saw to the disposal of their bags. The smaller, younger, of the boatmen cast off and powered up the motor as the kolek eased into the stream, first boat out of the day. Richard paused for a moment to look at the men who would be their crew and guides for the next two days and the intervening night. They were pale-skinned and almost Chinese in feature. But the lobes of their ears were stretched by weighty rings and the square-cut fringes across their broad foreheads gave them an almost South American look, as though they were members of some tribe long lost in the Amazon jungle. They were Dyaks, he realized; the best possible guides for this terrain.

'What are their names?' he asked Gabriella quietly.

'You'd never get your tongue around them,' she answered; though *she* had been able to, Richard noted. 'The tall one there is Father. The shorter one is Son. Father and Son. That's the best we can do, and they'll answer to them in English, if you call.'

Richard nodded, and looked as Father pushed the baggage into the mandi and Son opened the throttle a little wider, keen to be away up the river, now that they were off.

Above and behind them, as the dawn began to brighten the sky, excited figures bustled on the Kumai piers, beside the fading glow of the brightly lit Park Ranger office. While Gabriella had elected to lead the expedition from the lead boat, she had left Inge to oversee the others, and, no doubt, to bring up the rear. Not that the vessels would present an armada, or even a flotilla. As soon as possible, each would ease into its own unique channel and follow its own course through the all-but-floating jungle. That was the plan, at any rate, according to the briefings.

Richard forgot about the others as soon as he turned to look ahead. And a moment after that he was up with Nic on the roof of the mandi, with Robin like a tall electric charge sparking energy and excitement beside him, straining to see as much as he could as quickly as possible.

The sky was beginning to brighten rapidly and dawn light was filtering across the still surface of the Sungai, or River, Sekonyer. Richard had explored the great rivers of Africa and had been half expecting to be dwarfed by timelessly giant vegetation, such as Conrad himself had described in his *Heart of Darkness*. But this was altogether more intimate. The river was narrow and closely overhung. Nipa palm trees crowded the half-submerged banks like bushes with grandiose ideas, close-packed and seemingly trunkless, close enough to touch as they swept majestically by. As the light gathered, they faded out of blackness into gathering green. An avenue of bushy treetops seemingly floating on the still black water.

But if the emergence of the colours was slow and painstaking, almost elegant in its waking languor, the same could not be said of the stirring inhabitants within them. For with the dawn came the dawn chorus. Every bird in the forest woke with the uprising sun and began to twitter, hoot, sing or scream. Nor was it only the bird life stirring. Against the stained-glass brightness of the pale-blue sky, flights of bats went skimming, leather-winged, snub-nosed and tailless, adding a high-pitched, piercing shrilling to the cacophony of the birds. And, as the river-smelling jungle atmosphere of the place closed around them, seeming at the turning of the first river bend to jerk them back to the dawn of time, so the apes and monkeys, lemurs, sloths and orang-utans all joined in. The stirring of the jungle at dawn would have drowned out the loudest, most drunken and bellicose of football-hooligan crowds.

Only as the daylight filtered further down did Richard begin to see the activity the cacophony was drowning out. Here and there the palms parted widely enough to allow a pathway to approach the water and here tiny deer were stealing down to drink. But their nervousness was little to do with the near-silent passing of the kolek. For there, in the shaded deeps beneath the leafy overhangs, stirred great scaly bodies half as long as the boat. Long, angular heads peeped above the water, too long and narrow, seemingly, to belong to crocodiles – and yet fearsomely armed with teeth.

'What's that?' asked Richard, as one angular head reared right out of the water grinning

178

toothily at him.

'False gharial. Kind of crocodile,' answered Nic, as quietly as the storm of awakening songs would allow.

'There are real estuarine crocodiles here too,' added Gabriella knowledgeably. 'Big and very dangerous.'

'Most dangerous to them, I should expect,' added Robin, gesturing to another tiny deer. 'Is that a mouse deer?'

'I believe it is.'

As the daylight gathered, and the humid heat began to build, so the howling in the jungle began to die back. But the activity did not slow. Squadrons of monkeys came and went through the treetops on either side. Larger deer and wild pigs passed like shadows – or blundered like little tanks – through the undergrowth. The distant snarl of a hunting leopard came and went echoing into sudden silence; silence that passed again in an instant.

'Probably not as big or dangerous as it sounds,' said Nic. 'Clouded leopards and leopard cats is about it for this park. You're more at risk from inquisitive orang-utans, I'd say.'

'And the spiders, snakes and scorpions,' added Gabriella bracingly. 'But we'll talk about those in more detail when we go ashore for our first walk.'

The lazy flow of the river widened into lakelets where white herons stood, apparently admiring their perfect reflections in the obsidian mirror of the surface. Almost invisible, beside them, black on black, stood the occasional hornbill. At the bank of one such lakelet, where the low palm jungle was just beginning to ease back into more patchy forest, the kolek's crew brought the long blue hull to rest and they stopped for an early lunch of fruit and water. Although they ate aboard their still, near-silent vessel, they all soon climbed ashore to stretch their legs. And so it became obvious that the place and time of their landfall was no coincidence. For after the early and sustaining repast and enough exercise to loosen them all up, Son, the shorter of their guides, checked their footwear, clothing and equipment. Then Father, the taller, led them off across the clearing and into the scrubby trees. Almost instantly, it became obvious that they were following a path. There were bright markers on posts beside their way, and, at the first convenient stopping place, a shelter with a map and a set of instructions in a range of languages from English to Japanese, warning them to keep to the path and to beware of straying into the jungle. Robin for one was uncertain whether the vivid pictures of spiders, snakes, scorpions, cats of various sizes, deer of various sizes, wild boar and orang-utan were telling them what to look for – or what they should beware of.

Father held up his hand with fingers and thumb spread.

'Five kilometres,' translated Gabriella. 'That should take, what, two hours?'

'Allow three,' advised Nic. 'We may want to

dawdle a little.'

'I want to dawdle a lot,' insisted Robin gamely, patting her camera and her binoculars. 'I don't want to miss any of this at all if I can help it.'

'Fair enough,' agreed Nic accommodatingly. 'Tell the man, Gabriella.'

Gabriella pointed at her watch and held up three fingers.

Father shrugged accommodatingly and turned, the late-morning sunlight gleaming on the gold in his pendant earlobes.

Richard wondered why they bothered with the pantomime – he was sure they had been talking to each other when he handed Robin aboard in the darkness of the dawn.

The muddy path led out of the scrub and back into the forest almost at once. The taller canopy of the trees closed over them at once, keeping the fierceness of the noonday sun at bay. Not that the shadows or the thick air through which they seemingly half swam were actually cool or anything like it. Humid, enervating, but bearable, for all that their clothes were sodden within five minutes – soaked from the inside as effectively as if they were walking through a monsoon rainstorm. In the trees above and around them, they soon began to see families of monkeys lazing in the noonday heat: proboscis monkeys, macaques, gibbons, red-leaf monkeys or maroon langurs.

'We should be looking out for sun bears too,'

whispered Gabriella. 'And of course sambar deer, mouse deer like the one you saw drinking this morning, Robin, and wild pig. We heard a clouded leopard or leopard cat hunting too, but we won't see them at all. Anyone particularly interested in plants or trees? There's nothing of the first rank here. In the jungle proper upriver this afternoon we should see orchids, a range of other striking and endangered flowers and stands of protected trees. And that's where we'll find the orang-utans too. Especially if we time it well and join the others who'll be there for four o'clock feeding.'

No sooner had Gabriella delivered herself of this confident and authoritative speech, however, than an orang-utan dropped on to the path immediately in front of them. It was the creature's size that stopped them dead. It stood the better part of a metre and a half high, topping Gabriella's five foot four and nearly equalling Robin's five foot eight. It was broad, solid and enormously powerful-looking. It must have weighed in excess of two hundred pounds, the better part of fifteen stones. Its fur was shaggy and beginning to fade, but nevertheless still burned with the orange glow almost unique to the species. It was bare-chested, pot-bellied and balding, its long serious face lined and drooping into pendulous jowls. It opened its mouth and grunted, showing an array of yellow teeth almost as intimidating as the crocodile's this morning.

Robin gaped. She had been half afraid that

she would find the creatures disappointing, little more than lively versions of the King of the Apes in Disney's *Jungle Book*. But this didn't disappoint her at all. It terrified her. Its feral stench seemed to cow something timeless deep inside her, and perhaps fortunately, the shock of its naked ferocity so close so suddenly robbed her even of the ability to scream. Almost robbed her of the ability to breathe. Here in the wild, face to face, there was no safe limit to protect her. No cage or moat. The massive creature could do anything it wanted – and there was nothing any of them could do to stop it.

Such was Robin's relief when the huge orangutan reached for Gabriella with the terribly unnatural length of his right arm that she almost fainted on the spot. Nic made some kind of a noise and the orang-utan simply glanced up at him, too powerful, too regal, too much in charge of this moment, this clearing, this jungle to be disturbed. It reached out further with one massive pale-palmed, shaggy-backed, black-nailed hand and removed the bag from Gabriella's shoulder. With simply human knowledge and understanding, it opened the flap and reached inside. It pulled out the two-litre bottle of chilled Evian water that Son had ensured they were all carrying. It put the bag down. It pulled the top off. It drank until the bottle was empty. It threw the crushed plastic aside like the husk of some discarded fruit. It licked its lips appreciatively.

It vanished.

The somnolent silence of a jungle at noon lingered with nothing but the buzzing of invisible insect life to break it. Or rather, to emphasize its utter stillness.

'I know,' said Gabriella with a loud and sudden brightness that bordered on the hysterical, as she bent to retrieve her bag, 'when we've finished our walk here and sailed on up the river a spell, let's give orang-utan feeding time a *miss*!'

Seventeen

Ramin

After the scrub and more open forest where they had stopped for lunch and their first, almost disastrous, exploration, the jungle proper gathered in. Son and then Father guided the kolek with its shocked and silent passengers into the shaded sections where the tall walls of greenery began to close over their heads. Even in the shadows of early afternoon the huge lily flowers lining the banks seemed to burn at the hearts of massive pads seemingly large enough to hide even the largest crocodiles. Behind the big green puddles of lily leaf, the lower greenery blazed with huge bushes of great golden gardenias and ranges of male and female pandanus. These varied in size from small bushes to tall trees whose leaves joined the canopy overhead. They were covered in white flowers almost as beautiful as the gardenias and fruits the size of pineapples that reminded Richard irresistibly of the spiked maces carried by medieval knights. The fruits varied in colour from green through orange to bright red, and hung in series back into the green jungle darkness like Chinese lanterns suspended in the trees. The smell was disorientatingly complex, a mixture of garden, with fragrant flowers and compost, greenhouse and kitchen spice cupboard. The pandanus, like many of the water's edge trees, had support roots like mangroves reaching out of the black surface and halfway up their trunks. And these roots, filled with leaf-mould, debris and detritus, gave safe haven to a bewildering range of ferns, vines and orchids.

As the kolek eased past this dazzling array, as close as the giant lily pads would allow, so Robin and Richard began to see that beneath the flower-jewelled carapace of the bank, the roots gave refuge to other, less gorgeous life forms. Here, amongst orchids as purple as the robes of emperors, ran giant scorpions as red as blood and as yellow as bile. Under gardenias as bright as golden goblets crouched spiders as big as dinner plates, waiting to trap kingfishers and hummingbirds. Up vines as beautifully woven as hand-made tapestries crawled centipedes that looked as long as the quick green mambas and pythons hanging from the branches over-hanging above.

Kingfishers flickered in and out like flames capable of burning underwater. Darters of all kinds threw themselves like tiny bolts of lightning across the shadowy air. Hummingbirds hung like gorgeous hornets sipping fragrant pandanus flowers, and, like the massive insects that they resembled, carried the vital pollen between the male and female plants.

186

Dragonflies swooped, bigger than the droning hummingbirds, as bright as the darting king-fishers. Flying ants, mosquitoes and midges stirred as the afternoon wore on, making all of them grateful for the insect-repellent cream that was even more vital than the sunscreen; almost as vital as the cool sustaining water.

At last they came to a landing stage. 'Pondok Panggui. Ranger Station,' said Gabriella. 'We're actually in perfect time for the orang-utan feeding, if any of you want to go. Son will take you. I'll stay here. This is a good place to tie up for the night, in any case...'

'Naaaw,' drawled Nic. 'It'd be an anticlimax for me. Might as well be at Central Park Zoo, or San Antonio, Houston or Austin. I never want to see an orang-utan any other way than face to face like that again. I tell you, Gabriella, I came as close as *this* to having a heart attack! It was only after he'd gone I realized I was excited instead of terrified. I simply cannot imagine what it must have been like for you. You are one ballsy lady, if you don't mind me saying so!'

'I agree,' said Richard, calculatedly vague about which bit he agreed with. 'What about you, Robin?'

'I agree too. Especially with the bits about being terrified and not wanting to see another orang-utan up close again...'

'That's not quite what I said...' temporized Nic.

'But it's what I feel,' said Gabriella simply.

'Right, then,' concluded Richard. 'Gabriella, what is there if we miss out on this trek and the four o'clock feeding, and press on for another hour or so instead before we tie up and camp for the night? Anywhere more off the beaten track, so to speak?'

'There's Leaky Creek. That flows deep and clear. Most people don't get that far in on the first day. You'll maybe see some pretty spectacular aquatic life at sunset there. The jungle eases back into marshland and opens up as well, offering all sorts of new fauna and avifauna. I expect Father or Son would know a good spot there to tie up and camp. And we could maybe do a night trek. There's a lot to see after dark, when the apes and monkeys have bedded down. There are all the night hunters, owls, bats, moths. Lots of stuff when we get up into the ramin-tree woodland. Clouded leopards, which are not big enough to attack and are notoriously shy, little honey bears, deer of all sorts, luminous lichens, toadstools that glow in the dark. You name it. I've heard rumours that there may be a Dyak village somewhere up there too; and there's talk of a ancient ruined Hindu temple the better part of two thousand years old...'

'Right,' said Richard decisively. 'Leaky Creek it is, then! Leaky Creek and a midnight walk. That sounds like a plan to me!'

Father's hand on his shoulder woke Richard from the brief power nap he had elected to seize between the glories of Leaky Creek at sunset and their proposed midnight trek to the ramin woods. He sat up at once, wide awake and fizzing with anticipation. The adventure so far had exceeded even his wildest hopes, and this promised to be a fitting climax. He glanced out through the net-draped mandi door and froze. Surely there was some mistake. It was daylight out there. Father and Son must have overslept. He looked across at the pair of them, but they were busy waking the others, so he held his peace and tiptoed out on to the deck. Held his peace wisely, as it turned out.

Richard had never seen a moon so massive, hanging so near the earth, in all his life, not even in tropical oceans with the nearest landlights thousands of miles distant. There seemed to be a weight to the light that settled like silverdust on everything around. A weight and a welcome coolness, at strange odds with the sultry stirring of the air against his face and forearms. There was that strange almost savoury smell again. He recognized it now – it was pandanus. Father and Son had used a knot of the spicy, almost curry-flavoured leaves in the rich fish and vegetable stew they had cooked for dinner on an incongruous little Primus stove, and then offered the spiked red fruit as a delicious pudding afterwards. But the pandanus were a good way back behind them in the jungle groves standing along the banks of the main river. What stretched in front of Richard now was a long silver creek winding lazily between peaty banks that fell back into scrub-covered plains backed on low slopes in the distance by the woodland of die-straight ramin trees. Beneath its apparently shallow, glassy surface, Richard knew, there were unexpected deeps. In the shadow of the silently coasting boat he had watched strange fish that reminded him of sturgeon that Father had called *arwana*. He had watched more false gharials with their long bony faces, creatures for all the world like huge otters playing in the depths as they chased the silver-sided fish.

Robin was at his shoulder. 'I thought it was dawn already,' she whispered. 'Have you ever seen anything like that moon?'

'That's a good old-fashioned prairie moon,' added Nic as he joined them. 'I heard my grandpappy talk about them when I was a kid but I never thought I'd see one. Not one like he used to describe. "Bright as day; you could read a paper by the light of a prairie moon," he used to say. And I never really believed him. Until now at any rate.'

'You never have a paper handy when you really need one,' teased Robin, and Nic laughed a little self-consciously. Richard watched, struck by the way that Nic seemed uneasy at having let his guard down. He thought back to the dark look shot at Gabriella when Nic had not known about the Bugis harbour in Makassar. Of the odd coincidence that both of them had been missing during their one-night stay-over in Pontianac. Like the silver-surfaced river, Nic had hidden depths.

190

'We'll still need flashlights as well as binoculars and cameras,' warned Gabriella, arriving full of practicality and determination to be off. 'We'll lose the light pretty quickly when we get into the forest, though the moon's not due to set much before dawn. Father and Son will be coming with us this time, but we'll need to stick together and take all the care we can.' She paused until she was certain she had all their attention. 'We'll need to be very careful out there,' she said.

Father and Son added strong high-sided hiking boots to the more traditional clothing they had favoured so far. Clearly impressing the tourists came a far second to dying of scorpion sting or snakebite in the ankle. And it wasn't just the warm day, as Shakespeare had it, that craved wary walking, Richard thought as he followed Father ashore. As well as hiking boots the two men carried stout-looking sticks about two metres long – the closest thing to a weapon allowed in the national park, unless you were a ranger. Just as the little Primus stove was the closest thing you were allowed to an actual cooking fire.

Richard watched the easy, apparently casual way Father swung his stick across the path, sending the heavy end whispering through the shadows at his boot-tips as he walked. Beneath the more distant sleepy calling of birds and animals of all sorts that came echoing from the woods ahead, a much more sinister slithering, scurrying rustling close at hand warned that they would do well to watch where they were putting their feet. But with the tall Dyak guiding them across such open country beneath such a massive moon, there was no need for torches yet, and Richard for one felt that the closer they stayed to nature for the moment, the more the park would offer them.

The peaty bank soon settled back into the scrub-covered plain and a path through the scrub emerged, hardly more than well-trodden earth between bushes, where the grass had been worn thin. Father followed this, his quarterstaff a-swing. Richard stopped watching where he was treading quite so closely and began to look around. No sooner did he do so than a squadron of huge fruit bats swept overhead like monsters from a vampire movie. Beyond these, a pair of egrets swept across the moon, its brightness turning their whiteness to black in silhouette. A huge heron lazily shifted its roosting place, all long snake-neck and massive wingspan, looking like some kind of dragon in the moonlight. Lower, away across the scrub, little owls hovered like huge moths just above the night-closed flowers of the bushes, silently hunting on the still, warm air.

The ramin forest closed over them surprisingly quickly, seemed to gulp them into its shadowy throat. Father's footsteps did not falter; indeed, Richard felt them pick up pace as though they were beginning to hurry towards some secret assignation. He looked around, wide-eyed, before resorting to his torch, for as

Gabriella had promised, there was weird and wonderful brightness here. Fireflies and glow-worms whizzed and wandered through the trees. Luminous beetles crawled like deep-sea fishes hoping to attract some prey with their chilly brightness. Apparently radioactive lichens glowed on tree trunks to left and right, or swept in branch-shaped clouds above like tiny bolts of frozen lightning. And, at his feet, all along the path, glittering toadstools stood in little skeins and rings like discarded Christmas-tree lights, shining like something out of *A Midsummer Night's Dream*, waiting for Titania's fairies to arrive.

Richard drew in his breath to call Robin's attention to the beauty of the scene. And froze. For suddenly, in his nostrils there was the faintest odour. The one smell he did not expect in this utterly natural place. The one smell that warned of utterly unexpected presence of other men. Of destruction in this utterly pristine place. Of danger.

It was the smell of smoke.

Richard switched his torch on, shining its bright beam forward. Father was striding even more rapidly now, almost trotting, with his quarterstaff slicing ahead of him, just above the ground, as though testing the shadows for trip-wires instead of tarantulas.

The skin across Richard's belly tightened. Automatically, he was jogging forward too, his first thought to stay close to Father. He was in motion before any other thought occurred, and once in motion, he was not a man to hesitate. He glanced over his shoulder, though, and saw Robin and the others also jogging forward, their torches bright, beams swinging to and fro among the tree trunks, like a little group of Jedi knights rushing to confront Darth Vader's evil empire.

But what were they going to confront? Richard thought back to the second part of Inge's lecture all those hours ago. About the concerns of the founders of the biosphere here that their park was under constant threat. How the collapse of the strong centre of the Suharto regime had led to the shattering of power-structures in Indonesia, just as the collapse of communism had in the old Soviet Union. About how local people, long forbidden to touch their tribal lands, the mineral wealth beneath them and the commercial wealth – both forest and fauna – upon them, all too easily fell prey to the more ruthless corporate giants. And the return-ing of the lands to their natural environments also meant returning them to their native owners – which of course could compound the problem. There were Dyak settlements within these forests and jungles. Fixed ones which worked with the land and those striving to protect it. Villages full of men like Father and Son who could adapt their natural lifestyle a little. For whom a living could be made doing a little hunting, fishing, guiding of tourists. But there were others, Inge had warned, whose lifestyle did not fit in so well, the slash-and-burn farmers whose longhouses were moveable, who wandered at will through virgin forests given to them by their gods; damaging, perhaps even destroying them as of right. And on top of all this, there were the illegals – the hunters, the miners, the loggers, who bribed the guards and rangers, fooled the tribal elders and secretly ripped the heart out of the land.

The smell of burning could originate almost anywhere. Their hurrying footsteps, following Father's sensitive nose, might lead them to a Dyak longhouse with a legitimately roasting pig. But there was no smell of cooking – merely of burning. Dyak deforestation, then; one of the moveable longhouses Inge had described.

But then there came the unmistakable *whipcrack!* of a gunshot, from unsettlingly close at hand. Father was running full tilt now, his quarterstaff supplemented by the bright beam of a torch. Through the trees ahead there suddenly came the sounds of shouting, though Richard could make out neither words nor language. The crunch of feet running across dead leaves and brittle branches. The creaking and slamming of doors. Then almost blindingly, even at this distance, the dazzle of big headlights, and the jungle sounds were drowned beneath the full-throated roar of a big motor being fired up. Another, almost at once.

Father was going flat out now, heedless of everything else as he hurled through the juddering forest towards the weirdly dancing bars of brightness and shadow that no doubt originated with a couple of big trucks turning in a clearing. Richard powered up in pursuit. At his back, he heard Nic calling to the women to fall back. Richard knew Robin well enough to know the words would be wasted on her. And sure enough, she arrived at his left shoulder just as Nic arrived at his right.

Side by side, on Father's heels, with Son and Gabriella immediately behind them, they all exploded into the clearing. They arrived at the same moment as a pair of big trucks barrelled out down a track much wider – and newer – than the one Richard and his companions had followed. Wide enough, certainly, to have removed all the forest cover and receive full benefit of the moonlight. Richard caught a flash of distant tail-lights, high square rear-sections and great piles of logs lashed into place on top of them. Then the trucks roared round a bend and were lost to sight, except for the brightness of their headlights gleaming through the tree trunks. Striped black and gold like the flanks of tigers. Tiger-like also was the receding roar of their motors snarling away to whatever rendez-vous would relieve them of their contraband cargo.

Richard looked around their immediate vicinity and saw at once that the word *clearing* was exactly right for the place they were hesitating in now. A sizeable stand of ramin trees had been cleared with a vengeance. Chopped and trimmed. Their trunks stood forlornly to ankle height, like gravestones marking what

196

looked like the better part of a hundred trees: damaged, maybe dying. It was their useless leaves and branches that they could all smell smouldering in a great smoking pile in the middle of the clearing, the wood-stove smell somehow fresh and clean in contrast to the stench of powder left on the air by whatever gun had fired the shot. The last few naked trunks still remained laid down – ready, no doubt, to be loaded into another truck on another secret forest-stripping run. And lying on top of these was the orang-utan. Somehow all six torch beams found the creature at the same time and the rest of the clearing faded into spectral moonlight as he was lit up by the unforgiving brightness.

His size and power were only slightly diminished in death. His arms seemed somehow longer, spread wide as they were, along the tree trunks, as though he had been trying to protect them, like a parent guarding its children. Or a monarch defending his birthright. His mouth was half open, showing his teeth, and his pendulous jowls were creased in his dying snarl. His naked, almost hairless chest was marked by a hole in its centre the size of a fist. There was no blood to be seen, though the trunks he was lying on would be thick with it, Richard knew.

'You know what they use ramin wood for?' asked Nic, apparently apropos of nothing. 'Pool cues. *Pool cues!* That poor bastard of an ape just got slaughtered so that someone some-

197

where can clear a fucking pool table! Jesus, it makes you weep!'

What had happened seemed clear enough to Richard. The huge orang-utan had appeared here just as it had appeared this morning. It had reached over and taken someone's bag just as it had taken Gabriella's. But the reaction had been fatally different. A shot, followed by panic and escape. He was able to work so much out not only because he had an innate ability, honed by all-too-wide experience of violent death, usually among humans, but also because the orang-utan was still holding the bag that it had taken just before it was shot. Some attempt had been made to pull it from the death-grip of the massive red-furred hand. With no success. Its contents therefore had simply been pulled out by an owner desperate to retrieve whatever he could while his companions fired up the trucks ready to escape. The important things would be gone, of course – wallet, keys, ID – but other bits and pieces remained scattered around the pile of tree trunks. One of these, close enough to the dead orang to be bathed in the steady torch beams, was the flimsy of a fax. It lay spread wide open, held in place by the sap of the ravaged trees. Even at this distance, Richard recognized the lists down the main body of the paper. They were shipping schedules, detailing the ports of call of a company vessel of some kind. And beside them there were manifests detailing cargoes, ports of lading and destinations. But he didn't recognize the letterhead above the lists.

'Do you know whose logo this is?' he asked Robin, breaking the silence and the stasis, beginning to move forward towards the dead orang. Robin shook her head.

But Nic answered grimly, 'Yes I do. That's the Luzon Logging Company. You were right all along, Gabriella.'

And Father nodded, his pendant Dyak earrings chiming quietly. 'Yeah,' he said. 'That's Luzon Logging all right.'

Eighteen

Bambang

What saved them in the end was Sailendra's latest eco-friendly economic initiative. This was Baya Brand Hand-Fried Organic Red Plantain and Green Mango Chips: a mouthful in more ways than one. Or it would be when the red-plantain harvest was in and they and the green mangoes were sliced and deep-fried in the organic palm oil that was due for delivery soon.

In the meantime, the initiative consisted of an industrial-scale preparation and deep-frying facility housed in an underused section of the cannery. Alongside it was a state-of-the-art chip-packing facility with foil bags already stencilled with the initial logo, and an inert-gas system designed to pump nitrogen gas into the bags with the finished chips. This was guaranteed to keep the chips in an environment where flavour and freshness would last for the longest possible time.

But because inert-gas systems could be hazardous to those who operated them, there was a first-aid kit accompanying it, also of industrial size. It contained two oxygen cylinders designed to revive anyone who had breathed in sufficient pure nitrogen to choke them. And the oxygen cylinders would be equally effective in reviving anyone who had breathed in dangerous quantities of any other toxic gas. Carbon monoxide, for example.

Sailendra did not think this through. He had only the vaguest idea of what was actually happening to him. The bubbles in the paddies made him think of poison gas but what sort it was he had no real idea. He certainly had neither the training nor the experience to be able to say for certain it was carbon monoxide. But that was the only odourless, tasteless deadly gas he had heard of, and so he guessed. And guessed accurately enough. And it was upon that guess he acted.

There could hardly have been anything further from his mind than Red Plantain and Green Mango Chips as he stumbled down the hillside, falling from one paddy to the next. But he did reckon that if there was anyone left alive and capable of helping Parang and him on this side of the island, they would probably be in the cannery. And, somewhat vaguer, at the back of his mind lay the thought that if he made it as far as the cannery and found it empty after all, then the brother to the truck stuck on the hillside up above them was parked there. And he knew where the keys were kept.

Luck and several other factors favoured the dying prince and his all-but-dead friend.

Because of the dead men and women blocking the sluices, the paddies continued to overflow. The soil downslope was wet and slick, making the burden of Parang's inert body just that vital bit more manageable. The paddies gave way to banana groves nearer to the cannery and the lethal gas was less thick here – an effect blessedly compounded by the sudden arrival of an ozone-filled onshore breeze. The cannery itself was empty of workers. Alerted by the almost mystical mouth-to-mouth communication system that was all the island had left now that the radio station, phone masts, post office and exchange were under several million tons of landslide, they had taken the two remaining trucks. They had filled them with all the fittest workers from the banana groves and the fruit farms and gone to help in Baya City. They had left the elderly, the women and the children in the village near the point that serviced the farms. The paddies were run by mountain people who rarely came down here, so at the moment only Sailendra knew of the mysterious tragedy they had suffered on the upper slopes.

But the cannery manager, farmers and villagers had left the manager's son as watch-keeper. He was a natural choice for watch-duty, in spite of the fact that he was just entering his teens, because he knew every nook and cranny – he had been brought up there and was possessively protective of the place. And he was too small to be of much help in Baya City. A keen and ambitious lad, named Bambang after

Suharto's son for reasons of political insurance rather than paternal affection by an over-careful father, shortly before the general's fall from power, the manager's son saw the two men staggering down the muddy slope towards the cannery. He paused on his patrol. Looked at the clearly demarcated boundary and the notice announcing private property which they were clearly ignoring. Then, fired by all the righteous indignation of a young man who felt that the factory was not only his own private property but also his home, he ran out at once to confront them.

Fortunately, Bambang recognized Sailendra at once, and only an instant before he also recognized the symptoms of gassing. The details of the effect that nitrogen has on a victim of gassing may differ significantly from those of carbon monoxide, but the broad brush-strokes are the same. Certainly Bambang never doubted what he was seeing. Of course he had attended his father's lecture on how to use the first-aid equipment soon after it had all arrived in the cannery, he had helped the maintenance man put it all safely away in the organic-chip area, and he had secretly tested the oxygen on himself once or twice, marvelling at the sudden burst of energy the gas had given him. So he knew exactly what he had to do with the staggering, gasping man who also happened to be his prince.

'This way, Your Princeliness. You must come this way,' he said, taking the dead man by the arm and aiding the staggering Sailendra with all his wiry strength. Fortunately, the organic-chip area was the nearest of the cannery's rambling sections. It had a big sliding door that Bambang pulled wide, as though his prince was a Mac truck. He ran on ahead of the stumbling prince, heading for the security cage at the back of the hangar-wide space. It was never locked, in spite of his father's security consciousness. Bambang swung the wire door wide and grabbed the two red-painted oxygen cylinders. They were about the same length as the boy's arm, and too wide for him to grasp with fingers and thumb. So he tucked one under his arm and cradled the other like a baby, returning at a run to the kneeling man who seemed to be held upright only by the arm reaching back to the mud-crusted bundle of his dead friend.

Bambang pushed the triangular mask of the first against the prince's face and hit the button that released the gas. Prince Sailendra gasped a great breath. His left arm swung up and Bambang pushed the bottle into his hand. When he was certain that the prince could – and would – continue to hold it in place, Bambang went to check on the other man. He did not seem to be breathing at all, but because he seemed to be the prince's friend, Bambang persisted. And the pressure from the oxygen bottle filled Parang's flaccid lungs exactly as the nitrogen from the system was designed to fill the chip bags. Parang shuddered as though the oxygen held a considerable electrical charge.

Bambang took a sniff of the almost magic gas himself, then settled seriously to work.

Sailendra really realized he was alive when he began to feel the pain in his head. Dead princes do not feel as though they have been hit repeatedly with a heavy club. For some reason he could not quite fathom, his shoulder and arm were stiff and painful too. Some sort of recognition of his surroundings began to swim in through the mists. Not detailed, for he had never been in this section of the factory before, but an increasingly lively awareness of where he must be. And when, after some uncounted time, he felt able to look down, he recognized the lean, intelligent face of the manager's son. He said nothing for a considerable time longer, however, fearing that if he took the mask away from his nose and mouth, even to say thank you, he would pass out.

And so continued one of the strangest parts of Sailendra's life: the hundred hours – give or take – for which he was away from Baya City. The hundred hours in which on every level, things on Pulau Baya went from very bad indeed to incalculably, unimaginably worse.

To Sailendra it seemed that, trapped here as he was to begin with, the fight to save his island was reduced to its barest essential – the fight to save his friend. But then, as he began to get some freedom of movement, it widened into a fight to solve the terrible mystery of what had happened on the paddy fields. Then the battle to make sure the same fate did not overtake the elderly, women and children in the village beyond the cannery and the farms. The almost fatal effort to get the truck back on the road. And finally the fire on the mountain.

As soon as he dared, Sailendra pulled the mask away from his face. He took great heaving gasps of the air in the shed, confident that it must at least be wholesome or the boy would not look so bright. His head began to reel again, but he fought the dizziness and the nausea. It was clear that Parang was in a very bad way still. The less oxygen Sailendra needed, the more there would be to help his friend.

'You have saved our lives, young man,' he gasped at last. 'Thank you.'

'I am Bambang, son to the manager here. It was my duty, Your Highness. But your friend is still very ill, Your Highness. According to the health and safety manual we should summon a doctor.'

There was a glimmer of hope in Sailendra's heart powerful enough to ease his headache for a moment. 'There is a doctor? Where is the doctor?'

'He has gone to Baya City with the others.'

'A pity.' The headache thumped back. But then another thought: 'How would one summon him, however? Is there a telephone? A radio?'

'A telephone. But it has not worked for a couple of days. I can run to the village and see if anyone there could help but everyone strong, well trained and capable has gone to Baya City.

I could fetch my mother.'

Sailendra thought about it. Any contact would be welcome.

But Bambang continued his thought: 'Except that there are three dead dogs on the road to the village. I have never seen such a thing before, and I am concerned that what has attacked you might have killed them.'

'We need a meter or monitor. Did one come with this kit?'

'Yes! I had not thought of that! There is a clean-air monitor. I will fetch it at once.'

The monitor turned out to be a simple little hand-held battery-powered box with a needle designed to move across a scale marked in red and green. It measured the presence – or lack – of oxygen in the immediate atmosphere. And so was just as well able to check for carbon monoxide or for nitrogen. Sailendra took it at once and switched it on. The needle settled safely in the green. The prince pulled himself to his feet and crossed to the wide-open door with hardly a stagger or a stumble. He pushed the monitor to arm's length in the bright afternoon air outside and waved it around as best as he could, given the fact that he had pulled most of the muscles on that side by dragging Parang here. The needle stayed in the green. He stepped out and looked downhill to the narrow beach and the sea. The sea-breeze fluttered in his face and faded. He stepped right outside, turned determinedly left and crossed the front of the building to the car park. This wire-walled enclosure overlooked the road that led down to the village. A dusty track that split a kilometre or so away to send a branch up towards the pass and the upper road that he had driven along this morning. Thus he discovered the three dead dogs Bambang had mentioned. And learned that when the monitor's needle went into the red it sounded a piercing alarm.

Sailendra tested that alarm considerably during the next half-hour as he explored the outer limits of the bubble of safe air around the cannery. Then he returned to the nascent chip-packing facility and slid the door shut. 'We're trapped for the moment, Bambang. Can we move Parang to an upper storey? Is there a bed for the watchman or anything like that?'

They moved the still inert secretary with some difficulty to the offices on the upper floor. The upper offices seemed to be half after-thought, half ship's bridge in design, a set of clapboard prefabs sitting on top of the main factory building, accessible via a spiral stair that led through a rough-cut hole in its ceiling. There was a watchman's facility up here, a toilet, a basin, a grudging shower and a fold-away bed. Here the three spent the night. Sailendra paced restlessly, working his stiff shoulder and massaging his aching head until he collapsed into a chair and sank into a deep sleep, snoring gently and regally. While this was going on, the ever-amenable Bambang did the nursing, secretly and excitedly locked in a death-defying adventure fit for repeating to his grandchildren, in time. And his parents in the meantime. The fact that he was increasingly hungry simply added to the sense of adventure. There were several thousand tins of mixed fruit in the warehouse below so he could afford to luxuriate in the feeling, knowing he could easily sort things out if it all became too much. And the hunger distracted him from the worrying possibility, which the prince did not yet seem to have registered, that there might be more than dead dogs lying on the road down to the village. That the village itself, indeed, and all who used to live in it, might be dead.

The oxygen ran out at midnight, but the prince's friend seemed to be breathing more easily then. After a while, having checked and double-checked, Bambang went down and opened a tin of golden mangoes, eating and drinking as he climbed back to his lookout. In the distance he could see the fires and oil lamps that told him the village was safe for the moment. With his heart pounding with relief, he lit the big signal torch that told his anxious mother that he too was fine, and went to bed like a faithful hound, on the floor between the prince and the prince's friend.

Nineteen

Fire

The three were awoken by Bambang's mother. She was doing as she did every morning – bringing breakfast to her son. She had walked up from the village bearing a basket of flat breads and fruit with a screw-top jar full of fresh goat's milk. She had seen the dead dogs, but had noticed no ill-effects upon herself, and was surprised that they should expect her to have felt any. By the same token, if she was surprised to find her son sharing quarters with a prince and his secretary, she did not show that either – much to Bambang's secret chagrin. It was a bright, clear morning and the first promise of the southern monsoon had arrived, bringing a breath of fresh air to the whole of Pulau Baya's southern coast.

Parang was still weak and sick, coughing like a case of terminal lung cancer, but he declared himself strong enough to walk back to the village with Bambang's mother. So Bambang got to remain as a leading actor in the adventure. He locked the cannery carefully and sent the key home with Parang as a punishment to his unflappable, unimpressed mother, then he joined Sailendra when the prince, armed with the clean-air monitor, went off up the hillside once again.

With the breeze at their backs, they toiled up the slopes Sailendra had come crashing and sliding down yesterday afternoon, his path easy to see but impossible to follow as it was still running with overflowing water. Sailendra found Bambang to be a mixed blessing. On the one hand he was an interesting, energetic and enthusiastic companion, full of insight into his own small world and inexhaustible in his desire to impart it. On the other, of course, he could not be the equal in discussion that Sailendra needed. Bambang had none of Parang's knowledge or insight. He could not be expected to hold his own in anything to do with political necessities or practicalities. He could not be trusted to accept an opinion of political weight and guarantee to keep it secret at any price in order to protect his prince. And Sailendra needed to have that conversation and discuss those opinions, for he was all too well aware that Councillor Kerian would not be wasting these precious hours that the prince was absent from the political arena. Furthermore, the reason Sailendra was extending that dangerous absence was so that he could find out what had killed the people in the paddies. And here he found himself hesitant to expose the voluble but overpoweringly innocent child to the grosser horrors of mortality.

Sailendra found himself considering the corpses in the flooding paddies from a distance, therefore, allowing Bambang to catalogue little more than seeming bundles of sopping rags. Likewise, when they reached the truck, frozen in a half-slide towards a particularly precipitous series of paddy fields, he kept the pair of them far further back than he would have kept Parang and himself, had the trusted secretary been here.

The alarm on the clean-air monitor began to sound once they started following the road above the paddies, but every time Sailendra raised the shrilling monitor to check how far into the red the needle had moved, it fell back into the green once again. And the intermittent insistence of the new-born southern monsoon wind gave him the confidence to proceed. For this road led along the back of the paddies, just beneath the high ridge of the watershed to the jungle village housing the rice workers.

Sailendra found that the nearer he came to the village, the slower he moved, fearing that he would suddenly present Bambang with a sight so horrible that it would scar the ebullient youth for life. But the huts appeared with nothing more sinister than the occasional shrilling of the monitor. The occasions seemed closer together, but apart from that, there was little to worry Sailendra at first. The huts stood in an over-hanging jungle clearing around a central long-house, for the mountain people were of Dyak ancestry just as the coastal dwellers like Kerian claimed Bugis blood. The huts stood in a circle and the longhouse stood at the centre, on its long legs – in spite of the fact that there would be little flooding here. Beneath the longhouse lay the first warning sign, however. The legs of the longhouse itself were joined together by simple fences made of woven twigs. Within the little compounds these made there were pigs and chickens, the occasional goat. And they were all lying dead on the ground. 'Look in the huts, would you, Bambang?' ordered Sailendra, aware that the huts were used as storerooms by the people who lived in the longhouse and worked in the paddies. So while the boy checked whether the simple staples of the village, like rice bags and cooking fuel, had survived whatever had killed the livestock, the prince ran up the notched log leading to the veranda surrounding the building and looked into the darkness of the longhouse itself. Such was his concentration that he forgot all about the clean-air monitor in his hand. He stepped into the darkness utterly unaware that he was carrying it.

The longhouse was divided into areas exactly like the animal compounds beneath, only each area up here was designed to hold a family. There were reed mats. There were the possessions clearly belonging to men and women, the toys and games belonging to children. But there were no people at all. The whole place was eerily empty. Sailendra drew in a deep – if unconsidered – breath of sheer relief. And as he

213

did so, the whole structure seemed to shiver. The monitor began to shrill. A body crashed through the palm-thatched roof and smashed to the floor at his feet.

Sailendra was halfway down the notched-pole ladder before he really registered that the shaking had stilled again and the body was that of a gibbon. But the tremor and the shock were enough to get him in full retreat. The monitor continued to shrill, and he hit the blessedly still, solid ground, calling Bambang out of the nearest store hut. 'Back to the road,' yelled Sailendra, all too well aware that he was using up the last good air in his lungs, 'RUN!' In a sort of strange replay of yesterday's nightmare, Sailendra ran towards the road, heart pounding already, refusing to breathe, watching Bambang scurry fearfully in front of him, already beginning to reel like Parang had yesterday. But there was one vital difference. The promising monsoon. Out on the roadway, the wind blew sufficiently steadily in from the sea to stop the monitor shrilling. But Sailendra was still concerned at being anywhere near the paddy fields and so he urged Bambang to keep running and stayed at the boy's heels.

They had slowed to a jog by the time they reached the shallow valley across the track where the road had been washed away and the truck had crashed yesterday. It was dry now, and gave firm footing to half a dozen elderly men from the village who bowed formally to the prince and greeted Bambang with a great deal of affection. Parang was amongst them. 'I thought we should at least try to get the truck back on the road,' he explained, breathlessly after completing his greetings and his thanks to both for their parts in saving his life. 'If we can, it will speed up our return to Baya City.'

'We must take these people with us if we can,' added Sailendra. 'I don't like what's going on here. Did you feel that tremor an hour or so ago?'

'Yes. The villagers say there were other tremors yesterday. Do you think they have anything to do with what is leaking through the paddies?'

Sailendra nodded grimly. 'It's not just through the paddies. There are pockets of gas all over the place. But you're right about the truck. Have you any lifting equipment?'

'I have the stoutest of the remaining villagers and a good strong rope.'

The villagers remained on the road under Bambang's leadership. Cheerfully obedient to the boy's confident plans and orders – clearly familiar with both – they let the rope down to the truck so that Sailendra and Parang could use it to let themselves down the steep, slippery slope, and to pull themselves back up if need be. The two men slid down side by side until they could transfer their handholds from the rough hemp to the wooden slats of the lorry's tailgate. Here they looped the end of the rope round the tow hook on the rear of the chassis, planning nothing more complex than to put the

215

truck in reverse and get the villagers to pull her up.

But to get into reverse, of course, they would have to get down the length of the vehicle, climb into the cab and turn the engine on. So, like acrobats they worked their way round the corner until they were able to climb on down the truck's side. Sailendra was the first to lose both grip and footing, slip and start to slide. Parang grabbed at him, missed and followed suit. Luckily for the dignity – perhaps the health – of both of them, Sailendra had left the door open as well as the key in the ignition when he climbed out, so the pair were able to catch at the open door and heave themselves aboard, one after the other. Their arrival was enough to shake the vehicle, however, and it moved a good thirty centimetres further down the slope, until the villagers brought it to a halt. 'Good,' said Sailendra, grimly positive. 'At least it isn't stuck in the mud.' He wrenched the key round in the ignition and gunned the motor brutally as soon as it caught.

'Perhaps I should get out. My weight will only make things more difficult,' suggested Parang.

'Now that I have you beside me, old friend, I'd rather you stayed. At the very least you can stick your head out of the window and yell up at Bambang. But I missed you. I thought I'd lost you.' Sailendra spoke with unaccustomed directness as he swung round to glance over his shoulder. He eased the gear lever into reverse and eased his feet on clutch and accelerator until he could feel the biting point. Holding it there, he took his hand off the gear lever altogether, put his arm along the back of the seat and swung round further so that he could look up the length of the truck and on along the taut rope to the tug-of-war team on the far end of it. 'Tell them to pull, Parang,' he ordered.

Parang did as he was told, then settled back into his seat, feeling Sailendra's arm around his shoulders, like a father protecting his son. The accidental intimacy coming so soon after his near-death experience stirred something in the secretive young man. And the fact that it was Sailendra who had saved him in the end broke through his reserve. 'You must beware of Councillor Kerian, Your Highness.'

'Of course I must. I always have.' Sailendra eased the clutch up as he squeezed the accelerator, feeling the wheels begin to grip.

'He is more cunning than you know, Sailendra. He has bribed or blackmailed all of those around you. He spies on you constantly, trying to manipulate you. He will destroy you and take power if he can.'

Sailendra did not respond to this, apparently concentrating on easing the truck back, one centimetre after another, up the hillside. There was a distant chanting cheer as Bambang's tug-of-war team felt the movement. The rope groaned loudly enough to be audible over the growling of the motor. 'He has bribed or blackmailed *all* of those around me?'

'Yes. Even me.'

At first Sailendra thought it was the simple shock of his old friend's admission that caused the whole world to heave around him. The roaring in his ears could have been surprise as easily as the yelled warnings of the stunned and sprawling men on the road above. The screaming could have been the agony of betrayal inside his head as easily as the protesting of the motor as the wheels were simply shaken off the ground altogether while the whole truck seemed to jump up into the air like a startled cat. But then Parang was screaming himself, and Sailendra slammed back to reality to find the truck sliding wildly out of control down the still-heaving mountainside. Even the treachery of the prince's closest friend took second place to that.

Sailendra fought to keep the truck facing straight ahead. If it turned side-on to the slope then it would roll. If it rolled, then they would die. It was as simple as that. But keeping the leaping vehicle on anything like an even keel was incredibly difficult. The steering wheel leaped right and left with enough force to numb his hands as the tyres, wheels and axles smashed to bits. 'JUMP!' he yelled at Parang, but for once the secretary disobeyed him openly. Then it was too late. The bonnet kicked up as though a landmine had exploded under it. The men were lashed back into their seats, then whipped forward again like a pair of royal cobras striking. The bonnet exploded into smoke – which instantly turned out to be steam. And water droplets which thundered back against the windscreen like a muddy monsoon. The whole rushing wreck of the truck slewed across the topmost paddy and smashed into the solid concrete of its outer wall, sending a tidal wave of water and rice plants thundering down from one to the other below in a strange stepped-chain reaction. Sailendra's chest hit the steering wheel so hard he sounded the horn with his breastbone. Parang's forehead hit the windscreen sharply enough to send a spider's web of cracks across it. Then they slammed back into their seats again.

Sailendra couldn't breathe properly anyway, but the shrilling of the monitor in his pocket warned him that it was more serious than the fact that he was winded. He looked across at Parang. This time at least his companion seemed wide awake, if bleeding from a rapidly swelling bruise on his forehead. 'We need to get out again,' rasped Sailendra.

Parang nodded and opened the door, slopping down into the paddy immediately. Sailendra swung out also, moving like an old man, with the whole of his torso joining the muscle-torn ache of his shoulder. The crowd up on the roadway were picking themselves up, Bambang waving and gesturing. Without the dead weight of Parang, this time Sailendra elected to go upwards. Side by side he and his secretary pounded up along the trench the truck had ripped into the slope. By the last piece of good fortune they were to enjoy for a while, the rope had parted at the tow hook, so that once the labouring men had made it back to the point they had boarded the truck, they could pull themselves up to the road.

Here, with all the ebullience of a group of heroes who have stared death in the face and overcome it, they walked off down the road. Of course Sailendra wished to accuse Parang. To get the facts. To plumb the depth of his treachery and discover whether the secretary/spy would give up any of his councillor master's secrets. But the prince found it was simply not possible to ask the questions he burned to ask in the presence of Bambang and his good, honest friends. Besides, there were other matters which he could and should discuss with them all. Matters that took precedence even over Kerian and whether he was staging some kind of coup d'état even now.

As the group walked back towards the village with Bambang now in charge of the clean-air monitor, Sailendra discussed with the oldest there the pattern of earth tremors. Whether these had happened before; whether there had been any release of gas before. Whether anything had happened in the memory of the oldest, or in his memory of things he had heard about – reaching back to the moment when General MacArthur had stood upon Bandar Laut beach – that could give them some guidance now. But there was nothing. Pulau Bay had never before been subject to landslips, hot ocean currents, earth tremors or poison gas. Not since the Americans had bombed out the Japanese towards the end of the war – with almost all of these effects. In Sailendra's opinion, that made what was happening now all the more worrying. By the time the weary troop had straggled back into the village, he had decided that he should get these people to leave their homes, take whatever they could carry, and follow him into Baya City.

But General MacArthur's men had not died in vain. They had brought democracy to Pulau Baya. No mere man was going to order the villagers around – whether he be Prince Sailendra or Emperor Hirohito. Fortunately, the tug-of-war team comprised the majority of the village council, so it was easy and quick to summon a full meeting immediately they arrived at the village. And Sailendra had only to sketch his concerns, for most of them were already familiar with his thinking. Even so, it took some hours of deliberation before the charismatic young ruler got his way. And by the time the villagers had collected their most precious portable belongings and secured their homes against the distant threat of looting, it was sunset.

With Parang on one side and Bambang on the other, Sailendra at last turned to lead the procession of villagers along the road that would take them – eventually – into Baya City. On his back he carried a bundle of holy and historic things from the village's council chamber. In his right hand he carried a simple wicker cage in which a white parrot preened itself contentedly. The dusty road looked westwards along the length of the island. On their right, the low hills gathered towards the watershed ridge that was the gently curving spine of the island. In a couple of kilometres the road ahead would swing north towards the pass over which Sailendra had driven the truck nearly forty hours earlier. Now it just followed the slope up towards the shady, wooded ridge, perspective foreshortening the gathering hill-peaks until it seemed that the sharp top of Guanung Surat itself was close enough to touch, though it was the length of the island away. And as the big white disc of the sun slid down behind it, it seemed that the great rock tusk was casting its shadow down over them, even over the whole length of the island. Like the head of a saint or a god in a picture, like the head of the Prophet as described to Moslems, the great peak was bathed in a halo of pure gold fire.

And just then, at the very moment of sunset, came the loudest noise that any of them had ever heard. It was so loud that it seemed to be happening inside their heads. It was so loud that it seemed that it must be happening just beside them, beneath them, behind them. It was so loud that they seemed to *feel* it the merest instant before they heard it. It was so loud that they only heard the first sharp microsecond of it before their quaking ears switched off.

It combined the crack of a great artillery

weapon discharging with the first huge chime of the loudest peal of thunder. It contained the deepest cataclysmic crash of a cave-in just beneath their feet with the explosion of a jet liner smashing to earth just behind them. It was louder than the sounds of the bombs at Hiroshima and Nagasaki being detonated at once.

It was the loudest sound that had been heard since Krakatau had exploded.

It stunned the little band of villagers as utterly as it stunned their brave young prince. And in itself, in the instant of its existence, it explained everything that had happened since even before the landslide began.

And into the silence of the deafness that claimed them all for some time afterwards, Bambang said what they all were thinking. Though Sailendra was only able to understand him by reading his lips.

'The top of the mountain's on fire,' he said.

Twenty

Makassar

Richard, Robin, Nic and Gabriella only spent a couple of hours in Makassar and they never got to visit either Bira Beach or the Bugis harbour at Paotere. They were hurried on to the plane at the little airport five kilometres outside Tanjung Puting National Park a couple of days after finding the dead orang-utan and then stepped off some hours later at Hasanuddin Airport, twenty-five kilometres outside Makassar, a couple of hours after that. Two hours later still they were back aboard *Tai Fun* and the beautiful vessel was already easing out of Pelni Harbour with clearance for the fastest possible passage to Pulau Baya.

The minute Richard saw the orang-utan, he knew they were going to miss the boat. Literally. There was no way the national park's prize exhibit could be slaughtered almost immediately in front of their eyes without the authorities getting involved. And the involvement of every authority he had ever encountered led from dead slow to dead stop. And *Tai Fun* had a schedule to keep, which, like time and tide, would not wait. But even then, he did not realize how deeply the authorities would want to become involved. And how many different, occasionally unexpected, levels of authority would appear, and from so many increasingly distant places.

The park rangers arrived first, within a few minutes. Brisk and efficient, seemingly hardly surprised by the crisis at all, they left one team to guard the site and begin to question the witnesses while another team went off in pursuit of the lorries. For once – and indeed for the next couple of days – Richard had to take a back seat, something that neither suited nor amused him, and went a good way to explaining the speedier of his decisions and the riskier of his actions later. But, despite his usual accurate insight, an acuity which might have flattered the sharpest of fictional detectives, he had not really had the time or the opportunity to think through the full implications of his acute observations.

It came as little surprise to him, therefore, to find that Father and Son were not quite the simple, taciturn Dyak guides they seemed to be. Men such as Nic Greenbaum did not dash unsupported or unprotected into the wild. Gabriella had arranged the closest the park could offer to undercover ranger guides – men able to offer the most authentic of experiences combined with maximum security. Nic seemed amused if unsurprised by the revelation. He turned to Richard, including Robin in his wide grin.

'Guys like us're just too precious to risk, I guess. We've earned a kind of second childhood – nurses watching everywhere. It's like I said. No more fast cars or off-piste slopes for me.'

This observation was made while Father and Son were in deep conversation with the first team of rangers at the site, but it continued a couple of hours later at the ranger camp at Natai Lengkuas as they waited for a more senior team to come and talk to them. But the team could not arrive before the morning, so they slept the first night there and waited. Richard and Robin in one hut, Nic and his lovely nursemaid in the other.

Richard was woken in the dawn after only a couple of hours' sleep by the howling of the proboscis monkeys in the trees nearby. He rolled over and felt for Robin among the folds of mosquito netting but she was gone. He sat up at once. Very few things indeed got his lovely wife up before full daylight. In fact the only thing he could think of that did it was a cup of teak-dark English Breakfast Tea. She was standing by the slatted shutters of the window across the tiny room, looking out.

'What?' he asked.

'I'd hate to say I don't trust Nic Greenbaum – or Gabriella Cappaldi for that matter – but you know there's more going on here than meets the eye,' she said quietly, as though too well aware how easily someone could use the monkey noise to eavesdrop outside their window.

'I'd been working under the assumption that

he'd decided to outbid me or outmanoeuvre me for *Tai Fun* and the High Wind line.'

'Me too. With Gabriella nicely placed as his spy, looking for weaknesses and angles he could exploit. I mean, he has the reputation of getting pretty cut-throat when it comes to protecting his investments and expanding his empire.'

'More of a Caesar than a Christmas tree.' Richard had been aching to crack one of his puns on Nic's name for some time.

'Yup,' said Robin, without even wincing at the dreadful joke. 'But I think there's more to it now. I think we've been focusing on his reputation as a businessman so closely that we've overlooked some other elements of his reputation.'

'As a ladykiller? I mean, Gabriella seems more than...'

'No, you dope. As an eco-warrior. You know he gives a fortune each year to UNESCO? No, of course you don't. It's not a boy thing. Well, he does. And I'm guessing he's not the kind of guy who's afraid to put his mouth where his money is. More than just his mouth, in fact.'

'Uh-uhunh,' he said, as though he had the faintest notion where she was going with this. But then the penny dropped. 'And UNESCO is in charge of the Tanjung Puting National Park?'

'Funds it. Takes responsibility for protecting it as far as is needed at an international level.'

'OK, I read the article. I listened to Inge Nordberg, distracting though that Calvin Klein safari minisuit was. Protecting it from the collapse of strong if unpopular centralization into more fragile local controls. Against people on the ground who feel they have a right to get something out of it at last. But most especially against the international businesses all too willing to bribe them, blackmail them and just plain rip them off no matter what the ecological cost. Big mining, big logging. These Luzon people...'

'So, here we have a guy who's not allowed to race his cars any more. Or jump from choppers at the top of mountains wearing nothing but skis and a smile. Who's had to shelve his "Been There Done That" T-shirt collection. But who's gone into Indonesia the same way as Geldof and Gates went into Africa, with his own personal commitment as well as all the money he can manage. And now he might just want to get down and dirty to protect all the investments he has made in the environment out here.'

'The same as he would do to protect any other investment he had made. On the one hand Greenbaum International, Texas Oil and their state-of-the-art green refineries, on the other hand UNESCO and Tanjung Puting National Park.'

The next level of investigators arrived just after the four witnesses had enjoyed a late breakfast, but before Richard had really got to grips with testing Robin's theories on Nic himself. These were the authorities from Pangkalanbun, the local administrative centre with oversight of the park. The details recorded by the rangers were repeated, expanded, witnessed, notarized, as though some kind of contract was being drawn up here. The process took until about the time Richard estimated *Tai Fun* would be setting sail for Makassar, with all her passengers except four safely back aboard.

'May we leave now?' he asked when it became clear that the last of the local formalities was completed. But his question was answered with polite astonishment. Did the honoured captain not realize that even now, there were teams flying here from the local UNESCO offices in Jakarta, who were hoping to link up with a team from central offices in Tokyo? There was some talk of getting a group out from UN Headquarters itself...

'From *Manhattan*?' asked Richard, almost awed. This was a lot of heat for one dead ape. But then, he thought, remembering his conversation with Robin that morning, perhaps there was more going on here than the murder of one orang-utan. The wider the ripples spread, the more likely that this was more to do with Nic Greenbaum. Or Luzon Logging. Or both.

In actual fact the men and women from Tokyo and Jakarta wanted mostly to speak to Gabriella, and so Richard found out that there was more to the entertainments officer than the considerable amount which met the eye. And that her relationship with Nic was even more complex than even Robin had supposed. If UNESCO could be said to run secret agents, then Gabriella was one. And if they employed visiting experts, then Nic was one. And if spies and experts got together in pursuit of suspected eco-sanctions busters then that was what they had been doing.

'Look,' said Nic over a late lunch after the Jakarta contingent had left, but before the people from Tokyo arrived, a good few hours after the time Richard reckoned *Tai Fun* would have docked in Pelni Harbour, debouching her passengers via the immigration offices on Jalan Nusantara into Makassar itself, 'we might as well level with you guys.' He took a deep breath and sat back, eyes narrow as he looked at Richard and Robin through the fragrant steam of the after-lunch coffee. 'This place isn't anywhere near the Eden it should be, you know? There have been concerns about what's been going on out here for years. As far back as 2000 the Environmental Investigation Agency were publishing reports about this problem. Then there was the stuff from Greenpeace and all the rest. And, most importantly for us I guess, the article by some of the experts who set this park up alerting us to how much it was still at risk. We really had to do something, you know? *Tai Fun*'s cruise route was a perfect cover. It was taking us to every protected location Luzon Logging were supposed to be pillaging. Getting Gabriella aboard as entertainments officer was easy enough, because she's actually very well qualified indeed, and she's done really out-standing work on the last few circuits of the

230

track. Then when I arrived with full briefing from the guys at 760 United Nations Plaza, we were able to make contact and proceed. They have a case against Luzon Logging coming together, but these guys play dirty. They have illegal contacts with every shady business that has power or influence anywhere in Indonesia. Or all points east right around the world, from what I can gather. There's as much illegal logging in the Amazon as there is here, and cocaine fields planted where the forest used to be. Profit from both ends and pretty good contacts with the drug-lords bleeding poison in through Florida. They even support one or two terrorist militias so they have people who will literally stop at nothing. There are witnesses out here who have vanished *before* they even agreed to talk, with their families; and in at least one case, their whole damn village. I'm not holding myself up as anything special but I'm in a protected position in all sorts of ways. Also, I've put a helluva lot of time, effort and cold hard cash into the preservation and reconstruction of eco-systems and traditional social systems and micro-economies in this part of the world. And I'm one guy that'll stand up in any goddamn court in the world and testify against these scum whose one function in life seems to be to rip the heart out of all of it. And now, thanks to a lot of hard work by people like Gabriella here, it looks like I got something to say, even if it's only that I know who killed poor old Pongo the orang-utan. *Stealing wood to make pool cues!*'

'You'll have more than that, I promise you,' said Gabriella earnestly. 'I have a guy on Pulau Baya who's just solid gold from our point of view. And we're due to see him within three days at most.'

The Tokyo contingent arrived in the early afternoon with the welcome news that the guys from UN Headquarters were going to stay home at 760 UN Plaza on the corner of First Avenue and 46th Street, an address that, for one reason or another, Richard and Robin knew well. Their conference went on late into the night. Richard and Robin took the opportunity of one last trek through the moon-bright landscape in spite of a peal of thunder that seemed to come out of a clear blue sky near sunset, then retired. They were woken before dawn, not with the screams of the monkeys but by a courteous park ranger informing them that their flight to Makassar would leave from Lapandong Udara Airport within the hour. They joined Nic and Gabriella in a Land Rover and then a speedboat. Then another Land Rover. The plane took off at dawn and arrived in Makassar while it was still quite early in the morning. They were bundled straight into an air-conditioned car and driven straight to Pelni Harbour. All of their lively and intense conversation focused on the UNESCO mission, how Gabriella and Nic planned to push it forward decisively in Pulau Baya, and what Richard and Robin could do to help and support them.

At no time did any of them sense the

impending crisis towards which they were whirling so rapidly. And at no time did any of the men and women moving them through airport, air or city see fit to update them, even by putting the news on to radio or TV screen.

So they arrived at *Tai Fun* a little before lunchtime, still almost magically ignorant.

Tai Fun was riding at anchor, seemingly almost deserted. As soon as he stepped aboard, Richard realized something was wrong. Inge stood at the top of the gangway and so he asked her first. 'What is it? What's the matter?'

'It's the passengers,' she explained as the other three climbed aboard and clustered round her. 'Almost all of them have gone down with food poisoning. Well over one hundred and counting. There was a reception at the Makassar Surabaya Imperial Hotel and they all went to it. The first ones fell ill almost immediately and all the rest went down like nine-pins, while they were still there. The hotel was fantastic. It's blessedly close to the hospital on Jalan Penghibur, overlooking the bay there, and they're all tucked up in hotel accommodation but with medical attention from the Stella Maris.'

'Bloody lucky for us,' announced Larsen, suddenly appearing in the foyer beside the lifts, 'or there'd be no point in us setting sail at all. The captain wants to see you and the owner's with him. They're in the bridge and I'll take you up. Miss Nordberg, the sails are set. We're ready to go as soon as this final conference is completed. Make sure everything down here is shipshape as far as you can. Are the extra supplies stowed, do you know?'

The five of them squashed side by side into the lift. 'I'm confused,' said Nic. 'Most of your passengers are sick in bed ashore and that's a good thing? Your reaction to this crisis is to up anchor, set sail and leave?'

'There's something else going on,' said Richard. 'Something we don't know about. What is it, Larsen? What's happened?'

'It's Pulau Baya, Captain Mariner. Worldwide emergency called. Ten thousand trapped, in Baya City alone. They've had landslides, tremors, God knows what else, apparently, and now this. Guanung Surat. Anyone who can get there must get there to take them off as best we can.'

'Guanung Surat?' asked Robin, dazed by the speed at which things appeared to be happening all of a sudden. 'What on earth is Guanung Surat?'

The lift hissed to a stop. The doors opened. Larsen hurried them out towards the bridge where the captain and the owner awaited them.

'Guanung Surat,' said Larsen, as though simply unable to believe that they hadn't heard and didn't know. 'It's the main mountain in Pulau Baya and at sunset last night the whole top of the thing blew off. The bang was heard from Nome to Calcutta, Hobart to Colombo. It looks like they've a full-scale volcanic eruption on their hands.'

Twenty-One

Volcano

None of the villagers following Sailendra were people of the book. So it was only Parang who was able to see his prince as a young Moses, leading the children, the bedraggled, the halt and the lame towards the promised land of Baya City, guided by a column of smoke by day and by a column of fire by night.

Sailendra himself was far less heroic than the figure he painted in his secretary's eyes. He could hardly credit what was happening. He had trusted only two things in his life since his parents died. He had trusted his friend and he had trusted his island. Now neither, it seemed, was what he had believed them to be. Each, in their own way, had chosen to betray him. How foolish did this make him? The only, petty, consolation was that Parang's betrayal of Sailendra's hopes and dreams into the grasping claws of Kerian had been more than cancelled out by the greater betrayal of the very land he loved into the enormity of this eruption. Kerian was welcome to whatever smouldering wreckage was left after both of these betrayals ran their course. And whatever plot or power Parang had sold his soul for he was also welcome to, for it would be nothing more than dust and ashes now. But, petty though these first reactions were, Sailendra did have some greatness of spirit. Both as a prince and as a man he saw his duty clear enough. He must get these people Fate had cast into his control safely into Baya City. Then he must get whoever was left on his island safely to some kind of refuge the best way that he could. Or die in the attempt.

The column of smoke was the plaything of the winds. At first, the heat of whatever had caused the explosion was enough to force it almost straight up into the sky. But then it seemed that what held it erect was the airy confluence of the southern monsoon and the north wind. It was not until the column reached the cold, still troposphere that it began to spread out slowly, then it started blowing westwards, with the jet stream.

Much later, volcanologists such as Dr Hirai aboard *Tai Fun* would discuss how much force and matter were expelled during those first hours, and why the column remained almost entirely of smoke and fine ash, illuminated and occasionally infested from below by great eruptions of gaseous flame. The effect on the inhabitants of the island, for the time being at least, was that they were able to breathe and move without undue effort. The air at ground – and sea – level remained clear after an initial rain of hot pebbles, all that remained of the mountain's peak. And that when ash did begin

236

to fall, it came in the form of a cool grey dust like dirty talcum powder which settled like a mist and not, as yet, hails of red-hot pumice or bombardments of blazing magma.

So, as darkness all too swiftly changed the great grey trunk of smoke in the sky ahead into a column of restless fire, and the death of the blood-red sun gave birth to a great blue-green moon, Sailendra guided the straggling villagers up over the pass in the mountains. The lonely, embittered prince led them over the pass and down on to the road behind Bandar Laut Bay. Bambang ran between the village elders and the lone figure striding at the head of the column, demanding that the pace be slackened, that refreshment stops be taken, that the younger and fitter be allowed to raid the coconut groves for food and drink. That they be allowed to drive back the darkness with makeshift torches made of blazing banana leaves and the burning branches of trees. Sailendra answered the boy with gruff monosyllables, which Bambang indefatigably translated into whatever instructions he thought the elders wanted to hear. And so the villagers moved onwards through the night – for it was clear to the least among them that with the island on fire, stopping to rest was likely to result in a much longer sleep than they planned. And besides, even the most recalcitrant amongst them could hardly fail to be inspired by the solid, steady leadership of the man who was their true-born prince and sovereign.

The road before them was empty, even when

they reached the prawn fisheries, for they were a good three hours behind everyone else. It remained empty as they passed the spur on their left that led up to the foothills where Sailendra and Kerian had their homes, a spur that the prince strode steadily past as though there was nothing up there as important to him as the helpless people at his back. But after the spur, the deserted roadway became increasingly littered with discarded possessions, particularly when they reached the outskirts of the city, where people had set out for the docks carrying impractically heavy treasures. Still Sailendra led the villagers, a silent and bitter figure, perhaps, but a charismatic one if for no other reason than that he was a familiar face moving with clear purpose. And that so many had chosen to follow him; their numbers flattered in the darkness, perhaps, by the brightness of the flaming torches so many carried, as though this were some kind of religious parade or festival. So that, first in very occasional ones, but then in twos and threes, those who had stayed behind began to join the crowd at his back, able to see the straggling parade from far away because of its river of brightness. The terrified, lost and confused found light, companions, a leader. Waifs and strays found other waifs to join with. The elderly and recalcitrant saw others just like them moving forward, and they began to move forward along with them.

Sailendra arrived at the high point of the road just as the dawn broke. He paused on the ridge, looking down into the bowl that contained his city and saw only the wildest of confusion in the shadows. Ten thousand people, maybe more, had gathered around the docks, but the first great beams of eastern light showed the waters of Baya Bay and the harbour to be utterly empty of shipping. Not even the praus of Councillor Kerian's Bugis fleet remained. In the instant before the sun itself framed his figure like a halo, the men, women and children who had followed him gathered at their prince's back so that to those in the city below it seemed that the ridge was suddenly on fire. A wave of panic ran through the crowd down by the docks. Every eye turned eastwards to look at the new threat. But then Sailendra himself stepped forward. The sunlight framed him, making the solid silhouette of his body seem even larger than it was. His shadow seemed to reach across the still dawn air. And he seemed like a saviour to the terrified crowd, even before the first amongst them recognized who the man on the horizon actually was.

And so Sailendra's arrival in Baya City, an event that was to attain almost legendary status, was enhanced by two more elements that happened at the same time as the sunrise. The strange physics that held the column above Guanung Surat in a kind of stasis was upset by those massive sunbeams. The first great bolt of lightning leaped down the writhing column from the very roof of the heavens, the crackling of its thunderous brightness lost in the still

239

gathering roar of the intensifying eruption. And at that moment also, those westward-racing beams spread out across the whole of the Java Sea, to reveal a flotilla of rescue ships sailing over the northern horizon at flank speed.

The ragged cheer that ran through the exhausted and terrified crowd was accompanied by a push towards the promise of safety. From the hilltop, Sailendra could see the danger of the unregulated crowd pushing one way and another, quite apart from the probability of chaos and panic when the ships did arrive and started trying to get people aboard. He turned to look at the expectant faces behind him. 'Help is coming,' he said just loudly enough for everyone to hear him. 'But we must help the people who are trying to help us. I must go down and try to organize the people by the dockside. You must follow quietly, without excitement, and set a good example by waiting your turn. Some of you will find friends and family members down there. Tell them I ask that they do the same. It is our best hope.' He turned to the two who had walked closest to him so far. 'Bambang, what did your father plan?'

'To help with the landslide. He has a good team of men.'

'Could you find him?'

'I can find the cannery trucks. There are no others like them. They will be near the bridge across the river. He will be near them, I am certain.'

'Good. Try to find your father. Take your

240

mother too so that she can tell him you are a prince's messenger. Tell him this. I will be on Pier One. I will be trying to control the way the ships are loading and I will need the help of him and his men. If he can get to me I will be grateful. If he cannot then I need him to try and use his men to keep order and calm amongst the crowd. Is that clear?' Bambang and his mother nodded. 'Off you go then, and good luck.' Bambang turned away, then turned back. He held the largest of the flaming torches and was clearly at a loss as to what to do with it. On an impulse he was to bless for the rest of his life, Sailendra simply took it. Then he turned at last to Parang. All the things he wished to say were overpowered by what he had to say. 'I must go to the pier, as I said to Bambang. We must have order down there. I need you to go to the council. See who is there. Enlist the help even of Councillor Kerian. Tell them what I plan to do. Then find the head of the emergency services and tell him. We need leadership here, or I fear we may be lost even at the moment of rescue.'

Parang nodded once, turned and ran down the hillside into the shadows of the city's valley. Sailendra held Bambang's torch high as a signal to those behind him, and strode off down the road. It was another half an hour before the sun rose high enough above the ridge for its rays to reach right down to the dockside. But during that half-hour, Sailendra, with his flaming torch held high and his followers like a religious procession behind him, moved through the thinning shadows bringing leadership, light and calm. The crowds ahead of him parted to allow the procession through. To begin with, those who could joined on to the end of the procession. But down in the city centre by the docks, the bodies were already so tight-packed that all they could do was to ease back and let the men and women with their blazing torches through. So at last Sailendra came to the water front. But no sooner did he do so than the next set of problems became clear.

The pier head was packed with expectant people, looking hopefully northward. Behind their left shoulders the mountain stood seemingly joined to the heavens by the thick black trunk of smoke. Lightning was lancing down it almost constantly now, and the steady rumbling of the gathering eruption was like the approach of the largest imaginable express train. But from down here, the ships out on the horizon seemed to have made no progress at all. It was clearly going to be a long wait. Without food, water, latrines. With tens of thousands of people pressing forward towards the water away from the terrifying mountain. The first ships to dock would be simply swamped unless he could think of something. And the agonizing slowness of their approach was likely to be further complicated by one more fact. Baya Port was tidal, even under the new conditions dictated by the landslide partially blocking the Sungai Baya River. The ships might all arrive, he realized, going cold, only to find they had to wait for anything up to eight hours before they could actually get their gangways on to the pier. He needed to find the harbour master. But even as the thought occurred to the beleaguered prince, so the almost magical effect of the torch-lit procession took effect. The harbour master found him.

'Prince Sailendra? Your Highness!' Of all places, the voice seemed to be coming from behind and below where Sailendra was standing. He turned. There was nothing there but the edge of the pier with the curving top of a metal ladder rising to waist height before it plunged down over the side. Then the harbour mouth, the sea and the ship-crowded horizon. *The ladder*, he thought and stepped across to it. In the face of the crowds on his piers and his foreshore, the harbour master, naturally, was using his harbour to move about. There was a four-oared pilot boat sitting at the ladder's foot held in place by the firm hand of a rower while the harbour master swarmed up the ladder to the pier.

'There is much to discuss, Your Highness,' said the pompous little official as soon as he was standing on the pier. 'Do you wish to come to my office? We have maps, charts, tide tables and tea there. We have hand-held receiver/transmitters – walkie-talkies – that will, I am certain, soon be in range of the approaching vessels. Unfortunately our expensive and powerful new radio equipment went down when the masts went down...' He gestured with his chin at the brown mess of the landslide beyond the sluggish brown flood. 'And, of course, there is an enormous amount of electrical interference...' He gestured again at the volcanic discharge towering above the mountain, its huge grey trunk starred with lightning.

Sailendra was tempted. By the promise of tea if by nothing else. But his arrival had had such a powerful effect upon the crowd, he could hardly dare calculate what effect his departure might have. Even if he was only going as far as the harbour master's office. 'I will wait here,' he decided. 'But you are right. It is vital that I remain in contact with you – especially when you begin to make contact with the ships. Can you send me one of these walkie-talkies when you return to the office?' The harbour master nodded. Sailendra continued, hardly taking time for a breath, 'Have you many men at your disposal?'

'A dozen. And the harbour pilots. Some of the longshoremen have reported to me as well. A team of twenty-five in all.'

'You will of course remain in charge of the harbour waters. I will try and assemble teams up here. I must try and break the crowd into more manageable units. Then we must try and bring them fresh water at least, if not food.'

'Those at the rear of the crowd are of course near to the houses in the city. I believe there is still running water there.'

'An excellent thought, though we will have to

take care.' There was no time to explain about deadly gas permeating the water in the paddy fields. 'Is there anything else? It will be hot soon.'

'As chance would have it, Your Highness, there is a million litres of bottled water in one of my warehouses awaiting shipment to Yokohama.'

'The warehouses!' Sailendra looked across to the harbour's secure area. 'I had forgotten the warehouses. What else is in them we might use?'

'I will check, Your Highness, and alert you. In the meantime, the bottled water?'

'Leave it where it is until we get some sort of organization. As with the arrival of the ships, we could do more harm than good unless we have some kind of plan worked out. And to that end, get your people organized as soon as possible – then send someone to me with a walkie-talkie. And some instructions on how to use it, please.'

The harbour master bowed until the yellow buttons of his double-breasted blue-serge uniform met at breast and belly, then he heaved himself on to the ladder and vanished. He was replaced almost at once by Bambang. 'I have found my father. He was with the chief of the emergency services. They have a large number of men already organized to deal with the landslide. Now of course they have more important things. They are on their way here now, Your Highness. I came faster...' He ducked through the legs of the nearest people to show how.

And he nearly tripped up Parang, who was pushing through the crush towards his prince. 'This is Junior Councillor Nona,' he said without ceremony. 'He is the only councillor I could find. The others seem to have gone to their homes. Or to have gone with Chief Councillor Kerian.'

'With Kerian? Where has Kerian gone?' demanded Sailendra.

Parang gestured at the empty harbour at Sailendra's back, as though that in itself would supply the answer. Sailendra swung round, seeing once again the harbour mouth, the sea, the slowly approaching ships. And nothing in between. So that the gesture indeed did explain everything.

Even so, Junior Councillor Nona put into words what the shaken Sailendra suddenly came to understand. Everything he understood – and then some. 'Councillor Kerian and all his so called Bugis friends took to their praus almost immediately after the mountain exploded and sailed straight out of the harbour. Each and every one of them seemed to me to be armed to the teeth. They said the outside world was sending too little help too late. So they were going to take whatever they could from wherever they found it – in the old-fashioned Bugis way.'

Twenty-Two

The Bugis Way

'My grandfather was a soldier stationed on this island,' said Dr Hirai quietly to Richard. They were standing side by side watching the satellite TV image on the big screen that she had used to illustrate her talk on Krakatau. Pulau Baya swam in as much of a close-up as the pilot of the news company's plane could allow the cameraman, swinging as close as he dared to the huge column of smoke with its constant electrical discharge.

'Was he an expert on volcanoes too?'

'He still is. He is living in contented retirement with my grandmother in the city of Miyazaki. He was a doctor of medicine specializing in sports injuries but ceased practising some years ago. He says he stays because of the excellent golf. But the area is one of the most volcanic in Japan. Birthplace of the Gods. And he is working on a definitive history of volcanoes. He will be very jealous to know I am going to Pulau Baya under these circumstances. But he will also be a little surprised, I think. He was certain that of all the islands in the Java Sea,

Pulau Baya was the *least* likely to be volcanic. All the time that he was stationed in the jungle there before the Americans came, he kept a diary. And he noted nothing even faintly like volcanic activity.'

'Well, that sure as hell looks like a volcano to me,' said Nic, joining the pair of them in the cavernous lecture theatre. The whole of *Tai Fun* was almost empty now, a *Mary Celeste* with the vast majority of its passengers in bed in Makassar. Many of its contingent were also left in the safety of the city. Only the skeleton crew of volunteers were still aboard – all of them there because they felt they had something important to offer to the vessel's brave new mission.

'It is shaping up to be a powerful eruption, by the look of things,' agreed the doctor.

'Shaping up?' gasped Inge, coming in through the deserted – and currently managerless – casino. 'How much worse can it get?'

'Oh, very much worse,' explained the doctor earnestly. 'This is an early phase. Many volcanoes smoke and spit like this. Etna, for instance. It may carry on as it is or it may settle down. Or...'

'Or what?' asked Richard.

'Or it may go Plinian.' She looked around the blank faces and gave a little modest smile. 'Pliny the Younger wrote all about the eruption of Vesuvius in two letters written in 79 AD to the historian Tacitus so that he could accurately record the facts of the eruption in his famous *Histories*,' she explained. 'Pliny is the first person in Western science or literature to do such a thing. He observed it all across the Bay of Naples from Misenum, where his uncle, Pliny the Elder, was the naval squadron commander. Then, although he stayed with his mother – he was seventeen at the time – he talked to men who went with his uncle to try to rescue the people trapped by the eruption. He recorded how his uncle died in the attempt and how the rest of his command were lucky to escape with their lives. The record describes the classic sequence of events from the first explosion to the final nuées ardente or pyroclastic flows. Those flows were what finally destroyed Pompeii and Herculaneum. Though it was not until the 1990s before they finally discovered how many people actually died at Herculaneum, of course. When they opened up the long-buried waterside warehouses and found them full of two-thousand-year-old corpses.' She fell silent, but all of their eyes were drawn to the stippled, surging grey mass along the edge of the bright blue waters of the harbour which was the closest the picture could come to showing the better part of ten thousand desperate people waiting for them there. 'Or it may go up like Krakatau,' Dr Hirai finished. 'And simply blow the whole island to pieces.'

It hadn't taken much of a conference to convince Richard, Robin, Nic and Gabriella to join the rescue mission. Nic and Gabriella were hardly risk-averse and neither of them had much to lose in terms of family and responsibilities. Richard and Robin had been in situations like this before and were confident that their presence would add a good deal to *Tai Fun*'s effectiveness as a rescue vessel. Both kept their qualifications up to accident-and-emergency standard in first aid, so at the very least they could help Dr Hirai. But of course, both were fully trained ship's captains holding current certificates, so either could replace Captain Olmeijer if anything went wrong; both held the documents that would allow them to replace or support Eva Gruber as navigating officer; and Richard also held the same set of papers Larsen held, allowing him to double as sailing master if need be. The only thing they couldn't do was to replace le Chef in his oversight of the motors and mechanical equipment below. And that made all the difference in the end. Both of the men, however, had insisted on waiting until they contacted their respective head offices. Nic had fingers in a wide range of pies. There was a lot of action he could stir up – and stir it up he did. Richard also, as CEO of one of the largest shipping companies in the world, had a lot of tonnage he could send to the stricken island. And he was happy to do so – every vessel in the local area under his ultimate control was ordered to alter course for Pulau Baya. Except for the supertankers.

'Hey!' said Gabriella suddenly. 'Turn the sound up, somebody, would you?' The picture on the big screen had changed from a close-up on the island to an aerial shot of the rescue fleet powering into Baya Bay. All the ships had one central focus, whether they were heading east of south, due south or west of south. The only exceptions seemed to be a small fleet of native praus sailing close-hauled east of north. And, apparently by coincidence, a laden freighter steaming busily away from the island on a convergent course with the praus.

'Only the *Miyazaki Maru*, belonging to the Luzon Logging Company, seems to be ignoring the urgent call for aid,' the newscaster said, a little sententiously. 'And that's really a tragedy, because as we noted in our last broadcast, she seems to have at least one sizeable helicopter on her deck. What good use the poor people of Pulau Baya could make of that if it was all fuelled up and ready to be of help! But no! Just a minute, viewers! Even she is turning to reverse her course. Every ship in the Java Sea is now steaming to Pulau Baya, full speed ahead!'

'Miyazaki,' said Richard to the doctor. 'That's where your grandfather lives, isn't it? That's a hell of a coincidence.'

'Synchronicity. But Miyazaki is a large port,' she answered coolly. 'And the regional capital. It is also an important business centre as well as a leading centre for sport and recreation. There are many ships named for Miyazaki.'

'But it's interesting that she belongs to Luzon Logging,' added Nic thoughtfully. 'The only ship slow to get stuck in there to help is Luzon Logging's *Miyazaki Maru*.'

'You shouldn't be surprised, Nic,' said Richard without thinking. 'After all, you've seen her sailing orders.'

'Yeah. Until some guy in Manila decided to change them just now.'

Kerian brought his prau alongside *Miyazaki Maru*'s purposefully throbbing side. They ran in parallel, a little west of north for a moment, as though they were both heading for the ship's home port on the South Island of Japan. The prau was not a small vessel. Kerian did not have to do more than stand up on top of the traditional deckhouse to communicate with Captain Nakatomi, who was leaning over the edge of the starboard bridge wing. 'Make it quick,' the captain called down. 'The owners are about to come through, apparently.' He looked up at the vertical smudge of grey disfiguring the southern horizon and spreading like a mushroom cloud across the sky. He shuddered. Both sets of his grandparents had died in Nagasaki, leaving his father and mother to be raised in an orphanage, where they had met as children and married as young adults, and died of cancer twenty years ago.

'You have the timber aboard?' demanded Kerian. From the look of things everything he owned except his prau was about to be reduced to ashes. The timber from Guanung Surat's upper slopes that he had sold to Luzon Logging as a little perk of office now looked like a vital investment. But he wasn't due for payment until delivery had been made. He had acquired

252

the tastes of an expensive lifestyle and they would take some keeping up. Especially as there would be no more native forest girls to slake his lust. He suspected acutely that such pleasures as rape and bondage came expensive in the bordellos of Jakarta, Bangkok and points east.

'We have the timber, with some other cargo more recently acquired in Kalimantan. So what?'

'Are you in the market for anything else? Say, less traditional products. Knick-knacks and whatnots such as we might stumble across if we went aboard a ship or two?'

'Anything, Councillor. You know that. There is more to Luzon Logging than dead wood, as they say.' Captain Nakatomi turned away, summoned by a call from the bridge behind him. But then he turned back, looked down. 'But stay on course with us a while longer, Councillor. The owners are coming through. They'll have further orders for me, I expect; I haven't filled my holds yet. There's room for a good deal more, one way and another. And the choppers still have plenty of gas. So, more orders are on the way and it might be useful for you to know about them.'

While he waited, Kerian stood on the top of the deckhouse, leaned against the solid wood of the mast and looked away along his prau's invisible wake. His island was well below the horizon now. The smoke from the volcano hung in the air like a thunderhead, blocking a good deal of the sky down there. If the councillor felt a twinge of guilt for the thousands who had trusted him and who stood deserted now beneath that strange dark cloud, he dismissed it quickly enough. He had more important things to worry about than the fate of some worthless islanders. His own personal comfort and welfare, for instance.

'I'm on the television!' raged Captain Nakatomi as he came back out along the bridge wing. 'CNN or Fox News or some such. The only vessel in the whole Java Sea heading away from that fucking island except for you! You're on there too, but no one cares for a couple of scummy praus! *Miyazaki Maru* is different, however. The bastards in head office want the world to know they have a conscience. The word's come straight from Del Monte Avenue, or I'd think they must be joking! Luzon Logging with a conscience! But the Man from Del Monte he say *Go!* So I'm to turn round, if you please. Turn round, go back and at least pretend to help the pathetic rabble you left to fry and die!'

'What did they say about me?' demanded Kerian almost petulantly. 'Will they take anything I can bring them, no questions asked?'

Captain Nakatomi had had much more urgent business than discussing with the Luzon Logging Company of Del Monte Avenue, Quezon City, Manila, the doings of some self-important little Bugis pirate with ideas inflated far above his station. And, given his new orders, he had far more important things to do than to stand here chewing the fat with him. 'They say yes,' he lied therefore. 'You bring it, they'll take it. All part of the package with the timber from the island. Top dollar guaranteed.'

Tai Fun leaned easily across the northerly wind as she ran south in the wake of the armada bound for Pulau Baya. She was behind the bulk of the fleet, but beginning to catch them up, the great black sails driving her forward as swiftly as her motors would have done. They had no clear idea what to expect when they reached Baya Port, so they were preparing for the worst. All of those aboard not actively involved in shiphandling had joined the little team of stewards in making up all the bunks and filling the open entertainment areas with more mattresses, pillows and blankets. With everything out, and every possible place prepared, they could accept nearly three hundred people. And the next stage of the plan was to expect them to be burned, hurt, dying. Richard and Robin worked with the increasingly stressed and snappy Dr Hirai, good-humouredly making sure that all the ship's medication, supplemented like the mattresses with extra provisions loaded at Makassar, was in the best possible place and ready to go. Gabriella, Nic and Inge did not stand on ceremony either. They had no great medical expertise and were not needed to handle the ship. They helped in the galleys therefore, working under the tutelage of two chefs de cuisine whose normal professional manner made the stressed-out Dr Hirai at her tensest and rudest seem like the doyenne of the diplomatic service. But bullying, swearing and tantrums aside, there would be simple meals, cold water and a range of sustaining beverages ready from the moment the first refugee came aboard.

Because of her size and draft, *Tai Fun* had been anchored closest inshore at Pelni Harbour. Because of what had happened to her unfortunate passengers, she was already in contact with the hospital. Because she had the owner already aboard there had been no need to wait around for permission, clearance or head office bumbling. Because of her unique position, she was the vessel that could be loaded easiest and quickest with the most delicate and expensive of equipment, medicines, survival supplies. Because Richard and Nic had held her at anchor for the better part of a vital hour as they arranged things with their respective head offices, she was simply available for longer than the rest of the busily departing armada. Because of the urgency of the situation no one thought twice about putting so many vital and precious eggs into one undermanned insecure and all-too assailable basket. And, because of the urgency of the situation, not even the trenchantly old-fashioned and romantic Richard Mariner, who trusted these waters least of them all, thought twice about taking her out into Bugis waters with so much of worth aboard and so little in the way of protection. With no protection at all, in fact.

The two praus which were all that remained of Kerian's fleet now swung in behind *Tai Fun*, ready for an innocent reply to the watchman's hail. But there was no watch set here. Unknown to the pirates, Eva Gruber had further aided their cause by setting the collision-alarm radar to forward focus, so not even that fine instrument warned of vessels creeping up behind. Kerian slung the first rope himself and watched the grappling hook catch on the hoist that moved the hydraulic platform on the after section. The platform was in its 'rest' position, which coincidentally put it exactly level with the prau's deck. Kerian tightened the rope, secured it safely and stepped aboard *Tai Fun*. It was as easy as that. So disorientatingly easy was it, in fact, that the pirate captain was halfway towards the nearest gangway before he realized he was carrying nothing more threatening than a kris. He turned to the man behind him. 'Give me a gun,' he said.

Guns were forbidden on Pulau Baya. But then so were logging, rape and piracy. Kerian had supplied himself over the years with a range of firearms which he had kept in secret and used only on very special occasions indeed. These ranged from antique Japanese and American weapons discovered in the jungles after the war to more modern armaments supplied as part of his secret dealings with Luzon Logging and their like. He had brought it all aboard his prau, but remained very well aware that the Japanese bullets were almost all used up now and were no longer very reliable. The American stuff was more plentiful and reliable, though equally antique. The modern guns, on the other hand, had proved expensive to get hold of and incredibly expensive to load. But, as might be expected with organizations like Luzon Logging, even the apparently modern guns were not all they seemed. A man who was actually as expert as Kerian believed himself to be would have seen this. But Captain Nakatomi was right. The chief councillor's opinion of himself was over-inflated.

The Walther PPK, barrelled for 9mm load, was a cheap Chinese copy of the already venerable original made largely for the James Bond wannabe market. It looked the business and had fired well on the rare occasions Kerian had tried it but it was little more than a toy. The manufacture and the action were dangerously unstable. Much the same could be said of the Korean copy of the big Browning 9mm High Power that he was currently holding himself with what he fondly supposed was an expert hand. Kerian had never fired the Russian CZ52 that his nephew Bukit, the captain of the second prau, was holding. Which was lucky for Kerian because the Russian gun was genuine but chambered for Tokarev 7.65mm bullets – while it was Browning 9mms that were jammed into it. And all of them would have been very nervous indeed if they had fully understood just how ineffective the safety on the venerable Russian 9mm Makarov being carried by the last in the line actually was. All that was currently keeping him from emptying all eight shots into their backs was the fact that the trigger pull wasn't working properly. Fearsomely danger-ous-looking, and actually deadly in ways they couldn't begin to comprehend, the ten pirates crept aboard *Tai Fun*.

The first person they met was Inge. The own-er's daughter, deeply distracted by her calcula-tion of how much water in litres per hour they would need to hydrate three hundred sick and wounded people, simply came round a corner into the corridor leading to some storerooms and then the water-sports sections further aft. And there, immediately in front of her, were two men standing, stripped to the waist, wear-ing traditional island costume of short sarongs. Behind them stood eight youths dressed in T-shirts and jeans. Only their colouring dis-tinguished them from most of the youthful passengers aboard. And the fact that they, like the first two in traditional costume, were all carrying guns. The elder of the two in island costume, a wiry man of indeterminate age, with well-developed muscles turning scrawny under skin that seemed a size too big for him, stepped forward. He had a broad, long-eyed face with many wrinkles and no hair at all. There was something disturbingly feral about him; as though he had stepped out of a wild place in a much less politically correct era. It was the way his bottomless black gaze fastened so hungrily upon her cleavage then dropped unapologetically to look her right between the thighs. Only when he grinned at her did she think to scream. But by then it was too late. He did the safest thing he possibly could have done with the Browning High Power pistol he was carrying: he hit her in the head with it. She went down instantly and silently.

'Hostage number one,' said Kerian. 'Take her to my prau and tie her up tightly.' He licked his lips. 'Bukit, come with me. The next woman we take is yours. But the next person we find, man or woman, becomes our guide and shield. There is more to be taken from this pretty vessel than prisoners and playthings.'

Twenty-Three

Pliny

The second explosion was louder than the first. It was proved later that people heard it from Karachi to Chicago. Blessedly, as with the first explosion, the main power went upwards. It twisted through the upper air like a wave within the wind and many people later swore they saw it passing overhead like a distortion of the daylight itself just an instant before the sound came. It was as though the parallel lines of the sunbeams were for an instant twisted out of shape and then something huge exploded nearby. Sailendra was one of these; and he was in a good position to see it, for something flattened him as it flattened everyone else in Baya Port and many of the buildings in Baya City itself. Sailendra landed on his back on the rough stone of the pier, looking upwards. And so he saw the wave of twisting power spreading like a ripple through reality above his head. Then he heard the first microsecond of the sound before his ears gave out and refused to register the rest. Then, dazed though he was, he had the presence of mind to roll over on to his front and cover his head as a hail of red-hot pebbles came tumbling out of the sky like one of the plagues brought by the prophet Moses to Ancient Egypt.

The first thing Sailendra heard clearly as his ears recovered some time later was the screaming. He heard the tooth-jarring rumbling first, but believed that this was just the damage done to his ears by the explosion. Only when he began to connect it with the way the ground was trembling and the harbour water had gone strangely dark and choppy did he realize that it was something more. And a glance up at the mountain showed him that the column of smoke and fire had intensified immeasurably.

But the screaming worried him most immediately. Was it panic, he wondered, or were there people badly hurt out there?

Had the explosion happened much earlier than it did, Sailendra would have been able to do little more than listen, look and worry. But in the interim between the arrivals of Bambang, Parang and Junior Councillor Nona, Sailendra had also made contact with the chief of the emergency services, and the chief of police. One was controlling the fire crews and the ambulances while the other had teams of officers doing their best to keep order among the crowds. Both of these officers had walkie-talkies on their persons and spread out amongst their men. And both of them turned up in the company of Bambang's father, Mr Pelajar, the extremely capable manager of the cannery, though unfortunately he was without a walkie-talkie, as was Sailendra himself for the moment.

But then the harbour master's walkie-talkie arrived, brought across by Dr Nurul, the marine biologist from the prawn fishery, who had offered her services in case there was another unexpectedly marine element to the eruption to match the sudden rise in sea temperature that destroyed the fishery itself. It was the work of less than five minutes to check the wavelengths of the two other sets, and establish a four-way contact between the prince, the harbour master and the chiefs of emergency services and the police.

Sailendra was, therefore, at the very heart of the situation, with the ability to monitor and order events as necessary, when the second explosion came. With the screaming piercing the relentless monotony of the bone-jarring rumbling, he groped for the walkie-talkie. The channels were easy: 1 was the harbour master, 2 was the emergency services, 3 was the chief of police. He himself was 4. He pressed 2. He needed feedback from fire-fighters and paramedics first, he thought.

'Yes?'

'I hear screaming. Many badly hurt?'

'First impressions say not. It's mostly panic. Some buildings down. Some fires started, but surprisingly few casualties.'

Sailendra pressed 3. 'Chief? I hear screaming. It's panic, apparently. Any problems with crowd control?'

'Not yet, Your Highness. But it won't take much and my men are spread pretty thin.'

Sailendra frowned with thought. 'We need people to start taking responsibility for themselves if we can. Is there any way we can get them split up into village units? Or groups from streets or districts? Get a leader or an elder responsible for each. They can organize the smaller units and report to us if there are problems that they can't handle. That'll make it easier to distribute food and water too, as soon as we get the chance.'

And water at least was the next weapon in Sailendra's armoury. With the intuition of a leader, born and bred, he saw that his people would react badly to people in authority who did nothing but lecture, bully and threaten – even if it was all for their own good. But exhausted, frightened, thirsty people would do almost anything for men who handed them water and promised them food. He pressed 1. 'Harbour master, it's time to break out the water,' he said. And he turned to Bambang and Mr Pelajar. 'I have a job for you two, your men, and your trucks,' he added.

In actual fact, adding to the legendary status of those times and the young prince's part in the events, it was Bambang who found work for him. Forty minutes later, with the first of many blizzards of thick white ash-flakes beginning to settle over the increasingly panicky crowd, the indefatigable boy was back. 'The trucks are loaded and ready, Your Highness,' he said. 'But

264

I thought it would help keep the people calmer if you came with us when we started giving the bottles out. You could give out a little hope and comfort with the water. Bring everyone up to date about when the ships are likely to get here and what the plans are then...'

Sailendra turned to Parang. 'It's a good idea,' he said. 'I'll go in one. Why don't you and Councillor Nona go in the other. Dr Nurul, you have your own walkie-talkie; I am call number 4 so we'll make you number 5. You can stay here and update me as need be, especially as you can liaise with the harbour master.' He looked up at the rapidly darkening sky. 'We're losing sunlight and that's good, because it'll cool things down for a while. But if we lose daylight things will get pretty tense, especially if the fallout gets any thicker. Or hotter. I need to know the instant we have contact with the first ships.' Then he went off on Bambang's impatient heels, hurrying through the increasingly terrified crowd as fast as their fear would let him.

For the next two hours, Sailendra rode the back of the water truck, distributing water, calm and hope in equal measures, though he started to become increasingly tense himself as the pall of smoke from the volcano spread lower, thicker and faster than the first high plume. The light thinned and the blizzard of ash thickened relentlessly. As the unnatural shadows began to fill the air, so the flakes went from white to black, to white to orange. And it was only when an orange flake fell on the back of his hand that he realized the blizzard was no longer of ash but of fire.

But it was at that precise moment of transition from bad to worse that the walkie-talkie shrilled and Dr Nurul shouted, 'The harbour master is in touch with the first ships. They'll be here and ready to take the first nine hundred to one thousand aboard within the next two hours, maybe three.'

After Inge, the next people aboard *Tai Fun* unfortunate to come across Kerian and his Bugis pirates were Gabriella and Eva. It was because of Eva. Coming off watch for a while, as *Tai Fun* joined the more predictable and controlled stragglers behind the main rescue fleet, she went looking for Inge as she often did. The women had become friends, the owner's daughter unaware of the navigator's borderline worship. But when Eva could not find Inge, she went to ask Gabriella whether she knew where she was. As a matter of fact, Gabriella was fairly certain Inge had said something about finding some items down in the ship's storage area and so the two women set off together, running side by side down the gangways. Side by side still, they came round a corner and found themselves face to face with the would-be pirates. Gabriella was stunned. Not by the presence of the men so much as by the fact that she knew at least one of them. 'Councillor Kerian!' she said, in her fluent Indonesian *baha*

Indonesia. 'I thought you were on Pulau Baya! Is Prince Sailendra here? Or Secretary Parang?'

'We have come to ask your help...' Kerian stepped forward. 'There are many sick and dying...'

'Of course...' Gabriella stepped forward in response, moved by ready sympathy long before her brain actually engaged.

Up on the bridge, just at the very moment that she took her fatal step, a wall of force, twisting through the air just ahead of the sound of the second explosion, glanced off the clearview with enough power to split it from side to side. *Tai Fun* seemed to stagger. Gabriella lurched forward into Kerian's arms. He hit her on the side of the head with the massive Browning pistol and she dropped like a stone.

Eva Gruber gasped in a breath and let out a scream that would have shattered glass. But she screamed at the very instant that the sound of the explosion arrived, so the warning she tore out of her straining lungs was lost below the overwhelming rumble of the volcano's agony. And by the time the sound had faded into relative quiet, she also lay insensible on the deck.

'Take them to my prau,' ordered Kerian. 'We will find another guide.'

The next crew member that the pirates found was le Chef. One look at the fearsome array of weaponry and the state of the desperadoes who were armed with it, stopped the bellicose French engineer dead in his tracks.

'What are you looking for?' he snarled in his

267

thickly accented English.

By way of answer, Kerian pointed the Browning unwaveringly at his face. The chef was a pragmatist. He knew force majeure when he saw it. So he became at once exactly what Kerian wanted him to be – part guide, part shield. But le Chef was no fool. He knew that if he led the strange, not very sane, invaders to the central areas, he would more than likely lead them into confrontation with Captain Olmeijer, Mr Nordberg or – and this really did worry him – with Mr Greenbaum or Captain Mariner. The prospect of being trapped between ten well-armed pirates and the man who had taken on two blazing jet-skis with nothing but a hose and a bit of advice from the sailing master really made him think very hard indeed. He led Kerian and his men, therefore, to those sections of the vessel which he thought would be emptiest and quietest.

These areas were the storerooms midships on the lowest decks, surrounded with well-packed shelving and kept well away from heat and light, and he led them down. And the roiling darkness that swept so rapidly across the sky ahead remained something of which they remained in blessed ignorance, as they remained ignorant of what had caused the thunder and the fact that the clearview now looked as though it had been struck by lightning. As, indeed, these simply mesmerizing phenomena ahead kept the officers aboard *Tai Fun* in continued ignorance of the two praus grappled to the stern.

Kerian's eyes gleamed greedily at the sight of the supplies all around him. But he was wise enough to know there must be more aboard than the stock available from most ships' chandlers and dockside supermarkets. Still, when he saw the lengths of strong cord lying coiled on a shelf, he realized that he might avail himself of one or two more useful items to help with their plans after all. Five minutes later, the unhappy chef led the pirates into the next section of the storage deck on a short rope held in Kerian's fist, with his hands securely tied behind him, an oil-rag gag in his mouth, and the threat of a carving knife and a nail gun as well as the Browning and all the other automatic pistols at his back.

'The sequence Pliny the Younger recorded in his letters to Tacitus was this,' Dr Hirai explained. 'As the eruption intensifies, the smoke will spread at every level. The high smoke clouds will blot out the sun and the lower clouds will kill the daylight. The blizzard of ash-flakes will become a rain of burning flakes, then burning pumice and semi-molten rocks. The earth will continue to shake with increasing intensity, and the nearby water will become choppy at best but increasingly very rough indeed. It may be that lava flows will relieve pressure at the summit and may help the situation, though of course they will look extremely threatening and may well become dangerous if they spread down the hillsides towards any inhabited areas. Or if they come in contact with water. Herculaneum next to Pompeii was for many years assumed to have been buried by a relatively slow-moving lahar – a kind of river made of ash, molten rock, water and mud. That was how they explained how few bodies they found there at any level. The bodies in Pompeii of course were at roof-top level, showing that the end did not come until ash and pumice had fallen to a depth of two and a half metres or so. A long time after the initial eruption, you see. But the later research, as I said, suggests that, like Pompeii, Herculaneum was overcome by a nuée ardente or pyroclastic flow. These are walls of superheated rock, dust, steam and air that flow along the ground like tidal waves. They can move at speeds between one hundred and six hundred kilometres per hour and can have an internal temperature between one hundred and six hundred degrees Celsius. Modern research suggests that the people in the warehouse at Herculaneum simply smothered because the flow burned off all the oxygen as it went past. Then it vapourized their flesh and ... well, you don't want to know the rest. But it must have been instantaneous. Quicker and easier than roasting alive, I guess. The pyroclastic flow that came out of Krakatau burned people alive on the coast of Java more than forty kilometres distant and almost certainly annihilated all the life on the islands of Subesi and Subiku on the Sumatra side.'

'So these things can go over water?' asked Richard.

'Certainly. Ships recorded them the better part of one hundred kilometres out in the Java Sea in 1883. And of course when Mount Pele in Martinique went up in the famous eruption of December 16th 1902...'

But Richard wasn't listening any longer. 'We have to shore up the stern sections just in case,' he was saying to Robin as he hurried her off. 'If one of those things came through the windows into our stateroom, say, it'd simply blow the whole ship up. I think it would be a good idea to bring down the storm shutters there, in any case – keep things cool and shady if and when it gets used as a hospital ward. When we've secured ours as best we can, I'll have a word with Tom Olmeijer and Nils to see how we can protect the others back there.' Full of decisiveness, action and energy as usual, he punched the button to summon the lift and stepped aboard as soon as the door opened. Robin, frowning, went along with him.

'If these things are as fast and hot as the doctor says, Richard,' she observed, 'closing down some storm shutters isn't going to help much. But I guess you never know...'

She was still darkly thoughtful when she followed Richard into their stateroom. And collided with his shoulder when he stopped with no warning whatsoever. 'Well, I'll be damned,' he whispered. 'Will you take a look at that!' And, following his frowning glance, she

271

saw with a genuine frisson of shock, that there were two praus grappled to *Tai Fun*'s stern like massive leeches sucking on the back of an unsuspecting swimmer.

It was the darkness that was so unsettling, thought Sailendra. It was simply disorientating to have the sun snuffed out in the middle of the afternoon. It made even the broad reaches of the seafront at Baya City, the harbour and the sea-roads beyond seem like a constricted, claustrophobic cave. It emphasized the simple power of the eruption and the powerlessness of the people caught up in it. It blew heavy walls of smoke even across the harbour mouth and it hid the rescue ships from view. And it had been the sight of those ships which had added so effectively to the growing calmness of the crowds. It also made the rain of flaky sparks look even more threatening than it was. He stood thoughtfully in the back of the truck as it trundled back to the warehouse for the next load of bottled water.

Coming in through the compound gates, the prince was struck by how big the warehouse area was. Surely there must be something else there that he might make use of as well as water. He lifted the walkie-talkie to his lips and pressed button number 1. Twenty minutes later he was heaving cardboard boxes stencilled in Chinese characters on to the lorry beside the crates of water bottles. 'What have you got there, Your Highness?' asked Bambang, ever helpful.

'Battery-powered Olympic torches, from the Beijing Olympics,' answered the prince. 'Push the button and they light up. They're surprisingly bright. We'll give them out with the water to combat the darkness as well as the thirst.'

As he spoke, he thrust one into Bambang's hand and the boy flicked on the switch, illuminating the moulded plastic flame. He held the cheap plastic symbol high and it actually seemed to burn with a bright, undying confidence. Bambang used one of his favourite words from his American-English vocabulary. *'Cooool!'* he said.

'The Olympic torch certainly seems to be a success. And the first ship should be docking soon,' said Sailendra to the perspiring Mr Pelajar. 'That will really raise everyone's spirits!'

But even as he spoke, something made him look up at the lightning-wreathed column of flame-streaked blackness pouring upwards out of his mountain. And there, defining the lip of the new-formed crater, the first red river of molten lava came pouring out on to the upper slopes.

Twenty-Four

Heat

The first ships came in through the mouth of Baya Port an hour later on the back of the rising tide. The port itself was of a simple enough design. The harbour mouth opened into a wide bay which was divided from the mouth of the Sungai Baya River on one side by the levee that kept the river under some kind of control and prevented it from silting up the seaways. Opposite the levee right on the far side of the harbour was the warehouse section with its own deep-water access for loading and unloading. But the main port facilities consisted of the two long wide piers that projected straight out from the sea wall and port areas below the city itself.

It was rare that these piers were fully used – but today they were. The ships in the two parallel anchorages between the piers traditionally steamed straight in, and then reversed out. The vessels on the outer berths usually took advantage of the wider harbour waters, between berth 1 and the levee or berth 4 and the warehouse, to swing right round and berth ready to steam directly out again.

That was precisely what the harbour master directed – and it worked, hour after hour, from that first moment until the very end. While Sailendra and his team worked as the shoreside equivalent, moving between the patient lines of increasingly terrified people on to the piers, down to the berths and on to the boats, speeding their safe departure by quelling panic and spreading calming reassurance. Even after the lahar had come. Even when the deadly, glowing spectres of the terrible pyroclastic flows were on their way.

Each vessel could accept between three and five hundred. Each vessel took about an hour to dock, load and leave. The massive water-ballet that the harbour master choreographed speeded up the process as much as humanly possible, while Sailendra and his growing team of volunteers organized things increasingly efficiently on land, but the whole evacuation took between eight and ten solid hours. Hours the volcano had no intention of allowing them, any more than Vesuvius had at Pompeii and Herculaneum.

The next stage of the Plinian eruption of Guanung Surat was the rain of pumice. This started out as the occasional hot pebble and built towards an intense hailstorm of fragments heavy enough to hurt and hot enough to burn. Interspersed within this, right from the start, was the occasional heavier boulder of molten magma, still actually ablaze, which fell out of the roiling sky with the unexpected power and effect of a mortar bomb. It was one such bomb that exploded into the road immediately in front of Sailendra's truck just as the first four ships were docking. He was just pulling out of the warehouse section to go down on to the berths where the chiefs of police and emergency were organizing the expectant refugees. But the bomb made him tap his ingenuity for one last time before getting stuck in to simple crowd control. 'Stop the truck,' he bellowed and the vehicle stopped obediently. Sailendra looked up fearfully, expecting a bombardment. But what arrived instead was the hot hail of pumice. He could see it sheeting down through the smoky red air that was illuminated now not by the late afternoon sun but by the fires up on the mountain.

Sailendra's mind raced. There was nothing he could do about the bombs of molten magma. Anyone they hit full-on would die. He just had to hope that they would hit no one – or nothing – vital. But he could see all too clearly the effect of the hailstorm of hot pumice as the crowd seemed to shudder and heave as though it was one entire being. On the other hand, the numbers of people in that crowd holding Olympic torches gave him hope. If he could find in the warehouses something that would work as a fairly solid umbrella, they would add to each individual's sense of protection while distributing them would give everyone something to get on with while they were waiting to board the rescue ships. He opened his mouth to call on the ingenious Bambang or his equally acute father for some inspiration. But then he stopped himself. The warehouses of Baya Port were the cross-roads between Japan, China and Tai Wan on the one hand, Java, India and points west on the other. There had to be a warehouse full of golf equipment somewhere close at hand. Golf clubs, golf bags, golf balls, golf shoes.

Golf umbrellas.

The moment Richard realized there were two praus secretly secured to Tai Fun's stern, he took Robin – literally by the hand to begin with – and hurried straight for the bridge. The Mariners simply ran out of their stateroom on the uppermost deck and out into the smokily overcast afternoon, racing past the restaurant, beneath the tall shadow of one mast after another and straight into the bridge. But, unusually for people who had faced so many dangers so often in their lives, they were already too late.

The chef, leashed like a bellicose and ill-controlled dog, tried his best to keep Kerian and his men away from any important people or tempting cargo for as long as possible. But, finishing his repairs to the hydraulic platform, he had not really been well focused on what had come aboard at Makassar or where it had all gone. And so, inevitably, he eventually brought the pirates to a large storage area which he had last seen filled with a thoroughly mundane mixture of bedding and beach equipment, but which was now packed tight with near-priceless medical equipment and drugs. Kerian's narrow eyes swept across this treasure-trove while le Chef silently cursed himself and his luck.

He had good reason. For this area alone made Kerian change his plans entirely. It became instantly clear to the overpoweringly greedy man that he would never get all of this aboard his praus. And, indeed, he would never fit it all in his holds. And of course, this was only one storage area in a huge and unimaginably rich vessel. He must stop thinking about stealing the equipment and cargo she carried, therefore; he must steal the whole vessel. And as far as he could see, there was only one place aboard where such a feat could be achieved. 'Take me to the bridge,' he ordered, gruffly, in clear American-accented English.

Richard was too long in the tooth simply to run on to the bridge shouting a warning. But the simple fact was that when he checked the open bridge area everything seemed normal enough. Or it did so until he actually stepped into the command area. The moment he did so, a lean and dangerous-looking old man wearing a sarong and an evil grin stepped out of Eva Gruber's chart area and pointed a very businesslike Browning High Power 9mm pistol at him. Richard's first thought was of Robin, who was hard on his heels. And she was just behind him now, being threatened by, of all things, a Walther PPK – as though she was Pussy Galore

278

and he was Auric Goldfinger. 'Ah,' he said. 'I see you already know we have unexpected guests aboard, Captain.'

'Sit,' said the oldest of the pirates. He waved the Browning purposefully. Richard looked down and saw Larsen already on the deck with his back against the wall and a nasty welt across his head. The chef was seated beside him, trussed like a Christmas turkey. Richard made a meal out of obeying the curt command, his wise eyes busy. He had had dealings with a wide range of guns in his chequered past and could identify most of the major modern makes and models. As well as the Browning and the Walther, he saw a couple of half-familiar Russian models – Makarovs, maybe. Or Tokarevs – he wasn't *that* knowledgeable. Several venerable Colt .45 automatics, which he had last seen John Wayne carrying as he was winning World War II for Hollywood, battling his way past here and on to Iwo Jima. There were two other automatic handguns that he didn't recognize but which looked to be about the same age as John Wayne's Colts. Japanese war weapons, if the Colts were any guide. The Japanese army equivalent of the Nazi Luger. What were they called? Type 94s? Something like that. And there was another bulky, dangerous-looking pistol up on the shelving under the cracked clearview. He really didn't recognize that and wasted some tense moments in nervous speculation before he realized it was a simple nail gun. All in all, not the sort of weapons he would have chosen himself, but – other than the nail gun – quite enough to do the job, if they were all well maintained and in working order, he thought grimly.

Then he stopped thinking and concentrated on what was being said. 'This vessel,' said the old man, gesturing towards the radar screen and speaking in English. 'This vessel is the *Miyazaki Maru*? It has her identification code, you say?'

'Yes,' said Tom Olmeijer, clearly unhappy to be imparting the information, glancing at a stony-faced Nils Nordberg every time he spoke.

'How you know this? How you know for certain this is *Miyazaki Maru*?'

'All the rescue ships have unique identification numbers. We have logged them into our computers so we know which is which. Crucial for when we get right in close. So many ships, so little sea room, such bad visibility...'

'Bad visibility. Yesssss,' the pirate drew out the word, clearly deep in thought. 'We head for this *Miyazaki Maru*. Not obvious; no big change of course. Tell no one. We meet *Miyazaki Maru* close to harbour, under cover of smoke. I give more orders then. Now I need radio. I talk to Captain Nakatomi. In...' He hesitated, searching for the word. 'In secret...'

As soon as the leader vanished, Richard leaned over towards Larsen. 'Who's not here? Nic Greenbaum, Gabriella...'

'They have three women as hostages, according to the oldest one. I'd guess Gabriella, Eva

280

and Inge. That's why the owner's told the captain to play ball for the moment...'

'You shuttup! You shuttup!' A younger, more dangerously nervous version of the old man waved one of the Makarov pistols in Larsen's face and covered his beard with spittle. *Someone's going to pay for that*, thought Richard, easing himself back against the wall, apparently amenable. He glanced across at Robin but she had withdrawn, clearly wanting to think rather than to communicate for the moment at least.

The leader arrived back on the bridge positively aglow with excitement. He gave a decisive series of orders to his men in a rapid flow of Indonesian *baha Indonesia* that Richard could not begin to understand. He noticed that the young relative reacted to a word that sounded a bit like *bucket*, however, and guessed that this must be the young man's name or title. Other than that, Richard began to characterize his enemies by the weapons they were carrying. It was Bucket and his Makarov who was left on the bridge, with the two Colts to back him up. The leader took his Browning, the Walther, the other Makarov and the Type 94s with him – and le Chef like a guide dog on a leash jerked to his feet and pushed roughly forward. *More payback to come*, thought Richard, looking at the Frenchman's thunderous face.

But if he had thought the Frenchman looked murderous that was nothing to the way Nic Greenbaum looked when he and Dr Hirai were pushed on to the bridge ten minutes later, the

Browning held to Nic's temple and a Type 94 to the doctor's. 'I swear to God, Councillor Kerian,' Nic was saying in a voice and with a sentiment that Richard feared was probably as dangerous as it was satisfying to hear – it was, after all exactly what he himself was thinking, but far too canny to articulate, 'if you harm one hair on anyone's head here I will hunt you down.' As the man with the Browning, whose name was Councillor Kerian, apparently, gestured him to sit down beside Richard, unfazed by the American's bluster, 'I will pay you back for this one way or another,' Nic snarled, then, like all the rest of them, he fell into a brooding silence.

But the first part of the payback didn't come for several hours.

Twenty-Five

Lahar

It took a little while for the magma boiling out of the caldera at the top of Guanung Surat to attain a really steady flow. Only when the rock wall above the western slope collapsed did the lava really start to come down the mountainside at speed, pouring through the ever-widening spout caused by the enormous fissure. Although the molten rock was thick enough to form its own levees, solidifying on either side of the red-hot molten core as it rolled majestically down the steep mountain slope, these levees simply seemed to direct the flow of molten rock along the most disastrous course possible. The red-hot core of the lava river was the better part of a thousand degrees Celsius. It was moving with unusual rapidity because of the slope it was travelling down. It was an unusually heavy flow in any case because of the collapse of the rock-wall that had released it in the first place.

So that when it started pouring into the head-waters of the already flooding Sungai Baya River, it simply exploded. Superheated steam and boiling rock became a semi-liquid torrent

283

that went roaring down the steep-sided river course at many metres per second, in a wave that was sixty metres high, and in a slide that was still seven hundred degrees Celsius at its heart. And then it met the hot mud still pouring out of the mountain above the almost naked rock that was all that remained above the landslide. And all Hell was let loose in the form of a lahar.

The lahar boiled out of the mud-filled flood-channel of the river course and spread out across the mountainside. Its leading wall dropped to ten metres high, but it gained in weight and viscosity. At its heart it was still super-heated, riding on a slipway of steam as slick as any ice; but it had dropped to five hundred degrees and cooled further with every metre it hurled down the mountain, exchanging heat for mass as it gulped in more mud, exchanging heat for speed. By the time that it reached the upper point of the actual landslide debris which had buried the modern sections of Baya City, it was moving at sixty kilometres an hour. The debris slowed it only in so far as it seemed to hesitate, tearing more mud up out of the ground and into its hungry heart. It was nearly ninety per cent mud and debris now, with just enough super-heated steam to keep it moving. As its speed slowed, so its depth fell, to five metres. The mountain slope was easing, levelled by a combination of riverine plain and piled avalanche debris. Crucially too, the river itself spread wide here and was bound on its city side by the levee that led down along the harbour's side. The levee was designed to stand three metres above the top of the highest spring tide, but the avalanche had heightened it with yet more debris plastered there with walls of solid mud. And the tide had peaked an hour or so before the lahar came and had been a low one in spite of the fullness of the invisible moon. The combination of the flooded river's width, the tide and the levee kept the worst of the lahar out of the deserted city above and the harbour below. And away from the shocked and terrified crowds, therefore. But it sent the broad front of its massive, weighty power straight out into the ocean in a solid wall of boiling mud two metres high moving at seventy-five kilometres an hour.

The lahar came so fast that Sailendra never really understood what was going on until it hit. It added nothing appreciable to the shaking of the ground, and no distinguishable sound to the constant rolling thunder of the eruptions. The lahar itself glowed spectrally, especially high on the mountainside when it was still at incandescent temperatures, but it was disguised by the high-sided valley where it was at its brightest. And those who were looking closely at the lower mountain slopes and saw it coming thought their eyes were playing tricks on them – with a spreading ruby ghostliness seeming to cause everything around it to jerk out of focus. Most people witnessing the approach of the monster simply wiped their hands over their eyes, supposing their sight to have been affected by a blinding wash of tears.

Providentially, Sailendra had begun to clear the port area starting with the levee side. It was a logical decision, given the amount of work still going on around the warehouses on the opposite side. And, while one ship had just left the outer area of Berth 1, its passengers safely below out of the burning pumice hailstorm, the replacement vessel was still manoeuvring into position. So both vessels sat between the levee and the last few hundred Berth 1 refugees lined up on the dock. Because these were the last refugees this far along the dock itself, Sailendra had come down in person to see them off. When the lahar itself arrived, he was standing beside the main fire point with a bundle of umbrellas, torn between handing them out and putting them down to pull the hose out of its brackets to try and wash some of the burning pumice off the dock. The old man beside him made up his mind for him. 'Hey,' he snarled, with the lack of ceremony granted to old age in extremis, 'are you going to give me one of those or are you just going to stand there gawping?'

Sailendra opened the umbrella, but as he did so he heard a sound like an express train hitting the buffers at full speed. A great wash of darkness reared above the levee, only vaguely visible in the dull red glow of the eruption. The darkness seemed to leap up against the red-bellied burning smoke clouds above, then it fell like a breaking wave. Most of it seemed to tumble back beyond the quaking wall of the levee, but not all. The two ships out on the water so close at hand were suddenly soiled by a great rain of thick mud, filled with steaming debris. It spattered into the foaming water which seemed to start boiling from the first foul touch. And some of it spattered across the berth itself. Fortunately all the heavy debris fell into the water and it was only the outwash of mud itself which made it this far. Sailendra, standing foolishly frozen in the act of offering the golf umbrella to the impatient old man, felt the impact of the falling mud all but tear it from his grip. He staggered back and watched in horror as the man was beaten to the ground by a deluge of steaming mud as thick as molasses. In an instant the orderly line was reduced to filthy, shrieking anarchy. And it was only when he stepped forward and actually felt the heat of the mud like napalm on his leg that he fully understood. In an instant he had thrown down the useless ruin of the golf umbrella and grabbed the hose after all. He turned on the water and began to hose the burning mud off the people and off the dock. As he did so, the second ship pulled in and dropped its gangways into place. Sailors came running, slipping and sliding on to the dockside and started pulling the scalded refugees up into relative safety. Sailendra continued to wash the steaming, sulphur-stinking mud off everything and everyone nearby. It was only when he turned the water off at last that he realized his walkie-talkie was sounding urgently. He put it to his face. 'Yes?'

'Your Highness, we have to move as many as we can over to the warehouse side. Whatever it was that came down the river course has destroyed that whole section of the old river mouth approaches. It's ripped the outer end of the old levee right off. It's put a new isthmus out into the bay for the better part of half a kilometre and it's still growing. And it sent a wave outwards that some ships are reporting to have reached ten metres in height. And that's still going as well; it may even be still growing, I don't know. We won't find out until it reaches Kalimantan. In the meantime, it has caused mayhem out there. I think we may even have lost some ships.'

'We will meet with the *Miyazaki Maru* here, off the mouth of the Sungai Baya River,' said Councillor Kerian. 'He will wait for us there.' That was as much of the councillor's plan as they were to know. And during the next hours *Tai Fun* deviated from her planned course just enough to take her out of the main armada, and away towards the river mouth. The pirates may have been inexperienced and nowhere near as well armed as they supposed, but they were terrified and very watchful. And their prisoners could see that watchfulness and the nervousness. They had no way of knowing about the inexperience of the men nor the inefficiency of their weapons. So the stand-off stayed in place as the two ships drew closer to each other, to the island and to their rendezvous.

Richard breathed deeply and evenly, trying to keep the tension under control so that he could think clearly and predict what Kerian's plan might be. If he could guess it with any accuracy, he could plan his own countermeasures more efficiently. And the more he considered their position, the more vital it seemed to him that they would have to take countermeasures, no matter what the risks. Because they were not going to be allowed to walk away from this alive. They knew who Kerian was. Even if they hadn't known that, they still knew what he and his men looked like. And even if the old pirate was hesitant, Richard guessed that the men aboard the *Miyazaki Maru* wouldn't be. For, as the TV announcer had informed them earlier, *Miyazaki Maru* belonged to Luzon Logging. Nic and Gabriella had told them all about men who worked for Luzon Logging. Richard reckoned men and women would mean no more to them than orang-utans did.

Practically, thought Richard grimly, the best idea for the pirates and their ship-board fences would be to kill everyone aboard, and tow *Tai Fun* with her priceless cargo somewhere they could transfer whatever they thought they could sell, then scuttle her. The only imponderable Richard could see was the question of whether anyone involved would be clever enough to work out that if they kept them alive until they scuttled the vessel, they might get away with a simple loss at sea – and no comebacks. Not even for someone as notable as Nic Greenbaum. After all, there had been no great furore when Robert Maxwell went down. Bad things happen at sea – everyone knows that. But of course, under the current circumstances, it would be even easier to kill them all, strip *Tai Fun* and then bomb or burn her, blaming her loss with all hands on the volcano. But to get away with that, they'd have to move the cargo while they were still close to the island and safely under the deadly pall of smoke. Whatever way it was all supposed to pan out, everyone on *Tai Fun* was due to die. Richard decided to take that as a given and draw up his own plans accordingly.

The first hope of an edge Richard and the others got arose out of Kerian's greed. With his prisoners apparently cowed and quiet, the old pirate took the opportunity of scouting round the vessel in much more detail. And he soon discovered that there was jewellery in many of the cabins. Expensive watches. Loose currency. It didn't take him long to realize that the ship might have a safe, also. And that the safe on a ship with a large casino aboard might well be full of gambling money on top of everything else. And he didn't need to use Captain Nakatomi or his friends at Luzon Logging to fence watches and jewellery or to spend a fortune in good hard cash. Any hesitation that the owner or his captain might have felt to giving away the combination of the ship's safe was easily overcome by a simple threat to rape the captive women. Something he was looking forward to doing in any case. He didn't even need to use his fall-back of shooting the red-bearded sailing master in the head. Something he would also do later, before shooting the aggressive American in several slightly less fatal, infinitely more painful, places and feeding his bleeding body to the sharks.

The crew of Kerian's prau were suddenly no longer in evidence as they moved Kerian's personal plunder aboard. Then the magnanimous leader allowed Bukit and his men to make their selection of the remaining baubles and put them aboard the second prau. But Kerian was no fool and Bukit was scared of failing his uncle. They had discussed the American's fate and Bukit didn't want to share it. So the young man was especially careful when the old man was away. And so the night proceeded.

Tai Fun sailed out of the last of the rising moonlight and under the strange spreading cloud of ash and smoke with its seemingly abyssal black sections bounded by ridges of fierce and threatening red. And the red intensified sufficiently to give some real light. And that light throbbed, sometimes brighter, sometimes darker, according to how the eruption was going. But it seemed that each blast of brightness burned lighter and lingered longer the closer to Port Baya they came. It was exactly as though they were sailing into Hell itself, thought Richard.

As they came close enough to the burning island to receive the harbour master's signal, so Kerian came back on to the bridge and stayed. At first, he simply ordered Tom Olmeijer to remain silent. This was easier than trying to come up with some elaborate reason for the course they were following. Richard reckoned that Kerian would have to soon, however, or simply switch off the radio and swear – if it ever came to an enquiry – that the thing was malfunctioning. While Kerian was wrestling with this conundrum, the others joined him, one by one, until Richard was certain that all the guns were there. The chef was still missing, however, and Richard thought he must probably be down below with the rest of the crew, all tied up sufficiently to be left.

The light was not the only thing that intensified as they drew near the volcano, however. The fearsome up-welling of so much blazing matter set up its own microclimate. And as the red light gathered, so the wind strengthened, blowing steadily – then strongly – then fiercely – from the north, sucked ever more powerfully into the inferno above the mountain. The sea echoed the restlessness of the lighter element, boiling up into increasingly restless swells. But it lacked the wind's sense of purpose and instead set up a steep-sided, unpredictable chop that threw *Tai Fun*'s hull about quite brutally while her sails seemed set hard above her heaving deck. Soon, Captain Olmeijer was demanding the services of his sailing master. But even

Larsen could not be expected to trim the sails for these conditions. So, at last, as they came down towards their rendezvous with *Miyazaki Maru*, they had to furl the sails altogether and motor in.

Through the clearview, Richard could see the top of the volcano, well defined by outpourings of molten lava now, the unrelenting column of burning smoke occasionally brightened by what looked like showers of meteors sailing up in ballistic arches to bomb the slopes and the town below. There was a sulphurous stench, alleviated only by the fact that the wind was coming steadily from astern, over the fresh cool sea. Through the open door of the bridgehouse, he was able to see the lower slopes, the edge of the harbour, the levee stretching out into a groyne, and the width of the river mouth beyond. Over on the far side sat the dark bulk of a vessel riding apparently at anchor and without lights. Oddly, that was the only other vessel he could see, though he knew there must be others very close by.

Continuing to ignore the harbour master, Kerian ordered the radio operator to raise *Miyazaki Maru* and as soon as Captain Nakatomi came on, the Councillor began his final negotiations. But these did not run smoothly; and, fatally for many of those concerned, they were conducted at full-scream pitch by two angry men gabbling a mixture of Japanese and Indonesian *baha Indonesia*, but communicating mostly in English, for each was clearly ignorant of the other's native tongue. It was a combination that the men and women imprisoned on the bridge could follow quite clearly. Richard, as always, focused on the conversation with fierce attention, still looking for a way to use anything he heard to the advantage of himself and his shipmates.

Captain Nakatomi was increasingly nervous, it seemed. He wanted to be gone. He clearly understood the worth of *Tai Fun* and her contents but his own command was at serious risk. Either Kerian brought her alongside, threw him a rope and sat still while *Miyazaki Maru* pulled *Tai Fun* somewhere a good deal safer, or he could forget it.

Fine, decided the incandescent pirate, in the most basic and insulting terms. He had a sound ship, packed to the gunwales with priceless treasures, and two praus – all well crewed. The cowardly, double-dealing, motherless, fatherless Captain Nakatomi could take his precious *Miyazaki Maru* and dock her where the sun didn't shine.

Captain Nakatomi answered with actions rather than words. *Miyazaki Maru*'s propellers suddenly began to thrash the red water under her counter into a kind of bloody foam. Infinitely slowly, the big freighter began to turn away across the wide mouth of the river. Kerian replied by directing Tom Olmeijer to take *Tai Fun* back out to sea, but slowly – and cross by the end of the levee and into the harbour mouth. They would lose themselves amongst the shipping there.

'Up! Up all mans!' howled Kerian as soon as *Tai Fun* began to answer to his orders. He waved the Browning for emphasis.

Richard, Nic and Larsen obeyed. Richard at least did so with less trepidation than he had felt in a while. If Kerian planned to sail *Tai Fun*, then he would need all of them to do so. With any luck, they were going to Kerian's prau to release the three women. Even Kerian must see that what they needed here was a navigator like Eva Gruber. Such was Kerian's rage and excitement that he took his nephew and six men as guards for the three prisoners, leaving only a skeleton guard on the bridge. A skeleton guard all armed with US Army Colt .45s.

They were going to Kerian's prau all right, but not to get the women. The three stood on the heaving hydraulic platform in the steady blast of the wind under the guns of Bukit and two of his crew armed with Type 94 Japanese pistols as Kerian and a couple of his men, the Walther PPK and the Makarov, rushed up and down, gathering the most precious of the pirate's treasure. If Kerian was staying aboard *Tai Fun* for the time being, so were his ill-gotten gains.

Richard was standing on the outer edge of the platform, closest to a young guard armed with a Type 94, who was standing at the point where Kerian's prau was tied. Nic was beside him, with Larsen closest to Bukit in the middle of the platform. The third guard, with a Makarov, was on the deck of the prau itself, his gun wavering somewhere in the middle of the line of prisoners.

As Richard waited to be loaded with the bags and cases Kerian was piling on the deck of the prau, he had the opportunity to look around for the sight away to his left was one of awesome splendour. *Tai Fun* was moving past the point of the levee now, the concrete groyne reaching out into the restless water, spiked with shattered flood debris. The harbour mouth beyond the groyne was still hidden behind his shoulder but his view to the left was widened by the fact that the prau was pulling back against her tow rope as *Tai Fun* motored forward. The river mouth was wide and shallow, backed by the wild wreckage of the landslide that had obliterated half the city. Above this, the mountain slopes were walls of blackness festooned increasingly intensely by blazing fires, which were being added to minute by minute as individual magma bombs burst upon them. The upper slopes were already well covered with lava, what forest was left after the landslide, well ablaze.

But then Richard's attention was claimed by something so unutterably strange, he found himself blinking. There was a kind of brightness in the river valley. A spectral glowing that seemed to leap and pulse so wildly it made his eyes water. He rubbed his face with his hands and looked again. In the second his eyes had been closed, the brightness had leaped much closer. He blinked, still trying to comprehend what he was seeing. Closer still. Following the Sungai Baya's valley. Even out here, he could hear a throbbing that instantly became a rumbling, which was at once a roaring. And the roaring gathered with the awesome speed of an approaching super-train. Following the river down. Down towards *Tai Fun*.

'Get DOWN!' Richard threw himself at the nearest guard. His movement was so unexpected that the man had no time to react. Richard's shoulder hit him on the belly and he flipped backwards over the prau's rope and was gone. As he went, he threw up his hands and his Type 94 pistol described a ballistic arc on to the deck beside Richard's hand. He scrabbled at it, already starting to roll. Nic and Larsen were equally quick. The three men sprawled on to the deck, Richard on his side, the gun at arm's length, thumb seeking the safety. There was an instant of stasis. Then Bukit pulled the trigger of his CZ52. And the gun blew up in his hands. The bullet in the chamber was the wrong size for the barrel and it wedged in place. The explosion tore apart the back of the weapon, sending the shell-case and the firing pin back at bullet speed. As Bukit had been aiming down the barrel at Larsen, that was where the flying metal hit him, right between the eyes. Richard stopped looking for the Type 94's safety catch. He released his pressure on the trigger.

The noise the CZ made as it exploded was so shocking to the man on the prau's deck that he jumped and closed his fist. The Makarov he was holding rattled into automatic fire, its safety almost as seriously defective as its trigger mechanism. But because the boy was looking at the source of the gunshot that had surprised him so, that was where the eight bullets went, reducing the already deceased Bukit to a bullet-riddled mess.

The lahar hit the ocean then. All Richard knew of the event was a great surge of scalding water that washed up over *Tai Fun*'s stern as the game ship heaved up in a wild attempt to ride the wave the lahar threw out. The ropes securing the praus snapped loose and both vessels were whirled away by the wave. As the pirate vessels broke free, *Tai Fun*'s stern whipped up again in a wild action that seemed to glue the three splayed bodies on the platform into place while at the same time shrugging off the weight of the water that had washed aboard her.

So that Richard, one minute drowning in hot mud, found himself the next minute rolling over to look up. Where the river mouth had been there was now a massive mud-bank, awash with restless, steaming water. On the farthest edge, almost on her side and crazily aground, lay the *Miyazaki Maru*. And there, on the outermost edge of that great black tongue of destruction, but seemingly in reach of the wildly writhing water, were the two praus, mastless, half wrecked, half drifting, half aground.

The three filthy men arrived in the bridge together, with Richard brandishing the Type 94 pistol he had no intention of firing if he could possibly help it, to find Tom, Nils and Robin back in charge, each holding a Colt .45 just like John Wayne. 'We have to go and get the women off that pirate bastard's prau,' grated Nic.

But even as he spoke, the radio came to life, still at full volume from the screaming match between Kerian and Captain Nakatomi.

'This is the Baya harbour master. Will any vessel under power with any sea room at all please come into port at once. The final group of three hundred survivors including the prince and his entourage must be removed immediately, I say again immediately...'

And, as if to emphasize his desperate words, a new rain of magma bombs began to fall on the blazing city. And the largest landed directly on the harbour master's office, blowing the building and everyone within it to smithereens.

Twenty-Six

Hell

For Sailendra, the destruction of the harbour master's office was the beginning of the end. Scarcely able to believe what he was seeing, he ran along the steaming, mud-splattered road-way that joined the levee, the piers and the warehouse area, calling into his walkie-talkie, pressing Number 1 as though if he pushed hard enough the harbour master would be able to arise from the blazing wreckage and answer.

Instead, a completely new voice filled the airwaves. 'Hello, Baya Harbour Master, this is the captain of the *Java Queen* Berth 1. Five hundred aboard in various states of repair. Departing harbour. I have to warn you the channel is badly silted and getting worse, according to my radar. Whatever it was that hit the harbour just now has damaged the levee and fouled the bottom of the bay. All riverside channels likely to be closed soon. Will warn all vessels in my vicinity. Advise using inner harbour, and being as quick as you can. Good luck.'

Almost as soon as the *Java Queen*'s captain had reported, the outer end of the levee toppled decorously inwards and the great, glowing mud bank of the lahar began to spill straight into the harbour itself.

Sailendra thumbed all the other buttons in order, yelling instructions as he ran across the back of the harbour at full tilt. Thank Heaven he had agreed the fall-back position with the harbour master. His directions that everyone not going aboard one of the last ships be moved to the deep-water berth beside the warehouses now looked providential, though his main motivation had simply been to get as far away from the eruption as possible. As long as they could find a vessel nimble enough to get in there and get out, there was hope for the last few hundred. As long as the volcano would give them time.

The mud-soaked, scalded scarecrow of a prince hurled himself to the ground as the next set of magma bombs rained down on the shaking city. But when he looked up, Bambang was there with Parang at his side and his father at the wheel of the last working truck. 'The hospital has gone!' Parang shouted. 'That was the last place being cleared but the last rain of these bombs hit it hard and the whole lot went up. It was like Hell itself in there. The only people to survive were the ones who could run. The doctors, the nurses...'

'Send them to the warehouse dock,' ordered Sailendra. 'Send them all to the warehouse dock. It's our last hope.' He looked up at the next bombardment of magma bombs arcing overhead and shrugged hopelessly. 'It's our only hope.'

'It is my decision,' said Nils decisively. 'She is my daughter and this is my vessel.'

'And my command,' added Tom. Looking uncharacteristically fierce. 'We both agree with Captain Mariner. We must go in now. We are the only hope those people have.'

'But what about the women?' grated Nic, unwilling to give up without a fight. 'They're in one hell of a lot of trouble.'

'Three lives against three hundred, Nic,' soothed Robin. 'It's what we're here for. I guess they'd say the same. I know Eva Gruber would.'

Nic looked away from those still grey eyes. He knew Gabriella would as well. That was the kind of person she was – why she did the kind of work she did. And Nils must know his own daughter too. He shrugged. 'Let's make it quick, then.'

They were not standing idly during this conversation. Dr Hirai had gone below to release le Chef and the other prisoners, warning them to prepare for entry into the blazing harbour and for an influx of burned, scalded and probably terrified people. Then her post would be at wherever spot from which she could see the mountain most clearly – armed with a pair of binoculars and one of the ship's walkie-talkies. Now, if ever, was the time for her to use all her expertise as a volcanologist as well as a doctor.

Tom and Richard stood like statues, shoulder to shoulder, easing *Tai Fun* round into the busy harbour mouth. Larsen had taken over radio duty as his sails were not needed but, what with the static discharge and the state of communications in the harbour, that was a watching brief as well. Robin, looking away from the distraught and raging American turned to the navigation computers. Collision-alarm and depth warnings were both shrieking. And hardly surprisingly.

The whole ghastly panorama filled the clearview at last. On their right the towering mountain was extended by its relentless column of flame and superheated gases into a trunk that joined the earth directly to the sky. Blazing lava continued to pour out of the crater, some of it spitting over the edges like gold boiling in an alchemist's crucible. Most of it followed the track of the lahar down the ruined valley of the evaporated river. The upper slopes were darkest now, apart from the orange lava trails and pools. It was the lower slopes that blazed. Individual spots and pocks of brightness from the magma bombs were running together into lakes of brightness. But on the mountainside itself, there was nothing left to burn. On the lower slopes beyond where the river had been it was the same story. On the thick, dark mud, drifts of pumice were gathering as though there had been a black blizzard. The only brightness came from the magma bombs littering the place in a weird golden inversion of what the stars should have looked like, had not the sky been that red-bellied roof of heavy black smoke, still sifting the rain of pumice among the boulders and the bombs. This side of the levee was an inferno. Only the harbour itself was dark, for the water itself had not yet found a way to burn. Even so, the heaving waves glittered like golden blades as they took the brightness of the blazing city and reflected it out after the departing rescue vessels.

Suddenly they were the only vessel going into the harbour. In fact they had to rely on the almost psychic bond between Robin on the radar and Richard who took the helm, for the open bridge caught the rolling thunder and amplified it through every shuddering surface and reverberating space. They were skipping between vessels of various sizes in various states of repair, all of them desperately out-ward-bound, many of them flashing urgent warnings telling *Tai Fun* not to sail on into the stricken harbour under any circumstances. And none of this was any surprise to the tall, steel-jawed man at the helm, especially when he saw what had happened to the old levee – and realized all too swiftly what the swelling mud bank would mean for the harbour itself.

More than that, however, Richard remember-ed all too clearly a painting depicting Armaged-don he had seen once, long ago. It showed a city ablaze, reduced already to near annihilation, set against a flame-red countryside apparently being torn apart from below. Above it there was a low red sky, torn with lightning and patterned with flashes of sulphurous yellow and coruscating scarlet, frozen in what was clearly the wildest of wind-torn motion. Clouds of steam and billows of smoke were depicted, also frozen but obviously caught in the midst of the most violent activity. And through the whirling clouds was falling a wild bombardment of flaming meteors that exploded wherever they landed. In the midst of the picture, a huge fissure had opened in the earth and naked people, men, women, children alike, were being pitchforked by blazing, strange-formed demons into the jaws of Hell, most of them already on fire. All of them, like the burning city and countryside around them, obviously screaming in unending agony.

The only difference between that picture and what Richard could see now was that the harbour stood in place of the jaws of Hell, equally gaudy and threatening, lacking only the people being pitchforked down into it. Except, of course, that that was where *Tai Fun* and her little complement were going.

The sense of danger was overwhelming. Every fibre in Richard's being screamed at him to turn the ship around and get away from this dreadful place. The sound was indescribably deafening, so that he was only able to hear snatches of what Robin was bellowing at him with a voice that would have easily carried to the crow's nest of a tall ship. The buffeting of the following gale, sucked to storm force by the inferno ahead, threatened to pitch the vessel on its end. The heaving of the constricted waters in the harbour was simply made mad by the constant thrusting of the mudflow following in the lahar's tracks and over the top of the ruined levee. The bottom of the bay was actually moving up and down beneath the steady keel and the whole ship slewed and shuddered unexpectedly as it answered to forces far beyond anything it was ever designed to face.

A hand fell on Richard's shoulder. It was Larsen. 'They want us by the warehouses, I think,' he shouted, gesturing to a wall of bombed-out buildings, some of them still ablaze.

Richard nodded. 'More power,' he yelled, tearing his throat. Tom Olmeijer pushed the old-fashioned engine-room telegraph firmly forward. The electric motors responded.

The first magma bomb exploded on the foredeck. And Larsen was gone. Richard was already all too well aware of the sailing master's abilities as a fire-fighter; clearly they would have to rely upon these from now until they joined the rest of the rescue fleet away out in the Java Sea.

'C ... le ... fort ... fi ... deg...' called Robin. 'Bot ... fa ... ing awa...'

Richard came left forty-five degrees and hoped that it was the bottom of the harbour that was falling away. And not, for example, the bottom of the boat.

Sailendra had never seen a more beautiful sight

in all his life. The tall ship, with her four great masts, came out of the smoke like something out of a dream. The forecastle seemed to be ablaze but her fire-fighting equipment was hosing it down and everything else around it. A mixture of white flame and black pumice dust was pouring out of her scuppers as she eased in towards the dock. He looked down the exposed length of the warehouse berth, and realized that everyone there was cheering. Then a pain in his throat made him realize that he was cheering too. He swung round. Bambang and Parang were standing just behind him. He hugged them both, his embrace made clumsy by the difference in their heights. Then he turned back. There was still much to do. There were the better part of three hundred people here and they needed to be moved off the dockside and on to the providential vessel before the next set of magma bombs did a fatal amount of damage. Before the volcano thought up yet more lethal little tricks.

The ship swung into place. Sailendra saw the name – *Tai Fun* – and knew he would never forget it. Ropes came snaking shorewards, were caught and secured in record time. Immediately gangways slammed down, fore and aft. As they did so, the next set of magma bombs screamed to earth. Another warehouse, away in the bonded section, exploded. Half a million bottles of Suntory whisky burst into gaudy life and started flowing in a burning river down towards the harbour.

It was only the careful preparations Sailendra and his people had put in place that stopped a stampede. But everyone on the warehouse dockside knew what to do and more importantly they knew that if they did it, they all stood a much better chance of surviving even something as strange and terrifying as a river of blazing whisky. So, as soon as the gangways slammed down, they began to move up them in an orderly, carefully prearranged fashion, the doctors and nurses from the bombed-out hospital fitting as best they could. The next bombardment of magma began almost immediately, completing the destruction of the warehouses and, indeed, of the last of the harbour buildings. The last buildings in the city.

Sailendra was tempted to look back, and the sight nearly broke his heart. Behind the harbour, the Old City mounted the lower slopes of the timeless, traitorous Guanung Surat. And all of it was gone now. Blocks, streets, terraces, neighbourhoods, suburbs, all. In one great conflagration. Destroyed so utterly that there seemed no hope of any recovery. All lost. All gone. Forever. So many years of effort. So many lives and hopes. So much investment of money and effort and dreams. His princedom. He stood stricken.

Until Parang, his friend and secretary, took him by the shoulder. 'Come, Your Highness,' he said, as gently as the mind-numbing cacophony would allow. 'We are the last. And it is time for us to go. Let's get the hell out of here.'

Twenty-Seven

Jaunt

Sailendra walked heavily up the gangway and on to *Tai Fun*'s deck. As soon as he stepped on to the teak of the decking, the plank was raised behind him, the ropes were cast off from the ship itself and the sleek vessel surged into motion as swiftly as it was able.

The prince was not at first struck by this fluid urgency. Everywhere he looked there were numberless reasons for haste; this was not some leisurely jaunt up the river, after all. But even so, as the ship swung round in the last deep water of the choking harbour and powered towards the swiftly silting mouth, Sailendra followed Parang into the main accommodation area, where there was at least a slight diminution in the pounding roaring from outside. 'You know this vessel?' he demanded. He had seen it in the harbour himself, had talked to some of the people who sailed her, but he had never been aboard before and was surprised to find Parang so certain of his way.

'I have been on board before,' Parang confirmed. 'In fact I was expecting—' The secretary stopped suddenly, as if taking mental stock

309

of the situation. 'So much has happened, so swiftly,' he said by way of explanation, as though he expected Sailendra to have the faintest idea what he was talking about. Then he swung round and hurried forward, leading his prince up on to the bridge.

On the bridge itself, Sailendra was immediately struck by the concentrated sense of urgency and purpose that lay under the deafening noise tearing through the very fabric. He was a modest man, given his birth and upbringing, but he was not used to being greeted with grunts and nods when he was introduced to people. The only people who accorded him the courtesy he was used to were the two women, a Japanese doctor who was here, apparently, making her preliminary report of sick and wounded, but adding to it some kind of postscript on the state of the mountain itself, and a tall, golden-haired blonde with striking grey eyes, who was calmly and competently trying to ease them through the rapidly silting mouth of the stricken harbour. Every thirty seconds or so, she would bellow a set of headings, coordinates, depths and directions to the huge man at the wheel. He would never acknowledge that he had heard her, but the vessel would follow her orders to the centimetre; to the knot; to the degree, minute, second.

Left to his own devices by the apparent rudeness of his rescuers and suddenly feeling listless, Sailendra looked out of the clearview. He was struck anew by the velocity of the vessel as she headed at top speed for the mouth of the harbour. They were clearly running away from an incredibly dangerous situation, he thought. But were they also racing towards something he did not as yet understand?

Then another unfamiliar figure arrived. A small, dark-faced, tousle-haired individual in a blue engineer's overall. And he was carrying a tray half filled with something that smelt like olive oil, and laden with gun parts.

'The oil is the closest I could find to gun oil,' he bellowed to the tall man, Captain Mariner, at the helm in a thick French accent. 'It is first virgin cold pressing. The best. The chef de cuisine says he will take the Colts back when we have finished with them. He will fry them in the rest of the oil and serve them on a bed of young steamed palm leaves.'

Captain Mariner grunted. The French engineer carried the guns across to another man, one with a strangely familiar face who had been introduced as Mr Greenbaum, and together they started cleaning and assembling the weapons. Parang, who had seated himself beside Mr Greenbaum, started to help them, betraying a skill his prince had never suspected he possessed. Sailendra, who had never handled a gun in his life, went to join them.

Parang glanced up as Sailendra sat down, though the secretary's fingers did not slow in their urgent business with the gun parts. 'It appears that we have found Councillor Kerian, Your Highness...'

311

Under Richard's steady hands, *Tai Fun* almost felt her way forward out of the harbour. The currents and counter-currents within the water made the long vessel almost impossible to handle with the accuracy required by the delicate series of manoeuvres the rapidly silting mouth dictated. The influx of hot mud spilling across the harbour bottom was pushing the water out through an increasingly narrow channel so the speed of the current was building up as well. Nor was the water strictly liquid any longer. It was thick with churned-up mud and full of submerged and half-submerged debris, and the surface was clotted with increasingly thick rafts of floating rock. The fine pumice dust coagulated into chunks as soon as it got wet. Magma bombs were full of incandescent gas and they set on impact with the surface into sponges made of stone. Although the current was pushing towards the rapidly narrowing, steadily solidifying escape route, the wind was still blowing fiercely counter, pushing yet more floating pumice rafts into the sleek ship's way. The racing propellers were finding it increasingly difficult to ease the vessel forward, and the motors that drove them were beginning to overheat as Richard was forced to ask for more and more power as he fought to keep *Tai Fun* moving forward to Robin's dictates. But he had no choice. If they didn't get out of the harbour they were doomed. 'More power,' he grated to Tom, who pushed the ancient telegraph towards its limit, watching the needles on his engine monitors flick into the red.

But then behind them, another fusillade of magma bombs exploded across the burning city, half a dozen exploding into the water immediately aft of *Tai Fun*. As the great wave generated by their arrival surged the ship forward, so the racing headwind faltered. 'NOW!' shouted Richard. 'Give it all you've got, Tom.' His huge hand closed over Tom's hand with crushing force and rammed the handle of the ancient telegraph hard against its brass cradle at max revs. The needles settled into the red. The engines span more fiercely than they had ever done before. The propellers churned wildly, thrashing the muddy water, and the pumice into a kind of coal-dust glue. *Tai Fun* surfed over the mud bank of the lahar and slid safely out into the Java Sea. As soon as he felt her slip free, Richard wrenched his hand back with enough force to make Tom gasp in pain, his hand still trapped on the handle. But they were too late. The needles on the engine monitors flickered once and fell back. There was, if not a silence, then a sudden relative failure of noise. No headwind, no motor; even the volcano seemed to quieten. Richard turned to le Chef. 'Time for your diesel motors, Chief. I need power as quickly as you can give it to me, please. And bugger our carbon footprint.'

Fifteen minutes later, le Chef was in his engine room. The diesel motors were on line, switched in and delivering enough power to the main shaft to compensate for the loss of the electric motors. The Frenchman could feel *Tai Fun*'s long sleek hull gathering way again as she started to bash her way through the strange lumpy effluent that the volcano had rained down on them. The door behind him opened. 'Hey, Chef,' drawled Nic Greenbaum. 'Captain Mariner says can you lower the hydraulic platform, please. We'll need to take the Zodiac out for a little jaunt in a few minutes' time.'

Twenty-Eight

Flow

Fifteen minutes later, Richard was sitting hunched in the stern of the Zodiac, trying to protect his head and face from the constant rain of hot pumice. At least they seemed to be out of range of the magma bombs, he thought grimly. For this was bad enough. It had filled his hair and invaded his shirt collar like a combination of burning sand and firc ants. And that was only the start of it. Larsen had found out the hard way that the stuff set like concrete almost instantly when it touched water. And this meant that anyone who breathed it in would find his nose and throat immediately coated with hard-set clinker. What it might do to your eyes just didn't bear thinking about.

The Zodiac juddered forward over the thick, semi-solid heave of the surface. Richard risked a glance around. Nic Greenbaum sat midships opposite the Parang. They, like Richard, had the recently cleaned, checked, fully-loaded Colts immediately available. Richard also had the little task force's only walkie-talkie, for he was in command. As if to emphasize the fact, he was also the only one with a torch.

Prince Sailendra himself sat in the prow. Like all of them, his head and face were swathed in sheeting to keep the pumice at bay as best they could. Richard almost literally cracked a smile, feeling pumice trickle down his chest. The grimy cloth made the three of them look like extras from a cut-price remake of *The Mummy*. Sailendra looked like the star of *The Sheikh* or *Lawrence of Arabia*.

'Is he really going to be able to arrest this Councillor Kerian? He hasn't even got a gun,' Richard asked Parang.

'He is Kerian's prince. If he cannot, then no one can. But it is the prince's royal duty to try...'

They had had a lot of discussion along these lines already. Sailendra looked like being more of a liability than a help on this extremely risky venture. He was in no way sea-wise. He had no knowledge of or expertise with weapons – except, perhaps, with traditional ones such as swords. In the face of Colt .45s, Browning High Powers and what-nots, he was likely to be simply outgunned. But as the surprising young Parang pointed out, the prince might be an effective wild card. He was the one man on earth who might make Kerian stop and think about what he was doing. And if that approach didn't work, then there was the John Wayne approach to fall back on. And the rest of them were all well armed for that.

Parang was coming after Gabriella, as was Nic. An interesting situation, had anyone the leisure or the inclination to consider it, reckoned Richard. For Gabriella Cappaldi was involved with both men. She was Nic's contact as he looked into the illegal doings of Luzon Logging in Pontianac and Tanjung Puting. And Parang was Gabriella's contact as she did exactly the same thing on Pulau Baya. Parang's brief, apparently, had been to find out who was working with the illegal loggers, get close to them and find out as many damning facts as possible. And, as that man was Councillor Kerian, both of Gabriella's contacts had bones to pick with him independently of the fact that he had kidnapped her.

And those bones were due to be picked quite soon, for Kerian's prau sat, mastless, mud-washed and apparently semi-derelict, in the seemingly solid water dead ahead. It was a miracle, thought Richard, easing the throttle open a little wider, that the timeless little pirate vessel hadn't been beached on the sudden out-thrust of the muddy lahar like the *Miyazaki Maru*. For Luzon Logging's freighter lay half on her side and helpless on the far shore of the slick new isthmus that had been a river mouth before the outcome of the volcano's whim.

Because of the destruction of the Baya City hospital, *Tai Fun* was supplied with medical staff of all sorts well able to look after the hundreds of refugees now packed as safely as possible below. So Dr Hirai was able to put her medical responsibilities on the back burner for a while at least and concentrate on her secondary duties as volcano watcher. And, with her grandfather very firmly in her mind, she was glad to do so. The more likely it began to look that they might all survive this, the more detailed and accurate she wanted her account for the old man to be. As the sleek vessel sat motionless, bound in by rafts of floating pumice, like an ancient square-rigger in the grip of the fabled Sargasso Sea, she stood on the bridge deck in front of the bridge itself, therefore, right at the base of the foremast. She was dressed as though for the fiercest rainstorm in hooded yellow waterproofs, down which the pumice whispered like the voices of the dead. At which the wind seemed to tug with ghostly fingers. But she had long since stopped listening to the voices or paying much attention to the insistent touches, focused with absolute concentration on what she could see rather than what she could hear and feel. For her yellow-gloved fingers were tight-wrapped around the barrels of the most powerful pair of binoculars aboard. Like everything else aboard, they were state-of-the art; electronically enhanced and laser-focused, presenting her with a broad field of vision like a wide-screen television, with digital readouts for light and range.

Dr Hirai's vision was filled by the volcano's crater. Its pulses of fire and explosions of gas, giving birth to the meteor showers of magma bombs, sent the light-sensitive readout off the scale until she found a way of adjusting it to the minimum. But by the time she did so, the brightness and the frequency of the eruptions seemed to be lessening in any case. She frowned, trying to remember what that might mean. She lowered the binoculars and looked with her naked eyes. Yes. The fires were dying back a little. The whispering and the tugging seemed less insistent. That meant that the pumice-fall was easing and the wind was dying too. It was as though a damper was being slowly closed upon the massive furnaces up there. She frowned, suddenly hesitant, the binoculars level with her lips. Abruptly her nostrils filled with the stench of a sulphur pit. Her eyes flooded, and channels in the pumice she hadn't even realized was dusting her cheeks set into little levees as though the tears themselves were molten lava. The deathly stench came again, a little more strongly this time. The great red-streaked column of smoke above the crater seemed to settle, somehow. To lose something of its upward thrust. To gain weight – and a kind of middle-aged spread. Dr Hirai slammed the binoculars back against her face so hard she was lucky not to give herself two magnificent black eyes. But the wide-screen readout showed her all too clearly the full horror of what was going on. 'Oh God,' she said, turning to run back towards the bridgehouse, blaspheming in extremis, victim of too much Western culture, although she was herself a devout and thoroughly Eastern Buddhist. 'Oh God. Oh God. Oh God...'

* * *

Richard brought the Zodiac almost silently alongside the lower gunwale of the listing prau and cut the motor. Sailendra, with unexpected acuity for a landsman, caught the end of the snapped cable which had grappled the prau to *Tai Fun*'s stern until the lahar hit, and secured the inflatable in place. Nic and Parang were up on the deck like ghosts before he had finished. The instant Sailendra had secured the inflatable, he too climbed up on to the deck and Richard went up at his shoulder, with his big Colt ready, a .45-calibre bullet in the chamber, his thumb on the safety. His walkie-talkie was also at his belt but that seemed to be of thoroughly secondary importance at the moment.

It was impossible to cross the listing vessel's deck silently. There was no Larsen here to wash the pumice away; on the contrary, there was a good thick covering of mud to hold it in place. The pumice was augmented by splinters of wood and shards of glass from the all-but-flattened wreck of the deckhouse that lay half hidden under the rags of the sail immediately in front of the square black gape of the main hatch. And so each footfall crunched as though they were walking on cornflakes. The sound was made more audible by the fact that the wind was faltering, Richard realized suddenly. He looked up past the sail-wrapped deckhouse and over the rail on the up-slope of the deck. Were the fires on the volcano dying down? The brightness and the distant thunder both seemed to have eased a little. Reminded by the sudden gathering of shadows, Richard pulled out his torch and flicked it on. He shook his head as he followed Sailendra down the weird slope of the main gangway. Thank God these men weren't really under his command, he thought, or there would have to be some kind of reckoning. What kind of tactics dictate that the last man into a dangerous situation is the only one able to see?

Richard followed the bright gold puddle of the torch beam down the mud-crusted steps of the crazy gangway, frowning with thought, his gun at the ready in spite of the fact that he had heard no sound at all from down here. Then Prince Sailendra stepped out of his way and let him see. The main below-deck area of the prau was a mess. Everything Kerian had brought aboard lay scattered around, much of it covered with the thick mud that had washed down the open hatchway. A good deal of it was heaving sluggishly in the gathering wash of water leaking in through sprung and broken sides. The pillar of the mast seemed to have split – almost shattered – when the upper-works had carried away. Everything and everyone down here showed the most vivid evidence of having been thrown around by the wild movements of the lahar-stricken vessel. Ironically, the people who seemed to have suffered least were the three women lashed to the makeshift bunks. The rough rope bonds may have been designed as preparation for rape, but they worked as very effective safety belts. However, the fact that they had all been gagged and blindfolded must have made the experience almost unbearable.

Richard's torch beam swept over the sopping, heaving mess on what had been the lower deck. It found out the pale, faces of the women, wide eyes filled with terror flooding with tearful relief as the blindfolds came off. And, safe in the knowledge that there was no one else down here besides the men from *Tai Fun*, he said, 'It's all right, ladies, we've come to rescue you.'

'Where is Councillor Kerian?' asked Sailendra at once, stooping to loosen the knots restraining Inge. He dropped her blindfold and her gag beside her head, swept his headdress back over his shoulder, uncovering his long, lean face, and gazing earnestly into the eyes of the beautiful Nordic blonde girl he was freeing. He picked up a Bugis sword from the foul wash on the deck at his feet and started sawing at the ropes with its razor edge. As he worked, he glanced up, looking around the constricted area, where Nic was releasing Gabriella and Parang was busy with Eva. 'Do any of you know where Councillor Kerian has gone?'

But instead of an answer, Richard's walkie-talkie shrilled. He placed his torch on the bunk beside Inge's feet and pulled the radio transceiver from his belt. 'Yes?'

'You have to come back!' ordered Nils Nordberg, his voice cracking with tension. 'You've got to come back now!'

Richard knew better than to hesitate or start asking questions at a moment like this. 'We go,' he said, echoing Nils's urgent orders. 'We go now.' He shoved his fist through the walkie-talkie's wrist strap, grabbed his torch, turned and pounded up the gangway, exploding on to the deck just in time to see the lean silhouette of Councillor Kerian crouching over the line securing the Zodiac to the prau, busily untying it. Richard straightened, bringing the Colt up, left-handed. As he did so, one of Kerian's crewmen lurched drunkenly out of the wreck of the bridgehouse, where Kerian himself had clearly been hiding. He was waving a Type 94 and as soon as he saw Richard he pulled the trigger. Miraculously, the gun went off. The bullet smashed into the stump of the mast by Richard's head. Richard's Colt bellowed back. The pirate span away, howling. Richard drew a bead on the crouching Kerian, slamming his torch up alongside his gun so that both beam and barrel centred on the frozen man. Kerian stopped his feverish fiddling with the rope and turned to face Richard, still in a half-crouch. *I really do not have time for negotiation here*, thought Richard grimly. His finger tightened on the trigger.

'Councillor Kerian,' bellowed Sailendra from behind Richard's shoulder. 'I arrest you in the name of the people of Pulau Baya...'

Kerian's belly exploded in a tongue of red-gold flame. Sailendra staggered back with a shout of surprise. Richard shot once but the crouching figure with his half-concealed Browning still clutched to his stomach was gone over the side. 'Into the Zephyr,' shouted

Richard. 'No time to lose.' He caught the reeling Sailendra and nearly sliced his leg open on the prince's sword. Then Inge was at the other side and the three of them ran down the heaving deck, almost throwing the prince into the bottom of the sturdy inflatable. Inge leaped down beside him. Richard paused, raking the water's strange solid surface with his torch and gun. The others came out in two pairs, slithering down past him and into the Zephyr. When he was certain that Kerian was not lurking somewhere nearby, armed and dangerous still, Richard himself stepped down into the Zephyr and gunned the motor. Sailendra cut the rope with one slice of his Bugis sword and they were powering off towards *Tai Fun* as fast as they could go.

Tai Fun was already making headway as Richard brought the Zephyr in against the hydraulic platform with enough force to half-beach it. Le Chef was there to hold the short-cut rope as they bundled urgently aboard. Then, as Richard, last, ran past him he simply let go of it and turned. Side by side they pounded up into the after section of the accommodation area. Le Chef turned and secured the door behind him. Richard was struck at once by the strange scene. It was as though he were in a seaside morgue after some terrible maritime disaster. Everyone here was wet. All the patients looked like corpses with damp sheets pulled up over their faces. The doctors and nurses also were wrapped up and masked, like Richard, Sailendra and the rest had been aboard Kerian's prau. Sailendra was having a flesh-wound in his shoulder bandaged by a doctor with a bucket of water at his feet. But then Inge was there, replacing the doctor with quiet insistence. And Bambang appeared beside her, wide-eyed, with his parents in tow. 'I will be a doctor,' the boy decided, clearly at the end of a long discussion about his future.

Sailendra smiled and reached out with his good hand to ruffle the boy's black hair. 'I don't know,' said the prince, with a warm smile in his voice. 'When I get back on to whatever is left of my island, I fear I'm going to need a new chief councillor. And I can't think of anyone better qualified...'

'On the bridge, Capitaine,' said le Chef. 'Monsieur Nic and Mam'zelle Gabriella have gone. But time is short! Run!'

Still smiling at the little exchange, Richard took off at full speed. He burst out of the lift on to the top deck and sprinted down to the bridge itself. As he ran he registered that the sails were set – but at barest minimum. The tiniest triangles of flameproof, heat-resistant material were showing. Everything up here was awash with water, even the masts and sails themselves. The upper restaurant was as tightly closed as a seaside fish bar in February. Doors locked, shutters up. And the open bridge was no longer open either. Every opening that could be closed was closed. The instant he arrived and the last door shut – locked and bolted – behind him, a

325

sopping mattress was wedged in place and he stood dumbfounded, looking at what suddenly looked like an undersea lunatic's padded cell.

'Richard! Take the helm,' ordered Tom Olmeijer. Richard obeyed, gripping the ancient wheel like Mark Twain on the Mississippi. He looked ahead. Even the clearview had been padded – all but a little square which allowed him to see where he was going. But this padding was dry, for the instruments beneath it were electrical. Even the telegraph, which was set once again at full ahead.

'Do we know when it will hit us?' asked Richard, licking his lips. Although no one had said the words, he remembered all too clearly what Dr Hirai had told them about the Plinian eruption of Vesuvius. They had had the lahar. Now they were going to get the nuée ardente; the pyroclastic flow.

'Any minute now,' answered Robin and Dr Hirai at once.

'We shouldn't be facing into it?'

'No time to turn,' grated Tom. 'The High Wind fleet designs have been tested up to two hundred knots of wind. But never for two hundred degrees of heat. We're rigged for hurricane conditions and running away from the full force of the thing as best we can. Other than that, we pray.'

'Two hundred knots! That's superstorm stuff. Not even global warming has delivered speeds like that...' blustered Larsen, awed.

'Mount Washington, 1934, if memory serves,'

326

answered Richard. 'Two hundred and thirty-five miles per hour. But that was a wind-gust. It can go faster, so they tell me, in tornadoes and in pyroclastic flows...'

The flow hit then as though Richard had summoned it like a genie out of a bottle. It hit from behind at full-on hurricane speed. But it had come like the lahar along the river valley, and so it was dissipating its force already out across the big new mud-topped isthmus that had once been an estuary. *Tai Fun* was on the edge of it in any case, heading very slightly out of the main line of its colossal flow. It still picked up the ship and tore her forward, threatening to rip her sails to shreds and burn them like oil-soaked rags – flame-resistant, super-strong Kevlar woven with heat-exchangers though they were. It tried to tear the masts out of their sockets like some monstrous cousin of the Doctor wind of southern Africa – *the Java Dentist*. It hurled the miasma of red-hot dust particles against the rearmost sections of the vessel, stripping away fire-retardant paint that had shrugged off blazing jet-skis, pitting her imperishable fibreglass and plastic sections, setting all her soaking wood to steaming and smouldering. It forced its blazing breath, still in excess of two hundred degrees Celsius, into every tiny nook and cranny – until only the most incalculable of good fortune saved her. The blazing pumice dust that the deathly wind was hurling forward almost as fast as wind had ever travelled across the face of the globe was set solid by the soaking planes and runnels of the ship. A coating of lightweight black concrete formed all across the after sections. Formed and held and set hard. Shutting out the worst of it at last.

Tai Fun heaved, as the great jet-engine roaring enveloped her. She rolled increasingly wildly as the concrete formed even on her masts and sails. She pitched and heaved, all but tearing the Mississippi paddle-steamer's wheel out of Richard's hand. The mattresses rounded, like the sides of balloons, shivered and steamed, filling the bridge with foul-smelling, sulphurous steam until everyone was choking and coughing, faces red and eyes streaming. The air pressure within the bridgehouse rose and fell, flexing their eardrums until they screamed. Coughed and choked and screamed again. The clearview, stressed and strengthened coated glass that it was, starred in front of Richard's eyes like a windscreen hit by a stone.

But then it was gone.

Tai Fun was riding more easily. The battered, blackened ship was still alive.

They were all still alive.

Richard slapped the wheel with his open hand. 'I love this ship!' he cried. 'Nils. I want her. Like Nic says, MNO. I love her so much I'll take the whole damn fleet.'

'I'm sure we can cut a deal,' answered Nils. He sank into the pilot's chair, shaking a little.

'If that's all right with Nic,' warned Robin. 'He could still be after High Wind.'

'Naaw,' drawled Nic at his most Texan. 'I was only ever after Luzon Logging. And what Gabriella's told me, and what we learned in Pontianac, and Tanjung Puting, combined with what Parang's got, signed, sealed and delivered, I reckon it's a done deal there all right.'

'Then it's a done deal here.' Richard opened his right arm and Robin hugged his massive chest.

'Mind you...' said Nic. And paused, hanging on the silence as they all watched him suspiciously. 'If Heritage Mariner ever needs a friendly partner, then Greenberg International and Texas Oil are just at the end of the phone. You've got my private number, Richard. You be sure to use it.'

'I will,' said Richard cheerfully. Then he turned to Tom Olmeijer. 'Where away, Captain? What course shall we set?'

Tom looked at Eva Gruber.

And Eva, as unruffled as if they had just been safely boating on the Zuyder Zee, said, 'We will head due east, I think, and then due south. The nearest landfall is Java, and the nearest port is Surabaya. But we must go round the volcano to get there.'

Councillor Kerian pulled himself up the long rope left dangling when Sailendra cut the Zodiac free. He had lost the Browning in the water but he still counted himself pretty lucky not to have got trapped beneath the floating pumice like a swimmer under ice. The briefcase he had been planning to smuggle aboard the inflatable still lay on the deck precisely where he left it as he dived backwards to avoid being shot by the prince's massive friend. He picked it up and opened it, reassuring himself that the wads and wads of US$500 and $1,000 bills were still all safely there. He glanced across at *Miyazaki Maru*, trying to work out his best way of getting across to her. At least his prau was still afloat, sprung and leaky though she was. There must be a way in which a man as determined and ingenious as himself could work her over to the grounded ship before she actually sank. He looked a little wistfully the other way. The Zodiac was up with the tall ship now. She was so beautiful. It had almost been like ravishment to board her and strip her of her finery. A pity he hadn't had the opportunity to practise a more physical type of ravishment upon the women he had kidnapped. The blonde woman had been the most tempting, of course. But he had felt the darkest compulsion to make the dark one suffer, almost as though he owed her a debt of agony. Well, they had had a lucky escape. Now it was up to him to arrange his own escape. And to invest some of the fortune in his briefcase in evening the score with some screaming girls in Bangkok after all.

A hellish stench of sulphur and brimstone filled his nostrils, as though he had become in fact the Devil that his desires made him seem. His eardrums seemed to flex. He looked up at the volcano, more with a spirit of enquiry than with any kind of premonition or realization. There was a kind of glowing cloud rolling sedately down the river valley there. It gleamed and glittered, numberless points of whiteness seething against an almost crystal heart that made him think of rubies. The sea heaved massively beneath the creaking prau, pushing her out, away from the great slick hump of mud that lay like the back of some huge sea serpent between him and the *Miyazaki Maru*. He was surprised to see how far out he had drifted, how far inland the listing, grounded hulk seemed to be. It was almost as though there was an off-shore wind building up, he thought. That would be good. Better a southerly breeze pushing him out to give him some sea room than the relentless northerly gales that had made this a lee shore for the last few days. He looked up again and saw that the strangely attractive blood-red brightness seemed to have spread right across the north shore before him, seemed to be spreading out along the smooth back of the mud bank as he watched. He frowned. In simple wonder rather than in fear or comprehension. It was certainly moving at a fair speed, whatever it was! He reached into his briefcase and took out a bundle of bills, then he snapped it shut. Right, he thought, fanning himself with US$100,000 – the better part of ten million rupiahs in that one bundle alone – it was time to get busy. How was he going to get across to *Miyazaki Maru*? He looked across at her on the thought. Just as the pretty red mist swept over

331

her. She seemed to lie there, all aglow at the heart of it for an instant. Then the helicopter still secured to her forward deck exploded, a huge gout of yellow fire, expanded instantly by the barrels of fuel kept ready at hand. Before Kerian could blink, he saw that the whole of her deck was on fire. Every trunk of teak and mahogany ripped from the slopes of Guanung Surat ablaze like the merest kindling. Every stick of ramin torn out of Tanjung Puting National Park alight like a box of matches. Then the oil in the bunkers went up and blew the whole vessel apart.

All this happened so swiftly that Kerian hardly had time to register the vessel's terrible death, let alone associate it with himself. He never even really understood that the red cloud had crossed the mud bank in the moment it took the Luzon Logging freighter to die. But so it did.

A wall of superheated steam whipped over Kerian's head, driven by a wind moving well in excess of two hundred and fifty knots. A wind armed with grains of pumice that trembled on the edge of melting. The deck of his prau tilted up and he staggered back across it. He fell into the sea, but he was dead long before he hit the pumice-crusted water, choked and suffocated, boiled and burned all in a heartbeat. The prau turned over but it too was burned to charcoal before it could sink. It was all over in an instant; but that instant lasted a lifetime, like instants in Hell are said to do.

The steam was so superheated it seared Kerian's skin off his face and body before he could fall, let alone die. He gasped and the red-hot pumice, already driving like a million needles into his naked flesh, coated the wet planes of his nose, mouth, throat and lungs, filling his head and chest with boiling black cement. The skinless flesh was seared off his face, torso and arms, as though by the blast from the hottest of furnaces. The bundle of notes in his hand exploded into flames but the nerves in his hand and arm were burned away before he could feel it. The tendons clenched and set the naked bones like stone. His finger-nails and toenails boiled away. His eyes were poached blind in his head before he could see the brightness of ten million rupiahs burning. And his brain was boiled by the blast of nearly three hundred degrees Celsius before he could even realize it. The top of his skull exploded and the boiling matter spayed out into the wind. The barbecued muscles of his legs kicked spasmodically as his skin rolled down like stockings and vapourized – under the cotton of his sarong that remained moulded against him, apparently untouched. Then it simply burst into flames like the banknotes. The deck all around him steamed, split, splintered, dried and kindled in an instant. The briefcase full of money melted, its steel skeleton heated to cherry red and it all burst into flames.

What little was left of Councillor Kerian fell back into the boiling water. The charred sticks of his prau rolled over on top of him. The black rafts of pumice closed over them like floating gravestones. The pyroclastic flow caught up with *Tai Fun*, lifting her Zodiac into the air and bursting it like a toy balloon in a blast furnace before closing its ruby grip around her.

Then the burning, blazing, breath of the volcano passed over her like the highest of high winds; blew her and everyone aboard her safely away northwards into the heaving, steaming heart of the Java Sea.